Interdependency ; bk. 3

W9-AAK-470

# THE LAST EMPEROX

# THE LAST EMPEROX

# JOHN SCALZI

**THORNDIKE PRESS**
A part of Gale, a Cengage Company

Copyright © 2020 by John Scalzi.
The Interdependency Series.
Thorndike Press, a part of Gale, a Cengage Company.

Thorndike Press® Large Print Basic.
The text of this Large Print edition is unabridged.
Other aspects of the book may vary from the original edition.
Set in 16 pt. Plantin.

LIBRARY OF CONGRESS CIP DATA ON FILE.
CATALOGUING IN PUBLICATION FOR THIS BOOK
IS AVAILABLE FROM THE LIBRARY OF CONGRESS

ISBN-13: 978-1-4328-7961-7 (hardcover alk. paper)

Published in 2020 by arrangement with Tor/Forge

Printed in Mexico
Print Number: 01          Print Year: 2020

*To the women who are
done with other people's shit*

# PROLOGUE

The funny thing was, Ghreni Nohama-petan, the acting Duke of End, actually *saw* the surface-to-air missile that slammed into his aircar a second before it hit.

He had been talking to Blaine Turnin, his now-in-retrospect-clearly-not-very-good-at-his-job minister of defense, about the clandestine meeting they were about to have with a rebel faction who had promised to come to the duke's side in the current civil war. As Ghreni had turned to say something to Turnin, his peripheral vision caught a flash of light, drawing his glance toward the thick port glass of the aircar, where the aforementioned surface-to-air missile was suddenly very prominent in the view.

*I think that's a missile,* is what Ghreni intended to say at that point, but he only got as far as saying "I," and really only the very first phoneme of that very short word, before the missile slammed into the aircar and everything, frankly, went completely to shit.

In the fraction of a second that followed, and as the aircar suddenly changed its orientation on several axes, turning the untethered Blaine Turnin into a surprised and fleshy pinball careening around the surfaces of the aircar's passenger cabin, Ghreni Nohamapetan, acting Duke of End, formulated several simultaneous thoughts that did not so much proceed through his brain as appear, fully formed and overlapping, as if Ghreni's higher cognitive functions decided to release all the ballast at once and let Ghreni sort it out later, if there was a later, which, given that Blaine Turnin's neck had just turned a disturbing shade of floppy, seemed increasingly unlikely.

Perhaps it might be easier to describe these thoughts in percentage form, in terms of their presence in Ghreni's theater of attention.

To begin, there was *Shit fuck fuck shit fuck shit fuck the fucking fuck shit fucking shit fuck **hell**,* which was taking up roughly 89 percent of Ghreni's attention, and, as his aircar was beginning to both spin and lose altitude, understandably so.

A distant second to this, at maybe 5 percent, was *How did the rebels know, we didn't set this meeting until an hour ago, even I didn't know I was going to be in this car, and also where the fuck are the antimissile countermeasures I am the chief executive of an entire planet and there's a civil war going on you would think my security people would be a little more on the ball here.* This was honestly a lot to process at the moment, so Ghreni's brain decided to let this one sit unanswered.

Coming in third, at maybe 4.5 percent of Ghreni's cognitive attention, was *I think I need a new minister of defense.* Inasmuch as Blaine Turnin's body was now presenting a shape that could only be described as "deeply pretzeled," this was probably correct and therefore did not warrant any further contemplation.

Which left the fourth thought, which, while claiming only the meager remainder of Ghreni's attention and cognitive power, was nevertheless a thought that Ghreni had thought before, and had thought often — indeed had thought often enough that one could argue that in many ways it *defined* Ghreni Nohamapetan and made him the man he was today, which was, specifically, a man violently captive to forces both gravitational and centrifugal. This thought was:

*Why me?*

And indeed, why Ghreni Nohamapetan? What were the circumstances of fate that led him to this moment of his life, spinning wildly out of control, literally *and* existentially, trying to keep from vomiting on the almost-certain corpse of his now-very-probably-erstwhile minister of defense?

This was a multidimensional question with several relevant answers.

a) He was born;
b) Into a noble family with ambitions to rule the Interdependency, an empire of star systems that had existed for a millennium;
c) And which was connected by the Flow, a phenomenon Ghreni didn't understand but which acted as a super-fast conduit between the star systems of the Interdependency;
d) All of which were taxed and controlled by the emperox, who ruled from Hub, the system through which nearly every Flow stream eventually routed;
e) That was, until a great shift in the Flow happened at some point in the near future, and then nearly every route would go through End, which was currently the least accessible system in the Interdependency;

f) Which is why Ghreni's sister Nadashe wanted a Nohamapetan on End to usurp the ruling duke, but she couldn't do it because she was busy trying to marry Rennered Wu, next in line for the imperial throne, and Ghreni's brother Amit was running the House of Nohamapetan's businesses;

g) So fine, whatever, it had to be Ghreni;

h) Who went to End, and secretly fomented a civil war even as he publicly allied himself with the previous duke;

i) Who he then assassinated, pinning the assassination on the Count Claremont, who Ghreni assumed was just the imperial tax assessor;

j) And became acting duke by promising to end the civil war, which he could totally do because after all he was the one who was funding the rebels;

k) But it turned out the Count Claremont was also a Flow physicist whose research determined that the Flow streams were collapsing, not shifting;

l) Which turned out to be correct when the Flow stream between End and Hub, the only Flow stream out of the End system, collapsed;

m) The count then offered, in the spirit of pragmaticism, to join forces with Ghreni to prepare End for the imminent isolation caused by the collapse of both the Flow and also the Interdependency, which relied on the Flow for its existence;

n) Ghreni didn't take the count up on this offer for, uuuuuhhhhh, *reasons,* and instead disappeared the count;

o) This pissed off Vrenna Claremont, the count's daughter and heir, who rather inconveniently was also a former Imperial Marine officer with lots of allies *and* who knew the details of her father's Flow research;

p) Which she then *told* everyone about;

q) Who were pissed that the new acting duke had kept them in the dark concerning this whole "Flow collapse" thing;

r) And thus this *new* civil war;

s) Against *him;*

t) Which featured *new* rebels;

u) Shooting missiles at his goddamned aircar.

In Ghreni's defense, he had never asked to be born.

But this was cold comfort as Ghreni's aircar slammed into the surface streets of Endfall, End's capital city, rolling several times before coming to a full and complete stop.

Ghreni, whose eyes had been closed during the entire ground crash, opened them to find his aircar upright. Blaine Turnin's body was in the seat opposite him, quiet, composed and restful, looking for all the world like he had not been a human maraca bean for the last half minute. Only Turnin's head, tilted at an angle that suggested the bones in his neck had been replaced by overcooked pasta, suggested that he might not, in fact, be taking a small and entirely refreshing nap.

Ten seconds later the doors of Ghreni's shattered aircar were wrenched open and the members of his security detail — *none of whose aircars were apparently even targeted what the actual hell,* Ghreni's mind screamed at him — unclasped him from his seat belts and roughly dragged him out of the car, hustling him into a second car that would make a direct beeline back to the ducal palace. Ghreni's final view into his ruined vehicle was of Turnin's body slumping to the floor of the cab and making itself into a human area rug.

"Don't you think it's suspicious that none of the other aircars were targeted?" Ghreni said, later, as he paced back and forth in a secured room of his palace that lay far underground, in a subterranean wing de-

13

signed to withstand attacks for weeks and possibly months. "All the aircars were identical. We didn't file a flight plan. No one knew we were going to be in the sky. And yet, *bam,* the missile hit one car, and it was mine. I have to assume that my security detail is compromised. I have to assume there are traitors in my midst."

Jamies, Count Claremont, sighed from his chair, set down the book he was reading, and rubbed his eyes. "You understand my sympathy for your plight is somewhat limited, yes?" he said, to Ghreni.

Ghreni stopped pacing and remembered to whom he was spinning his dark conspiracies. "I just don't know who to trust anymore," he said.

"Probably not me," Jamies suggested.

"But am I *wrong*?" Ghreni pressed. "Doesn't it sound like there's a traitor in my security?"

Jamies looked wistfully at his book for a moment, and Ghreni followed his gaze to the somewhat tattered hardcover with the title of *The Count of Monte Cristo.* Ghreni assumed it was a historical biography and wondered idly what system Monte Cristo was in. Then he looked back at the count.

"No, you're probably not wrong," Jamies said, finally. "You probably do have a trai-

14

tor. At least one. Probably several."

"But *why*?"

"Well, and this is just a hypothesis, it might have something to do with the fact that you're an incompetent who assassinated his way to the dukedom and has lied to his subjects about the imminent collapse of civilization, which, incidentally, you have to date done nothing to prepare for in any meaningful way."

"Nobody but you knows I assassinated the duke," Ghreni said.

"Fine, then that leaves 'an incompetent who lied to his subjects about the imminent collapse of civilization,' and so on."

"Do you really think I'm incompetent?"

The count stared at Ghreni for a moment before proceeding further. "Why do you come to see me, Ghreni?" he asked.

"What do you mean?"

"I mean, why do you come see me? I'm your prisoner and a political liability to you. Your capture and disappearance of me is one of the primary reasons you're fighting this current civil war of yours. If you were smart . . . well, if you were smart you wouldn't have done pretty much *any* of the things you've done. But in the context of me, *now*, if you were smart you would have kept your distance and let me rot in quiet.

Instead you come here and visit me every few days."

"You offered to help me, once," Ghreni reminded him.

"That was before you decided the best course of action was to shove me down a hole," Jamies countered. "Not to mention to continue to frame me for an assassination *you* performed, and to use that assassination to disenfranchise my chosen heir. How is that working out for you, by the way? You think Vrenna has been slowed down any by being stripped of her titles and lands?"

"I don't understand your daughter."

"How so?"

Ghreni motioned toward the Count Claremont. "You're a scientist. You're not . . . *rebel* material."

"I wasn't," the count agreed, "until you made me one. And as for Vrenna, you never met her mother. If you had, you'd understand better. Not that it matters, since, as with me, *you* were the one who made her into a rebel, and a pretty effective one."

"I don't know that I would agree with that."

"Yes, of course, you're correct, an entirely *ineffective* rebel leader managed to infiltrate your security detail, plant at least one traitor, learn your secret travel itinerary and send a missile directly into your aircar and no others. Sorry, I was confused about that." The count reached again toward his book.

"I need someone to talk to," Ghreni said, suddenly.

Jamies looked over toward the (acting) duke. "I beg your pardon?"

"You asked why I keep visiting you," Ghreni said. "I need someone to talk to."

"You have an entire governmental apparatus to talk to," Jamies reminded him.

"Which has traitors in it."

"Let me remind you that I'm not exactly on your side."

"No, but" — Ghreni motioned to the room — "you're not going anywhere."

The count paused again, as if to consider how best to respond to the reminder that he was a prisoner, then picked up his book. "Maybe you should just get a therapist."

"I don't need a therapist."

"I'd get a second opinion on that if I were you."

"I'll take that under advisement."

"At the very least, don't you have *friends*, Ghreni? Even fake ones?"

Ghreni opened his mouth to retort to the fake friends crack and then paused.

Jamies, book open, studied Ghreni carefully. "Come now, my usurping duke," he said. "I used to see you surrounded by an entourage, back in the days when you were the duke's advisor. A whole tranche of schmoozers and flatterers. You could schmooze and flatter with the best of them. Now that you're the duke you should be able to pick and choose your hangers-on."

"I have friends," Ghreni asserted.

"Indeed." The count raised his book. "Then maybe you should bother them."

"You don't want anything from me."

That got a raised eyebrow. "Actually, I want you to resign your dukedom and let me go home."

"That's not what I meant."

"I understand that," Jamies said, dryly. "I'm just pointing out to you that your assessment is inaccurate. But, yes. In terms of your dukedom, there's nothing I want from you."

Ghreni spread open his hands. "Which means I can talk to you."

"I still vote for the therapist."

"You could still help me," Ghreni said. "Help me prepare for what comes next with the Flow."

"You mean, despite the fact that I am your prisoner and you are fighting a civil war

18

against my daughter, who you would kill if the opportunity presented itself."

"She just tried to kill *me.*"

"The fact you are trying to reduce a civil war to 'she started it' does not fill me with confidence," Jamies said. "And besides that, it's too late. The moment I could have helped you was months ago, when I made you the offer despite the fact you had murdered the duke and framed me for it. Dealing with that would not have been comfortable, but it could have been navigated. This civil war is something that neither you nor I can navigate anymore. You've angered too many people who were inclined to be your enemy, and too many of the people who might have been inclined to be your friend. Even if you produced me now, and even if I were inclined to help you, no one would believe after all this time that I was being anything other than coerced. And even if Vrenna believed it and changed sides — which she *wouldn't,* by the way — the others would continue on without her."

"So what do you suggest?"

"I believe I already mentioned you resigning and letting me go."

"Besides that."

"I suggest you work on your escape plan and disguises," Jamies said. "Because I suspect the remainder of your time as duke is going to be short and violent. You already have traitors in your midst. Unless you can make some new friends fast, you're finished." The count returned at last to his book.

"For the last time, Your Grace, the Imperial Marines are not going to get involved in a domestic dispute," Sir Ontain Mount said to Ghreni, after the (acting) duke had summoned the imperial bureaucrat from the space station where he and, incidentally, the Imperial Marines Ghreni wanted were stationed. Mount and Ghreni were taking tea in the (acting) duke's office, which was furnished almost completely as it had been when the previous duke had used it, because Ghreni hadn't bothered to swap out the accoutrements. "I do not need to remind you that current imperial policy dictates that the marines are to be used strictly for defense of interstellar trade, and for initiatives determined on the imperial level. That means the emperox directly."

"There is no interstellar trade," Ghreni said, "and no way to contact the emperox about any initiatives. Your marines are sitting idle."

"The Flow streams coming *into* the system are operational for now, so trade is still incoming, and the emperox may still deliver orders," Mount said, blandly. "And for the latter part, sir, Imperial Marines do not get involved in domestic disputes in order to get a little *exercise.* In any event, when I agreed to your taking the mantle of Duke of End in an acting capacity, it was on the understanding that you were to quell the civil war here on the planet."

"I did!"

"For roughly three weeks," Mount observed. "One might say that wasn't so much an end of a civil war as a breather between campaigns." He sipped at his tea.

Ghreni ground his teeth because he knew Mount was not actually as obtuse as he was pretending to be; the imperial bureaucrat knew full well that the players in the current civil war were entirely different and had different goals. But neither was he interested in getting his precious marines muddy with exertion on Ghreni's behalf. This was Mount's not-exactly-subtle way of saying, *You got yourself into this mess, you get yourself out of it.*

"At least allow me to borrow from your armory, then," Ghreni said. "Inasmuch as the material there is currently *resting.*"

" 'Borrow'?" Mount chuckled a bit, discreetly, into his tea. "My dear duke, one

21

does not *borrow* bullets or missiles. Once they are used, they are spent."

"I'll be happy to purchase what I need."

"What happened to that shipment of weapons you rescued from those pirates all those months ago?" Mount asked. "The shipment that was meant to come to the previous duke but found itself waylaid? My understanding was you had liberated it from the pirates' perfidious possession."

Ghreni indulged in a bit more teeth grinding; he knew Mount knew the answer to this question as well, and was additionally annoyed by the bureaucrat's snide alliteration. "Some of that shipment was destroyed in an attack. Much of the rest was stolen by the current rebels."

"That's unfortunate. That shipment really appears to have been cursed."

"I agree," Ghreni said, and sipped his own tea to avoid an outburst.

"It's possible the missile that knocked you out of the sky was part of that shipment, Your Grace."

"The thought had occurred to me."

"How ironic." Mount set down his tea. "It was unfortunate that your predecessor was not able to finish off his civil war, and that you therefore inherited some of his troubles, and perhaps added some new troubles of your own. But what stood for him stands for you. The Imperial Marines must remain neutral in this dispute. I am sure you will understand."

The door to the (acting) duke's office opened and an assistant came through bearing a tablet, which she presented to Ghreni. "A high-priority message, Your Grace," she said. "Encrypted. Your eyes only. It's meant to be read immediately on receipt."

"Something serious?" Mount asked.

Ghreni looked at the public headers of the message. "Family business," he said, to Mount. "Please excuse me for a moment."

"Of course." Mount reached for his tea.

Ghreni confirmed his biometrics and the message opened, in text, from his sister Nadashe.

Ghreni —

If you're reading this then things have gone poorly on this end. What it is I can't tell you because this was written in advance. But whatever has happened, I've put the backup plan into effect.

Which is: I'm sending you a troop carrier, the *Prophecies of Rachela.* It is fully armed and carries 10,000 Imperial Marines. Its commander and most of his executive team are ours; those who aren't probably won't survive the voyage. It should arrive not long after this message.

If you haven't finished up your little civil war on End, the *Rachela* will help you mop up. It would be helpful if you were the Duke of End by the time the *Rachela* arrives, but if you aren't then you will be by the time the *Rachela* is through.

Then the commander of the *Rachela* will take command of the Imperial Marines there, whether the current command structure helps or not. Then the two of you will take control of the Flow shoals and prepare for our arrival, which will happen one way or another.

You have a lot to do, little brother. Get it done.

And don't fuck it up.

See you soon,
Nadashe

Ghreni grinned at the note and closed it, which deleted the mail and then reformatted the tablet, and then bricked it, because you could never be too careful.

"Good news?"

"Excuse me?" Ghreni said, to Mount, setting the now-inert tablet on the table.

"You were smiling," Mount said. "I was asking if it was good news from home."

"You could say that."

"Well, good," Mount said. "You could do with a spot of good news, if you don't mind me saying so." He took a sip of his tea.

Ghreni imagined Sir Ontain Mount as the dead man he would be when the *Rachela* arrived, and smiled.

And while he did that several thoughts ran through his head, sequentially rather than plopped there, this time. They were:

*Fucking hell, I'm saved;* and

*The* Rachela *better get here pretty damn soon;* and

*How in the world did things go poorly for Nadashe?* And, finally,

*What the hell is going on out there, anyway?*

# BOOK ONE

BOOK ONE

# CHAPTER 1

"Let's be clear about what's going on," Deran Wu said. "It's the end of civilization as we know it. And it's going to be great for business."

On the top floor of the Guild House building, in the great conference room set aside for the use of the governing board of the House of Wu, where Deran Wu stood at the head of the immense table and offered this opening line, the governing board of the House of Wu, to a person, stared at Deran as if he had just ripped an enormous fart directly into their faces.

*Come on,* Deran thought, *that was a great line.*

Deran gave no outward indication that he was displeased his line fell flat. There was no need to. For the first time in his career with the House of Wu, Deran was not particularly concerned with what the members of the governing board of the house —

29

each of them one of his cousins to varying degrees of separation — thought about him, or his plans, or his snappy lines. This was because Deran was now managing director of the House of Wu.

And not just managing director. That role had been previously contingent on the sufferance of the board of directors, whose opinion about *anything,* from the competence of the managing director down to what should be served for lunch, could be most charitably described as fractious. Deran Wu's managing directorship, on the other hand, was immune from board disapproval, because Jasin Wu, the previous managing director, had attempted a coup on the emperox. The emperox, quite reasonably, believed this cast suspicion on the entire governing board of the house.

At least, this was the excuse.

More accurately, Deran Wu made board noninterference in his managing directorship a condition of handing over every bit of information he had on said coup, which he had been an active participant in, up to and including the assassination of one of the managing directors of one of the other great merchant houses and the attempted murder of one of the emperox's closest friends and rumored lover. The emperox, pressed for time and preferring the devil she knew, gave her assent.

And here we were, at the first full House of Wu board meeting since the recent unpleasantness, with Deran, previously not necessarily in line for the managing directorship, ever, now running things, whether the board liked it or not.

Standing there, it occurred to Deran that they probably didn't like it at all. Which might explain why the line went over so poorly.

"Why are we here?" came a question, from far down the very long table at which the directors, the cousins of Wu, sat.

"Pardon?" Deran said, looking down the table to see which cousin it was.

It was Tiegan Wu, who ran the small arms division of the House of Wu armaments concern. "I said, 'Why are we here?' " she repeated. "You are now the dictator of the House of Wu. This is the governing board. *Former* governing board, I should say. Now it's powerless. What was the purpose of calling us here?"

"Besides to gloat," said Nichson Wu, who ran the automated security concepts division, i.e., robots with guns.

"Yes, the gloating part had occurred to me," Tiegan said, staring at Deran.

"My cousins," Deran said, gesturing in a way that he hoped conveyed reassurance. "I remind you that these are extraordinary times. Jasin, our former managing director, tried to overthrow the emperox. She was not convinced that the governing board was not complicit in the coup attempt. She does not know you as I know you."

"Does she know you're completely full of shit?" asked Belment Wu, who ran warship construction. Belment had never been Deran's biggest fan.

"She knows I, at least, can be trusted," Deran replied. This got a snort from Belment.

Proster Wu, to the immediate right of Deran, cleared his throat. Proster was arguably the most powerful person in the room because, among other things, he oversaw the entire security division. Which meant, quite literally, that he had the most guns. Traditionally, the Wus who headed up the security division never stood for the general directorship. They didn't have to. They were the powers behind the throne, as it were. When Proster cleared his throat, everyone, including Deran, shut up and looked at him.

"Deran," Proster said, "let's not waste each other's time, shall we? You're managing director because you betrayed Jasin and

32

blackmailed the emperox into giving you the job. She also let you cut all of *us*" — Proster nodded to the board — "out of the decision-making for the House of Wu. Well played. But don't pretend that *we* don't know that, or that we don't know you were just as complicit as Jasin in that stupid attempted coup. Don't insult our intelligence. Fair enough?"

"Fair enough," Deran said, after a moment.

Proster nodded and turned to face the rest of the table. "As for why we're here, it's simple." He pointed at Deran. "Our new managing director is not entirely stupid. He knows that even if the emperox has given him complete control of the House of Wu, that 'control' is an illusion. He doesn't have a power base in this room. He doesn't have enough allies outside of it. And as he correctly notes" — Proster swiveled back to Deran — "the end of human civilization is coming. He doesn't have *time* to wait us out. Not if he wants to implement the plans he so clearly has and needs our cooperation to realize. Accurate?"

*Not quite,* Deran thought. He was not nearly as unprepared as Proster thought. Deran had quite a little list of people, mostly other Wu cousins, who would be delighted

33

to cut throats if it meant they were put in charge of an actual division at the House of Wu. Hell, *Proster's* head was first on the chopping block if it came to that. There wasn't a Wu cousin in this room who wouldn't strangle their own grandmother — and *several other* grandmothers, why be stingy — in order to run security, especially now that the managing directorship was locked up for the near future.

Proster had been in his directorship too long; he'd forgotten how hungry an ambitious cousin could be. He should have remembered this. He'd railroaded Finnu Wu, the previous security director, right out of her chair, and well done that had been, too. Finnu ended up retiring to another system entirely, so as not to be reminded, on a daily basis, of her ignominious unseating. Deran knew more about Proster's own set of vices and missteps than probably anyone else, Proster included, and would be happy to share that information with whatever Wu cousin would step up.

So, no, Deran was not *quite* as without a power base or allies as Proster was attempting to posit. More accurately, Deran was confident he could acquire both, in time.

But time wasn't on his side. Proster was right about that.

34

Time wasn't on anyone's side, anymore.

So Deran nodded at Proster and said, "Accurate."

"We all understand each other," Proster said. "Good. Then tell us, Deran, how the end of civilization is somehow going to be good for the House of Wu."

"It's simple, really," Deran said. "The House of Wu has monopolies on shipbuilding and armaments and security. What are the things that are going to be needed as the Flow streams continue to collapse?"

"Food," Tiegan Wu said.

"Water," said Nichson.

"Medical supplies," added Belment.

Deran waved these away impatiently. "You're missing the point."

"People starving is not the point?" asked Tiegan.

Deran pointed. "Close. People starving is not the point. People who are *afraid* of starving is. Over the next few years the Flow streams are going to collapse. People are going to be scared. This empire is called 'the Interdependency' after all. Every human habitation is by design dependent on others. This was fine when the Flow was stable. As it becomes less stable, so do the political and social systems of the Interdependency. Those systems are going to need

35

to be propped up."

"By security forces and arms," Proster said.

"That's right."

"Until the security forces get scared too, because their food is running out like everyone else's," Tiegan said.

"Well, actually, we have that covered," said Nichson, i.e., the "robots with guns" cousin.

"The point is, unrest is coming," Deran said. "Heightened unrest. Sustained unrest."

"And we want to make money off the chaos," Tiegan said.

"We want to offer the ability to hold off chaos as long as possible," Deran replied. "The unrest will happen. It's already happening. It's inevitable. But 'inevitable' doesn't have to mean *immediate.* We can buy time for system governments. Or more accurately, they can buy that time from us. Because, yes, we want to make money off of that."

"For as long as the money is good," said Lina Wu-Gertz, near the far end of the table. Lina ran the resale division, which sold used spaceships or the ships that were built but never used because the intended owner never took delivery. "When civilization ends, money's not going to be any use."

"Civilization isn't going to end," Deran said.

"Did I miss something?" Belment said. "Did you not just stand there and say civilization is ending?"

"I said, 'civilization as we know it.' " Deran reached down to the table, picked up a remote, and pressed a button on it. The wall behind him came to life, showing a green and blue planet.

"That's End," Proster observed.

"That's civilization," Deran corrected.

Proster chuckled at this. "You haven't been to End, then."

"End is where our civilization is going to survive," Deran said. "It's the one system in the Interdependency that has a planet that's capable of sustaining human life on its own. And from what the emperox's scientists tell us, it's the last place that will have a Flow stream going into it from Hub. Civilization will continue there." He looked down the table to Lina Wu-Gertz. "Along with its money."

"Civilization will survive there," Proster said. "As long as it can *get* there."

Deran smiled at this. "Rumor is, we build starships."

"Not *that* many starships," Belment said. "We need to save civilization. Not every single person in it. Although I'm sure every-one in this room, and all the people they care about, will find their way to End, sooner or later." This comment gave every-one a momentary pause.

"So your plan is spaceships for some, and riot control for the rest," Tiegan said, after the moment had passed.

"I'm not the one who is making the Flow collapse," Deran replied. "I'm just aware of what comes because of it. And no, the *plan* is not about the spaceships and the riot control. The plan, and what I need this board to support me on, is to start *building* the spaceships and riot control *now,* on a massive scale, before the orders come in."

"That's presuming the orders come in," Proster said.

"They're coming," Deran assured him. "And *we* don't have to wait for govern-ments and the rest of the merchant houses to realize the end is near. We have a sales force. They will *remind* them. I want to build the ships and arms *now,* so that our salespeople can say to our clients that we have the stock ready to go. No delay be-tween order and delivery except shipping. These days that will make the difference between a sale, or not."

"Offer them easy terms on the sale and

they'll take it," Belment said.

Deran shook his head. "No. Cash on the barrelhead from now on. For everything."

"That's crazy," Belment said.

"It's not crazy. It's the end of civilization as we know it; we don't have *time* to collect on installment plans."

"That's showing our hand," Proster observed.

"The *point* is to show our hand," Deran said. "If they think *we* don't think there's time for installment plans, they're going to prioritize the short term, too. They have the money; they just have to decide they need to give it to us, first." He looked over to Lina Wu-Gertz. "And if they think civilization is ending and money is going to be worthless anyway, they're not going to mind as much giving it away. They'll think they're getting one over on us."

Proster nodded. "So we build ships and arms now —"

"While it's still cheap and easy, because as more Flow streams collapse, it will be more expensive to get materiel, and harder to source as well," Deran interjected.

"— and take as much as we can get up front, and then as the Flow streams collapse, move our base of operations to End, where the money will still have value and the remainder of civilization will still need arms and spaceships."

"That's the plan," Deran said. "Basically. Broad strokes."

Proster nodded, and then looked down the table, where there were other nods, even from Belment and Tiegan. Then he looked back at Deran.

"Looks like you're right: the end of civilization is going to be good for business," he said.

"Yes," Deran said. "I think so."

"That was a good line, by the way."

Deran beamed. "Thank you, Proster."

The door to the conference room opened, and Deran's assistant Witka popped her head in to announce lunch; the rolling tables came in, stacked with food and drinks. The board got up and served themselves, talking to one another as they did so. Deran's assistant came over to him with a cup of his favorite variety of hot tea, which she kept for him in a stash at her desk.

"How did it go?" Witka asked, handing him the cup.

"I think I may have just pulled it off," Deran said, and took a sip. "They seemed to understand what I wanted to do with the plan."

"Well, it's a good plan."

40

"I thought so," Deran admitted.

"I'll get you something to eat." Witka wandered over to the tables of food.

Deran took another sip of tea and basked in his accomplishments for the day. He didn't need the board to do all the things he had outlined to them — indeed he had already started the process of moving much of the house's financial holdings to End — but having their agreement made things better. Easier. Simpler. He wouldn't have to fight them as much, and he wouldn't have to replace as many of them in their jobs as he'd suspected he would have to. Not yet, at least. He did have a little bit of time. Or at least he did now.

*Yes, this is all coming together nicely,* Deran thought, took another sip of his tea, and collapsed dead, teacup tumbling beside him.

Witka, turning back to him with a plate of food, screamed, dropped the plate to the floor and ran to Deran's body. The rest of the board stood there, silently staring at the spectacle. After a minute Witka fled from the room, calling for medical help.

The board members continued staring at Deran's body.

"Well, *I* didn't do that," Belment said, eventually.

"Did anyone else?" Proster asked.

41

There was a general murmur of denial.

"Huh," Proster said, and took a bite of his bread roll.

"So, are we still going through with his plan?" Tiegan asked.

Medics burst into the room before anyone could answer.

# CHAPTER 2

At the same time Deran Wu was dropping dead on the highest floor of the Guild House, several stories down, Kiva Lagos was fighting the temptation to throw someone through one of its windows.

"The *fuck* did you just say?" Kiva said to the man sitting on the other side of the desk from her.

The man, Bagin Heuvel, senior trade negotiator for the House of Wolfe, didn't blink. "You heard me perfectly well, Lady Kiva. The House of Wolfe intends to renegotiate our contracts with the House of Nohamapetan, of which you are the administrator. We would prefer those negotiations be handled positively and in the spirit of cooperation and mutual benefit. But if that's not possible, and by your response I can see that it might not be, then we'll be more than happy to file a suit in the Guild Court to seek relief."

43

"On what grounds, exactly?"

"On the grounds that civilization is collapsing, Lady Kiva."

Kiva glanced over at Senia Fundapellonan, who was a lawyer for the House of Nohamapetan — well, had been one, until the Countess Nohamapetan accidentally had her shot while trying to assassinate Kiva, at which point Senia had switched sides and come to work for Kiva, who was now in charge of the House of Nohamapetan because the countess was in jail on a count of treason. Kiva had put Fundapellonan in charge of the House of Nohamapetan's legal department, and also Kiva and Fundapellonan were totally doing it and doing it *well* — really, it was *all* kind of sudden and complicated — and Fundapellonan read her glance perfectly. "The contracts between our houses have no clause for any alleged collapse of civilization, Mr. Heuvel," she said.

"They do, however, have clauses regarding force majeure," Heuvel said.

"Force fucking majeure?" Kiva exclaimed.

"I didn't put the word 'fucking' in there, but otherwise, yes."

"Force majeure is for when an unspotted space rock suddenly destroys a whole fucking habitat," Kiva said.

"That is one example," Heuvel agreed. "We argue the collapse of civilization is another."

"The key word is 'suddenly.' "

"Actually, the keywords are 'collapse of civilization.' "

"Lady Kiva is correct," Fundapellonan interjected. "Force majeure is about unforeseen and unexpected events."

"Yes, like the collapse of our entire civilization," Heuvel said.

"Fucking years from now," Kiva said.

"During a time span in which significant elements of the contracts between our houses will not be able to be executed, exposing the House of Wolfe to significant civil and financial liability," Heuvel said, raising a finger for emphasis. "If the current best estimates for the condition of the Flow streams within the Interdependency are correct, then the House of Wolfe will, through no fault of its own and entirely contingent upon forces that are not within its control, begin to default on its contractual obligations in ways that expose it to unacceptable levels of risk."

"Which is your problem."

Heuvel nodded. "I agree it is a problem. I don't agree that it is only *our* problem. And the House of Wolfe is willing to go to court

45

to make that argument."

"The Guild Court is not exactly known for its receptiveness to novel interpretation of contractual law," Fundapellonan pointed out. "There's several hundred years of case law that strongly suggests that if you file this suit, what will happen is that you're laughed out of court and your client will end up paying our legal fees plus a significant penalty."

"That's one possibility," Heuvel said. "The other possibility is that the Guild Court will recognize that several hundred years of case law means nothing when the Interdependency is confronting an existential threat to its existence that literally has no parallel in all of recorded history."

"You're expecting a lot from the Guild Court."

Heuvel shrugged. "They are trapped by this collapse just as much as any of the rest of us. We're off the map entirely." He turned his attention back to Kiva. "But as I said at the outset, we don't actually want to have to go to court at all. We're ready to renegotiate in good will, to the benefit of both of our houses."

"That's not what you said." Kiva stared back stonily at Heuvel. "What you said was, the House of Wolfe intends to renegotiate these contracts, or go to court."

"Yes," Heuvel said. "So?"

"So, you came here to tell me what was going to happen, not to ask for my help to make it happen."

"Obviously we will need your help to make it happen —"

It was Kiva's turn to hold up a finger. "But you weren't *asking* for it. You were telling me what was going to happen, and expecting me to go along with it like it was already a done deal."

"I'm not sure why that matters."

"It matters because you've fucking pissed me off," Kiva said. "I don't like when people come into my office and tell me how I'm going to do things, as if I don't have a say in the matter, and preemptively threaten to drag me into court to try to coerce my compliance."

"Lady Kiva, if I came across in such a manner, I apologize, it was unintentional —"

"And now you've just fucking pissed me off *twice,* because you're pretending like you did this shit accidentally. You're a grown adult and the senior trade negotiator for an entire fucking house. And yes, the House of Wolfe is a truly minor fucking house —"

"Hey —"

47

"But even a minor fucking house has the resources to hire someone competent. So either you've managed to hide your absolute fucking incompetence from the House of Wolfe long enough to shit yourself upward into your current position, or you knew what you were doing the moment you sat down in that fucking chair and decided to insult my intelligence. So which is it?"

Heuvel blinked, and then asked, "Why do you care?"

"About your competence? I don't, but I'm sure your boss might."

"No, I mean why do you care about *this*? This contract."

"What do you mean?"

"The Countess Nohamapetan tried to murder you, Lady Kiva," Heuvel said. Fundapellonan shifted uneasily in her chair at this; she had been the one hit by the bullet intended for Kiva, and it was only in the last week that she'd been cleared to go back to work. Her shoulder was still fucked up and in the slow process of healing. "The House of Nohamapetan is a house of traitors. Its head is in prison and its heirs are missing or dead. You're in charge because it was assigned to you by the emperox. You have no allegiance to this house, my lady. *So what* if this contract is renegotiated? The

48

worst-case scenario is that the House of No-hamapetan makes a slightly less immensely large pile of money than it did before. This traitor house. I don't understand what the problem is here."

Kiva nodded at this and stood up, and came around the desk to Heuvel. Heuvel glanced over to Fundapellonan uncertainly; Fundapellonan shook her head ever so slightly, as if to say *Too late to escape now.* Kiva bent over to put herself eye to eye with Heuvel.

"Well, since you asked," she said, "I care because the emperox told me to care. I care because aside from the fucking Nohama-petans, this house employs hundreds of thousands of people who now have to rely on me to look out for their best interest. I care because although *you* will never know this, running a whole fucking house is an immense responsibility, and maybe, I don't know, I would like to be seen as *good* at my fucking job. I care because despite the name on the door, this is *my* fucking house now. I care because when you come into my house, into my office, and tell me what is *going* to happen, you insult me and you insult my house. And since I can tell you're not the sort to show any actual goddamned initia-tive on your own part, you fucking cognitive mudfart, I care that your shitty little house is insulting me and my house — both of my houses, since I am still of House fucking Lagos. I care *because I fucking care.* And you and your shitty little house have picked the absolute wrong fucking individual to try to push around. Is this clear enough for you now, Mr. Heuvel? Or should I use smaller fucking words for you?"

"No, I get it," Heuvel said.

"Good." Kiva straightened up and leaned up against her desk. "Then here's what you're going to do. You're going to go back to your bosses and tell them that the House of Nohamapetan thanks them for the offer, and our counteroffer is that the House of Wolfe goes and fucks itself sideways, because we're not agreeing to change a single fucking comma in our current contracts. If the House of Wolfe wants to file a suit with the Guild Courts, they can go right ahead, because the House of Nohamapetan will tie that shit up, not only until the collapse of the Flow, but until the actual heat death of the observable fucking universe." Kiva turned to Fundapellonan. "We have the resources for that, right?"

"Oh, yes," said Fundapellonan.

Kiva turned back to Heuvel. "So if you want your great-great-great-grandchildren

50

working on this as the oxygen leaks out of their habitat, go to court with this force majeure crap. We'll be there, watching them turn blue. Until then, get the fuck out of my office."

"I enjoy watching you work," Fundapellonan said, after Heuvel got the fuck out of Kiva's office.

"This isn't the last time we'll see this," Kiva said.

"The force majeure strategy? Probably not." Fundapellonan gestured toward the direction that Heuvel had fucked off. "The House of Wolfe isn't known for innovative legal strategies. I don't think they thought it up on their own. If they didn't, you can bet that someone else has already filed a case with the Guild Court. I can have someone follow up on it."

"Do that."

"Okay." Fundapellonan made a note. "Of course, this *does* raise the question of why you care."

Kiva squinted at Fundapellonan. "Not you, too."

Fundapellonan smiled at this. "I know why you cared when it involved you and this house," she said. "You caring when it doesn't involve you is notable."

"That doesn't sound great."

51

"You're supremely self-interested. That's not bad or good; it just is. So if you're interested in this, you're thinking about how it's a pain in the ass for you."

"It's a pain in the ass for me because that odious shitbug isn't wrong," Kiva said. "The collapse of the Flow is coming. If the Guild Court decides that the collapse of civilization means contracts are null, that's chaos."

"You suddenly don't like chaos."

"I don't like it when it's not working for me."

"See, this is what I mean by self-interested."

"In this case it wouldn't be working for *anyone,*" Kiva said. "If the Guild Court lets one of these suits get by, it'll kick the legs out from our entire economic system."

"Not like, say, the collapse of the Flow."

"The end is coming," Kiva said. "I'm not sure why we want it come *faster.*" She pointed in the direction Heuvel had left. "People will fucking starve because of him or someone like him."

"To be fair to poor Mr. Heuvel, he was only following orders, and he was fulfilling his fiduciary duty," Fundapellonan said. "If you told me to go to some other house with the same foolish plan, I'd be obliged to do it."

"I hope you'd punch me in the face first."

"My shoulder is still messed up. I'd have to kick you in the ass instead."

"You'd still do it."

"At this point I don't think I'd have to. You're self-interested, but it seems your self-interest has expanded somewhat. At least temporarily."

"Don't get used to it."

"I won't." Fundapellonan got up out of her chair, using her uninjured arm to steady herself as she did so. "In the meantime I'll head back to legal to get a team together to respond just in case the House of Wolfe hasn't had the fear of Kiva Lagos sufficiently instilled into it. What about you?"

Kiva looked at her desk clock. "I have to catch a shuttle to Xi'an in half an hour. Fucking executive committee meeting."

Fundapellonan smiled. "You can't fool me; you love being on that."

Kiva grunted at that. The executive committee consisted of three ministers of parliament, three members of the Church of the Interdependency and three members of the guild houses. Kiva had been drafted to it after a coup attempt against the emperox ensnarled roughly a third of the houses. The emperox decided she needed a safe vote on the committee, and Kiva was it. Kiva was aware of the irony of her, of all people, being a safe vote.

"You should bring up your concerns about this force majeure nonsense at the meeting," Fundapellonan said. "Either Grayland or the parliament can cut it off at the pass."

"The Guild Court wouldn't like that," Kiva said. The Guild Court was notoriously prickly about its perceived independence.

"No they wouldn't," Fundapellonan agreed. "But that's not your problem." She left, and Kiva watched her go, in part because she was enjoying the view and in part because she was still thinking about the showdown they'd just had with fucking Heuvel.

Senia Fundapellonan was not wrong about Kiva; Kiva was *extremely* self-interested. Senia thought that was neither good nor bad, but Kiva was of a different mind about that. She thought it was pretty much the only way to be in a universe that didn't care about anyone's life one way or another, and in a civilization that was designed to keep the rich as rich as possible and the poor from actively starving so they wouldn't think to rise up and behead the rich. An uncaring universe and a fundamentally static civilization would smother anyone who didn't keep themselves and their

54

own concerns front and center.

Kiva wasn't wrong about this, at least as it applied to her. Her policy of "fuck you, what's in it for *me*" had taken her in the space of a couple of years from being the mostly superfluous sixth child of an only moderately influential noblewoman to being the de facto head of one of the most powerful houses in the Interdependency, as well as having a seat on the executive committee and the favor of the emperox. Admittedly Kiva's philosophy of pragmatic, committed selfishness wouldn't work as well for just about anyone else as it had for her, but fuck them, they weren't Kiva. Which, again, was right to the point.

For all that, the higher Kiva ascended the steps of power, the more she realized that her policy of selfishness had, shall we say, certain limits. Perhaps in a different era, when in fact civilization was not just a few short years from falling down a deep, dark fucking hole, she could have contentedly continued on a path of self-regard, secure in the knowledge that ultimately it wouldn't matter what she did anyway. She was just a speck of animated carbon that would be eternally inanimate soon enough, so might as well go ahead and have another muffin, or lay that cute redhead, or whatever. The universe was not intentionally designed to absorb Kiva's selfishness, but it certainly wasn't *hurt* by it in any noticeable way.

But Kiva was aware that *her* time now was not *that* time. *Her* time was human civilization fucking imploding, taking the individual humans with it — including her. The time span she was likely to be around (barring assassination, unintentional overdoses and falls down flights of stairs) now exceeded that of the civilization she lived in. Which meant that some portion of her life — possibly decades — would become *exceedingly fucking uncomfortable* unless things were done by people in positions of power to avoid that.

The thing was, it was turning out that people in positions in power were, well, *extremely* self-interested. Just like Kiva was.

Which, again, would be *fine,* if human civilization was not coming to an actual fucking end.

But it actually fucking was.

So it was a problem.

And it was how you got things like Bagin fucking shittoad Heuvel and his similarly feculent amphibian bosses, happy to throw the economic underpinnings of society under a bus in order to save a few marks that wouldn't matter anyway when civilization collapsed and their plump, soggy asses started looking tasty to the starving crowds. Bagin fucking shittoad Heuvel and his bosses weren't thinking about anything other than what was in it for them in the very short term.

Kiva couldn't say that she was fundamentally any different — or hadn't been until possibly right around the time Heuvel opened his smarmy little mouth — but she did realize that at the moment, the number of fundamentally selfish and self-interested people that human civilization could tolerate, particularly in the social tranche that could actually have an impact on the fate of humanity, had shrunk considerably. Kiva had been struck by a realization that, if not exactly an epiphany, was certainly enough to make her stop in her tracks:

Either she was going to have to become less fundamentally selfish, or she was going to have to find a way to make others less so.

Obviously, *she* didn't want to become less selfish. To reiterate, being fundamentally selfish had worked out great for her, and she saw no reason to change things up. To be completely honest about it, what she really wanted to do at this very moment was take Senia home and fuck her brains out, because if Kiva was going to try out this whole monogamy thing for a change, and she was, then she wanted to get full value out of it. And while, yes, Senia was likely to get some benefit out of that (and, well, *had,* if her testimonials were to be believed), that's not why Kiva was doing it. She was doing it for herself. Doing things (and Senia) for herself was working out great for everyone.

Therefore, it had to be *others* who were going to have to make a change.

Which was going to be a challenge. It's not like anyone else who was fundamentally selfish wanted to change what they were doing, either.

More relevantly, Kiva recognized something else: Things had reached a certain tipping point for selfish and self-interested human beings. As far as Kiva could tell, whenever selfish humans encountered a wrenching, life-altering crisis, they embarked on a journey of five distinct stages:

1. Denial.
2. Denial.
3. Denial.
4. *Fucking Denial.*
5. Oh shit everything is terrible grab what you can and run.

Bagin Heuvel's appearance in her office, and his strategy of attack, suggested that phase five was well and truly underway.

This would make things more difficult for Kiva, as people committed to grabbing as much as they could before everything went to shit were resistant to a sudden shift to altruism.

Which was fine. Kiva liked a challenge.

The door to Kiva's office opened and Bunton Salaanadon, her executive assistant, came through. "Lady Kiva," he said.

"Time to head to the shuttle," Kiva said to him.

"No," Salaanadon said, and then held up a hand to correct himself. "Yes. But that's not why I came in."

"Then why did you?"

"News from the House of Wu."

"What is it?" The emperox was a member of the House of Wu even if she didn't involve herself in its day-to-day affairs. It was possible this had something to do with her. "Is this about the emperox?"

Salaanadon shook his head. "It's Deran Wu."

"Oh, *that* piece of shit." Speaking of the self-interested, Deran Wu was a real piece of work on that score. "What about him?"

"He's dead."

"Dead?"

"Murdered."

"That wasn't me."

"I . . . was not aware that anyone would suspect you, Lady Kiva."

"Do we know who did it?"

"Not yet."

"Well, does the emperox know? About *any* of this?"

# CHAPTER 3

Cardenia Wu-Patrick woke up a half hour before her alarm was set because her lover, Marce, was a snorer. Normally Cardenia was able to filter it out, background white noise that the brain knew to discount and disregard. But for the last couple of days Marce had been fighting a cold, which made his snoring both louder and more random. When it woke Cardenia up, Marce sounded like he was two cavemen having a very urgent conversation with each other about discovering fire, or hunting a feral hog, or something else along that line.

Cardenia didn't mind. She found it endearing. She and Marce were still early enough in their relationship that their faults were still endearing rather than annoying to each other; or, at least, Cardenia still found Marce's faults endearing, and Marce was either too gallant or too circumspect to say anything about hers. Cardenia idly won-

61

dered if they would ever get to the point where faults *weren't* endearing, and rather than amusedly tolerating his snoring, she would seek to smother him with a pillow. She had never been in a relationship that lasted that long. She imagined that even as she was smothering her beloved she would be delighted that they had managed to get to that point.

In the meantime, she lay there, arm draped across Marce's chest, as the conversation between the two cavemen that he was snoring out came to a conclusion and the participants decamped, perhaps in search of a mastodon. Marce quieted down to his usual low level of snore. Cardenia lightly ran her fingers across his chest, not so lightly as to tickle him but not heavily enough to wake him, and not for the first time marveled that the two of them had gotten together. It was unlikely for several reasons. And yet, here they were.

She stayed there for a few minutes more, resting in that liminal area between dozing and full wakefulness, enjoying the warmth of Marce radiating into her. Then five minutes before she knew her alarm would wake them both, she sighed, grumbled slightly, and slid herself out of bed, careful not to wake her lover. The slippers and robe were where she had placed them the evening before; she put herself into each, and then whispered at the clock to dismiss the alarm. She needed to go to work, but there was no reason Marce couldn't sleep in. Maybe the cavemen would come back for a further conference.

Cardenia showered, toweled, brushed her hair into submission, and then in her dressing room put on undergarments and a dressing gown. At this point, she had two options: One, walk through a door to her immediate left, behind which waited her wardrobe, hair and makeup crew, along with Nera Chernin, her morning staffer, who would go over her day's itinerary, which would go from the instant she stepped out of makeup to some as-yet-indeterminate point roughly twelve to fifteen hours in the future, and possibly later than that.

Two, walk through another door entirely and have a conversation with those who lay beyond it. Going through this second door would not allow her to avoid dealing with Chernin and all the rest of her minions; it would just delay the inevitable by however long it was she chose to stay.

And either way, it would not change the fact that, through the mere act of stepping through a doorway, she would stop being

63

Cardenia Wu-Patrick, and become Grayland II, Emperox of the Holy Empire of the Interdependent States and Mercantile Guilds, Queen of Hub and Associated Nations, Head of the Interdependent Church, Successor to Earth and Mother to All, Eighty-Eighth Emperox of the House of Wu.

Cardenia looked at both doors, sighed, and walked to the second one, which opened for her without prompting. Grayland II stepped through.

The room into which Grayland had entered was large, and sparse to the point of being almost featureless; only a long bench, molded straight out of the wall, offered a break in the room's clean and almost antiseptic lines. It was, perhaps, a room not meant to be loitered in. Nevertheless, Grayland sat herself on the bench, made herself as comfortable as it allowed, and called for the room's primary occupant.

"Jiyi," Grayland said.

Hidden projectors flicked on, and in the middle of the room a sexless, genderless humanoid being was called into existence. It looked to Grayland, walked over to her sitting form, and nodded.

"Emperox Grayland II," Jiyi said, as it always did. "How may I assist you?"

Grayland considered the form standing

before her. This room was called the Memory Room. The thoughts and emotional states of every single previous emperox were in it — down to the very first, the Prophet-Emperox Rachela I — recorded by a neural network that each emperox, including Grayland, had embedded in their brains. Jiyi was the interface each living emperox used to access their predecessors; all one had to do was ask to see one, and Jiyi would bring them out, one at a time or together, as many as the living emperox wished to speak to.

All the previous emperoxs save one thought that had been all there was to Jiyi — an interface to other emperoxs, with some basic AI for other general information retrieval. But Grayland had recently learned that Rachela I, the first emperox, had built Jiyi with another function entirely: to seek out and find hidden information throughout the Interdependency.

In this task, Jiyi was neither fast nor efficient — some hidden information could take years or even decades to come to Jiyi's databases — but what Jiyi lacked in speed and guile, it made up for in relentlessness. Sooner or later, everything hidden was revealed to Jiyi.

And now, because she knew, to Grayland as well.

"Deran Wu has been dead for twelve hours now," Grayland said to Jiyi. "Do you know who did it yet?"

"I do not," Jiyi said.

"Have you discovered anything that might suggest a specific culprit?"

"After his murder became public there was a surge of communications from high-ranking members of important noble and mercantile houses," Jiyi said. "These communications were all encrypted, as is standard with nearly all their communication. It will take me some time to access them either through decryption or other means."

"Define what 'some time' means here."

"If I need to use brute force decryption, it can take decades. This is usually not necessary because there are other routes to get the information, such as accessing security cameras that show the screens with the information."

"You read over their shoulder," Grayland mused.

"Yes," Jiyi said. "At the moment, none of the secure messages I've seen indicate certain knowledge of events, save for the communications from eyewitnesses themselves."

"And none of them have written anything

about sending final payments on a contract."

"No."

Grayland scrunched up her face. "Because that would make my life easier, you know, if you found all that *today.*"

"I understand," Jiyi said, and Grayland wondered, not for the first time, if Jiyi really did. Jiyi was, by design, as aggressively blank as the Memory Room.

"Is there any new information that you have that I should be aware of?"

"About Deran Wu's assassination or in a more general sense?"

"About both."

"No other information about Deran Wu. More generally, several of the noble houses have secretly begun to transfer some of their wealth to End, and are planning to have key and critical members of each house follow."

Grayland II nodded at this. She didn't need a secret-sniffing millennium-old artificial intelligence to tell her that it had finally sunk into the heads of the noble families and the mercantile guilds they controlled that the Flow was actually collapsing, and that maybe they would want to preserve at least some of their wealth and send it to the one place in the Interdependency that, in theory, had the capability to survive beyond a few decades at best. She had enough legitimate security and financial reports to signal that. They would take up at least some of her day today, and she suspected progressively more of her days to come.

*Worry about that later,* she thought. She was in the Memory Room for the death of Deran Wu, and what the implications of that were. Jiyi, for all its usefulness, was not the person she needed to speak to about that. She needed someone who had actual lived experience dealing with the Interdependency, and the noble houses, and specifically, the House of Wu. She asked Jiyi for one person in particular.

"Dead from his *tea,*" said the Emperox Attavio VI, or more accurately, the exquisitely rendered simulation of him. In addition to being the former emperox, Attavio VI also happened to be Grayland's father.

Grayland nodded, and then grimaced. "Well. We don't know if it was Deran's tea. The teacup itself might have been poisoned. Or there might have been components in both the tea and the cup that would become a poison when mixed together. The investigators are still looking into it."

"But it was definitely poison," said Attavio VI.

"Oh, yes."

"There was no effort to disguise the poisoning, as a heart attack or a stroke, for example."

"No."

"There are no obvious suspects."

"Deran's personal assistant Witka Chinlun served him the tea and was questioned about it. They're keeping her in custody, but as I understand it no one considers it likely that she knew about the poison. She's apparently in shock, and is cooperating fully."

"You feel bad for her?"

"She poisoned her boss unintentionally, Dad. That's a lot."

"Yes it is," Attavio VI agreed. "You're telling me all of this for a reason. What is it?"

"I wanted to know what you thought about it."

"I don't think anything about it. I don't actually think."

Grayland bit her cheek for a minute, holding back a thought, as it related to Attavio VI, Jiyi and all the other emperoxs. And then, remembering that the Attavio VI in front of her was indeed a simulation, she said it anyway. "I don't think that's true."

"That I don't actually think?"

"Yes. We've been doing this too long and I've had too many conversations with you

69

where you ask questions and offer advice. You couldn't do that if you didn't think."

"That's not accurate," Attavio VI said. "At least in the way you think about thinking. This simulation is very good at heuristic approximation. I can offer supposition informed by my life experience and based on the stored model of how I thought when I was alive."

*That's pretty much what thinking is,* Grayland said to herself, but stopped herself from voicing the thought. She was aware that once again she was getting pulled into the teleological weeds about the fact she could have a conversation with her dead father, or a facsimile thereof, and that this was not going to help her with her current set of issues.

Grayland sighed. *Our civilization is collapsing and yet Deran Wu still got poisoned,* she thought. If nothing else, it marked a commitment to nefariousness that Grayland could almost respect if it hadn't also made her life more complicated.

Attavio VI, or the facsimile thereof, stood patiently while his daughter ran all of this through her head. He would stand patiently for years, if necessary. The reanimated dead were nothing if not patient.

"Let me rephrase," Grayland said to the

apparition of her father. "What *would* you have thought about it, when you *could* have thought about it?"

"Deran's death is meant to send a message," Attavio VI replied.

"How do you mean?"

"Your cousin was openly assassinated. Poisoned with his favorite tea. There was no attempt to hide the fact that he'd been poisoned, which would have been relatively easy to do. Whoever killed him wanted it known that he had been killed."

"Terrorism," Grayland suggested.

"Possibly," Attavio VI agreed. "Or it could be something else. Has any organization claimed the death?"

"The usual groups who claim anything awful that happens," Grayland said. "My security people say none of them had anything to do with it."

"So, no serious claims for the assassination."

"No."

"Then it's possible that it's not terrorism," Attavio VI said. "Or if it is, that its goal is a long-term one, not one for immediate gain."

"Like what?"

"I don't have enough information to go on. Who would want Deran Wu dead?"

Grayland smirked at that. "Roughly half

the noble houses, a large number of military officers and ministers of parliament, and probably every single member of the former governing board of the House of Wu."

"And you," Attavio VI said.

"Excuse me?" Grayland blinked at this.

"If memory serves, Deran Wu was part of the conspiracy against your rule."

Grayland smiled briefly at this comment, and at its implicit acknowledgment that a simulation of a dead man would have knowledge of an event that took place long after his passing. "He turned against the conspiracy and gave up all its members," she said.

"As may be. You wouldn't be the first emperox to benefit from a turncoat's information, only to move against him later."

"Did you?" Grayland narrowed her eyes at her father. "Assassinate anyone like that?"

"No."

"Did you have anyone assassinated?"

"Not openly," Attavio VI said.

" 'Not openly'?"

"Assassination was not a tool I preferred to use. That said, there may have been times when I wished that someone would rid me of a turbulent priest."

"You had priests killed?" Grayland was not aware of her father having any trouble with the Church of the Interdependency, which he would have been the (nominal) head of, as she was now.

"It's an expression," Attavio VI said. "You can look it up. My point is that I chose not to have assassination as part of my statecraft. You might ask your grandmother her thoughts about it, however. She would be likely to give you a very different answer."

Grayland thought of Zetian III, her paternal grandmother, and gave a little shudder. Zetian III would not be remembered well by history, what little of it remained at this point.

Attavio VI noticed the shudder. "I am understanding that you also choose not to indulge in assassination."

"No, I don't."

"That's probably wise."

" 'Probably'?"

"Assassination is never clean and always has consequences. But you rule in turbulent times," Attavio VI said. Grayland noticed the reappearance of the word 'turbulent.' "You have survived two near-successful assassinations and one near-successful coup attempt. You might not be judged too harshly if you, as emperox, decided to speed up the justice that those who conspired against you deserved."

Grayland considered the list of people who might be on her list, if she had one. It would be enough to keep her security forces busy until the Interdependency definitively collapsed. "We have other, more pressing concerns," she said.

"Probably wise," Attavio VI repeated. "If it wasn't you who decided to end your cousin's life, then it's best to start going down the list of the people who would, and see where that leads." This got a nod from Grayland. "This is presuming that you have any interest in discovering who assassinated him," Attavio VI added. "Aside from a natural pro forma investigation."

"Of course I do."

"I repeat: He was part of a conspiracy against you."

"Yes, but aside from anything else, his death does *me* no good," Grayland said. "He was meant to control the House of Wu and keep it in line. Now he's dead and the members of the governing board are already fighting among themselves for control. If Deran is the only Wu cousin who is assassinated in the next few months, we should count ourselves lucky."

"Technically you are the head of the House of Wu," Attavio VI pointed out.

"*Technically* the emperox hasn't tried to

run the House of Wu for centuries," Grayland said. "I was already out of my cousins' good graces for cutting out the board and putting Deran solely in charge, and I got away with that only because Jasin Wu had moved against me, so I had pretext to be suspicious. Unless there's obvious evidence someone on the board murdered him, I have no political pretext to be involved. If I insert myself again, the resistance is going to be impressive. I can't afford that. Not now."

Attavio VI cocked his head. "You have recently crushed a rebellion. You should have political capital to burn."

Another smile from Grayland, this one rueful. "You would think that, Father. But as you said. Times are . . . *turbulent.*"

"As you knew they would be. As I warned you when you took on the crown."

"Yes you did," Grayland said. "You also said that you thought I wouldn't be ready to deal with it all. Do you remember that?"

"I remember," Attavio VI said.

"What do you think now?" Grayland held up her hand. "What I mean is, what would you think, if you could think, now?"

Attavio VI paused. Intellectually Grayland was aware that this pause was unnecessary, and inserted into Attavio's simulation because the Memory Room was aware that at a moment like this, when two humans were having a conversation of this sort, there would likely be a pause while the responding human organized their thoughts to reply coherently. The pause was there to give Grayland a more psychologically authentic human experience. Nothing more.

It didn't keep Grayland, in the space of that brief pause, from having a rush of feeling. A feeling she was being judged, and found wanting, and that her father — or the facsimile thereof — was trying to find a kind way of telling her that she wasn't up to it, sorry.

"You're not up to it," Attavio VI said, bluntly. Then: "But then again, who could be?"

Grayland exhaled and in doing so was made aware she had been holding her breath. "Thank you for putting in that last part," she said.

"I didn't do it out of sympathy."

"I know. You're not programmed that way. Thank you anyway."

"You're welcome," Attavio VI said. "With respect to your cousin's assassination, what do you intend to do next?"

"Nothing directly," Grayland said. "My security and the other investigators are already working on it. As I said, I have more pressing concerns."

"You still came to talk to me about it."

"I figured another emperox might know something about assassination."

"I'm not sure that I told you anything you didn't already know."

"You didn't," Grayland agreed. "But you don't exist. So you could be dispassionate about it. And I think you're right. This was meant to send a message. We just need to decipher to whom."

"That would depend on who was behind the assassination," Attavio VI said. "And as you said, there are no obvious suspects."

"There aren't," Grayland said. "But I can guess."

# CHAPTER 4

Nadashe Nohamapetan woke up full of hate, as usual, these days.

And who and what did she hate today? Oh, let us count them down.

To begin, she hated the stateroom she was in, "stateroom" being an excessively generous description of the box — three meters long, two meters wide, two meters high — that she now found herself living in. It was smaller than the prison cell she'd resided in for several months, and smelled worse. The stateroom featured a fold-up bunk that included straps to secure the occupant when the push fields went out, which was not infrequently. The mattress on the bunk was two centimeters thick and apparently made out of particleboard and despair, and the sleeping bag she was provided, despite assurances that it had been cleaned and sanitized, smelled like decades of lonely spacemen had diddled themselves in it and left the remains to stew.

The stateroom had no windows, no decorations, was apparently only fitfully connected to a ventilation system, and there was a *sound* — occurring every few minutes but maddeningly random within those bounds — from somewhere in the room that reminded Nadashe of a baby choking on a metal lolly. On the first night in the stateroom Nadashe searched in vain for the sound's origin, growing slightly less sane the longer she did so, until she was finally reduced to zipping herself inside of her sleeping bag, hands over ears, huffing the residue of spaceman spunk until she more or less passed out.

It was, the captain had assured her, the best stateroom on the ship.

Which, to continue: She hated the ship the stateroom was in, the *Our Love Couldn't Go On,* a freighter that plied a route between the planet Hub and Orleans, a medium-sized habitat that orbited Hub's star, slightly closer than Hub itself. The *Our Love* was a century old if it was a day, and from the looks of it was maintained every decade or so if that; when Nadashe came on board she'd looked at the walls and bulkheads and wondered not *whether* she would catch diseases from them but which ones. Inas-

79

much as she had hacking bronchitis within a week of her arrival, she wasn't wrong.

The *Our Love* was an independent freighter, which was a polite term for "smuggler." It carried a thin veneer of legitimate inventory that would allow it access to berths at Hub and Orleans, and below that veneer lay a deep and limitless ocean of inventory both banal and insidious, all illegal. Cheap knockoffs, contraband, goods produced outside of legal monopolies, copyright and trademark violations, everything from guns to rum and back again. Everyone knew what the *Our Love* was and what it was doing, and also, no one cared, because the money was good and Captain Robinette spread it around, not to crew, of course, but to port officials and stevedores and bartenders and imperial tax assessors alike. Captain Robinette was very popular.

And to Captain Robinette, Nadashe was just another thing to be smuggled on the *Our Love,* with the exception that she was never offloaded, just charged an exorbitant rate for every leg of the journey, from Hub to Orleans and then back again. All Robinette was out was a stateroom, which had been used by the ship's two unlicensed sex workers, Jeanie and Roulf, for their appointments — which, now that Nadashe thought about it, probably explained the sleeping bag. Jeanie and Roulf were reassigned to Doc Bradshaw's stateroom, and Doc Bradshaw was left to hotbunk, which made her grumble fiercely at Nadashe every time she went to get medicine for her bronchitis.

Not that Nadashe had to worry about Doc Bradshaw ratting her out, either on Hub or Orleans. Like nearly every other crew member on the *Our Love,* Doc Bradshaw was hiding out from the law herself. The ship rumor was that she had stabbed a former lover square in the kidneys. Doc Bradshaw wasn't really named "Bradshaw" — that was just the name she was given when she berthed on the *Our Love,* from a list of names Captain Robinette kept on a board. Bradshaw wasn't really "Bradshaw," Jeanie and Roulf weren't really "Jeanie" and "Roulf," and Robinette hadn't been "Robinette" when he originally shipped out on the *Our Love* three decades earlier.

Even Nadashe had a ship name, for what good it would do in anonymizing the former fiancée of the crown prince of the Interdependency, who also happened to be the current Imperial Enemy Number One. *Rules are rules,* Robinette said, and dubbed her "Karen."

Nadashe fucking hated that name. And hated the stupid rule that everyone got new names. And hated that the *Our Love* had given her bronchitis. And hated that while being on the *Our Love* kept her out of prison, being on the *Our Love* was itself a prison sentence, in that she couldn't leave the ship, ever. Unlike "Doc Bradshaw" or "Jeanie" or "Roulf" or any other member of this ridiculous misnamed crew, the very second she popped her head out of the ship she would be spotted and taken. The *Our Love* crew could be relied on to not rat her out; no one else in the system had the same obligation.

Which was another thing: She hated being a fugitive at all.

*Intellectually,* of course, she could understand perfectly well why she was in this position. When one has fomented a planetary uprising, murdered one's own brother while attempting to murder the emperox, escaped violently from prison and become complicit in a plot to overthrow royalty, obviously being a fugitive is not only a likely consequence, but honestly the best-case scenario. She got it.

But that didn't make being sequestered in a smelly stateroom on a rusting ship filled with kidney-stabbing miscreants any better, either on an existential or a day-to-day basis.

There was no way Nadashe could avoid the fact that, in no uncertain terms, she had *come down* in the world. There was a time — not long ago! — when she was in line to be the imperial consort and mother to a future emperox. Even if that had not worked out perfectly (and as it turned out it hadn't), she'd had a backup plan to install her brother Ghreni as Duke of End prior to the shift of Flow streams, assuring that after the shift the Nohamapetans, not the Wus, would be the new imperial line.

Except *that* hadn't worked out either. Ghreni was still on End and may or may not have become the duke by now, but it turned out that the Flow streams were not doing what Nadashe had wanted them to do — that she had been told by her pet Flow physicist Hatide Roynold they would do — and that rather than shifting they were collapsing entirely. Nadashe had been furious when she learned that Roynold had been incorrect and would have had her dealt with, had her mother not already and inadvertently had her blown up in space, along with dozens of other people, in an ill-advised revenge attempt against the emperox.

*Her mother!*

Which was *another* thing she hated.

Not her mother — well, hmmm, let's table *that* one — but that her mother, the Countess Nohamapetan, had fomented her own coup attempt against the current emperox. It was bad enough that the coup attempt had failed; but *then,* after it had failed, her mother decided that the *smart* thing to do was to shriek at the emperox that she, the Countess Nohamapetan, had murdered the former crown prince, whose death had been previously thought to be an accident.

It was, in fact, not the smart thing to do at all. Nadashe hated that not only was her mother in prison for treason and murder — the same prison that Nadashe had been in for treason and murder, how was *that* for family irony — but now the Nohamapetan family had been permanently removed from the administration of their house and its commercial monopoly, which was currently being run by a minor member of a much less successful noble house.

That would be fucking Kiva fucking Lagos, as the extraordinarily filthy-mouthed Kiva herself would no doubt put it, and who, incidentally, Nadashe entirely hated. Kiva and Nadashe had first crossed paths at university, where, save for the stretch of time Kiva had used Nadashe's brother Ghreni as

84

a sex toy, they'd mutually decided that the best thing for both of them would be to stay out of each other's way — Nadashe because she didn't want to spend any time consorting with her inferiors, and Kiva because she was too busy fucking her way through everyone else at the university and couldn't care less if Nadashe was in her path or not.

This avoidance had also worked in the subsequent years as well, until Kiva had somehow apparently and literally banged her way into discovering Nadashe's involvement in the assassination attempt against the emperox and the murder of her own brother. For this she was awarded temporary control of the local House of Nohamapetan business. This led to, shall we say, *further issues* as Kiva combed through the Nohamapetan finances with a fine-tooth comb, discovering rather a lot of incriminating money trails.

Kiva was foul-mouthed, low-class trash, as far as Nadashe was concerned, which would have been enough for Nadashe to hate her. But the fact that this foul-mouthed, low-class trash was now in control of her family company and fortune, while Nadashe was reduced to a 2×2×3−meter box while nursing a persistent cough, took things over the top for her, hatewise.

For all that, Kiva Lagos did not hold the top spot on the Nadashe Nohamapetan Hate List. Neither did the *Our Love,* its crew, her stateroom, her fugitive status, her mother's stupidity or bronchitis. The top spot was held — and was held by a considerable margin — by the current emperox, Grayland II.

Of course there were all sorts of reasons for this. Starting with the fact that she was emperox at all, which had not been expected and which, due to the emperox's heterosexuality and apparent unwillingness to be flexible about it, had definitively robbed Nadashe of her chances to marry an emperox or birth another. Continuing with the fact that the emperox then refused to seriously consider Nadashe's brother Amit as a consort, shutting the Nohamapetans out of the running for marrying into the imperial line in any way. And then, that her response to the House of Nohamapetan's repeated treacheries was to disenfranchise it entirely. Which, while eminently reasonable from a legal and dynastic point of view, was decidedly inconvenient for Nadashe, who was currently bearing the brunt of these decisions.

But more than anything else, Nadashe hated Grayland's persistent unwillingness to just simply *die,* whether from bombs or runaway shuttlecraft or explosive decompression into the vast depths of space, or, hell, she was not picky, a wodge of pie crust stuck in the trachea or something banal like that. Pie crusts would do! Honestly, anything that dropped Grayland dead to the floor would be satisfactory to Nadashe at this point.

Nadashe was well aware that in having this opinion she could be accused of crossing fully into the category of one-dimensional villain with regard to the emperox. Her defense, such as it was, was this: how much the emperox had cost her. She had cost her a brother and a mother and a noble house and a future entwined with the imperial line. Whether the emperox had initially set out to do all these things — and the extent to which both Nadashe and her family had been the coauthors of their own misfortune — was immaterial to this. When everything came down to it — to the bare, rusting stateroom walls of it — Nadashe had very little left to her *but* hate for the emperox, and the continuing frustration that the aggravating naïf who held the title continued to exist.

At this point, if Nadashe did nothing else but bring down Grayland II, she'd consider herself even in the game of life.

But of course she — still! — had other, grander plans than that.

There was a knock on her stateroom door, and shortly after that the door moaned open to reveal First Officer Nomiek, who as rumor had it burned up several of his friends trying to make homemade, and evidently highly flammable, illegal substances in a bathtub back in his home system.

"Karen," Nomiek said, and Nadashe visibly winced at this, "your visitor is here and in the mess. I'll take you to him."

"Thank you," Nadashe said, coughed, grabbed her tablet and then followed Nomiek through the passageways of the *Our Love*, which smelled of metal and mildew and old.

"I was told I have to refer to you as 'Karen,' " her visitor said, as she entered the mess. First Officer Nomiek scowled at the flippancy from the visitor and left. "Does this mean I need a code name as well?"

"Would you like a code name?" Nadashe asked, sitting at one of the cramped, dingy tables in the cramped, dingy room and motioning at her visitor to do the same.

"Not really," her visitor said. " 'Proster

88

Wu' is a good name. I think I'll keep it for now." He sat, and looked around. "Not your usual surroundings, Karen."

"It's temporary."

"Is it?"

"If you didn't think so, you wouldn't be here. Which reminds me, were you followed?"

Proster looked annoyed at this question. "I'm currently the highest-ranking surviving member of the House of Wu, save the emperox herself. Of course I was followed." Nadashe tensed. Proster put up a hand. "But as far as anyone knows, the reason I'm here is to pick up a pallet of off-house brandy and port, which is currently being tended to by my driver. All very banal contraband. You're safe."

Nadashe relaxed. Then: "So now are you convinced that I am still a force to be reckoned with?"

Proster smiled. "I have to admit that it took me a minute to realize that you had poisoned Deran. I was expecting something else."

"What else were you expecting?"

"Well, I don't know," Proster admitted. "But you were the one to send a shuttlecraft barreling into a cargo bay to kill the emperox. I suppose I was expecting something . . . *louder*."

Now it was Nadashe's turn to smile. She pulled out her tablet, fired up an application and then placed the tablet in front of Proster.

"What's this?" he asked.

"It's the trigger for the bombs I had put into the House of Wu board conference room," Nadashe said. "They've been there for at least as long as the poisoned tea was in Deran's assistant's little drink stash."

Proster looked doubtfully at the trigger app. "And how did you get those there anyway?"

"Come now, Proster," Nadashe said. "You don't expect me to give away my corporate secrets, do you?"

"Actually, if you want me to keep talking to you, I do."

"Fine. When you get back, look for a member of your custodial staff who hasn't come in to work since the day Deran died. When you find their name, have your people look into their background and whereabouts. You'll discover that they don't actually exist, despite having worked on your custodial staff for years." Nadashe motioned around her. "This dingy little ship isn't the only place where fake identities are the order of the day."

"Corporate espionage," Proster said.

"Oh, don't pretend to be shocked. It's not like the House of Wu doesn't do the same damned thing."

"Where is this person now?"

"Back home," Nadashe said. "Or on their way, anyway. Everyone wants to be home these days. Apparently civilization is ending."

Proster pointed to the tablet with the trigger. "What's the point of showing me this?"

"You said you were expecting something louder. I wanted to make the point to you that I could have been *much* louder, if I thought it suited my needs." She took the tablet, closed the application, and handed the tablet to Proster. "Here. A souvenir. A little reminder that I didn't have to just get rid of Deran. I could have taken out all the important Wu cousins and thrown the entire house into chaos. I had that option. I didn't take it."

Proster took the tablet. "I don't know why not. I would have, in your situation."

"Well. Perhaps if you weren't in the room, Proster, I might have."

Proster was momentarily startled. "Me?"

"You said it yourself. You're the most senior Wu at this point. I don't think you have plans to let anyone else have the general directorship after all this nonsense, do you?"

"It's tradition for whoever holds the directorship of security not to run for the general directorship."

Nadashe snorted, which then caused her to cough, ruining the moment. "Come on, Proster," she said, nevertheless. "Things are a little past that now."

"Nadash — *Karen.* Just because I thought Deran was a grasping fool who had no business running the House of Wu doesn't mean I want that job for myself."

"Who else is there?" Nadashe said. "You know your cousins. Do any of them fit the bill? Especially now, when there's nothing to look forward to but crisis after crisis?"

Proster was silent at this, as Nadashe knew he would be. Proster might have been willing to let Nadashe poison Deran — and Nadashe was delighted to do so, as the two of them had a history that she felt obliged to revenge — but at the end of the day he was for the House of Wu through and through. He had been a power behind the throne long enough to know there was no one else among the Wus who merited that throne right now. Nadashe enjoyed watching Proster semi-grudgingly admit that to himself and picture himself — finally, irrefutably —

running the most powerful house in the Interdependency.

Or, at least, the most powerful house for now.

"Come to your point," Proster said, finally.

"My *point* is that right now, we can't afford chaos." Nadashe pointed to the tablet now in Proster's possession. "Blowing up the directors would have caused chaos, but poisoning Deran potentially restores order. Restores the directors to their rightful position running the House of Wu. Offers you, who understands the need for order more than any of the other directors, a way to return things to how they're supposed to be."

Proster smirked at this. "I'm not buying the idea that you did this out of the goodness of your heart."

"Of course I didn't," Nadashe agreed. "I had my own scores to settle. But I settled them — and *only* them. Doing anything else would have been ruinous. We're at the end of days, Proster. What we do now determines whether we — whether any of us — survive what's coming."

"And how do I fit into this?"

Nadashe nodded again toward the tablet. "I've earned a little credit with you?"

"A little."

"It's fair to say your dear cousin the emperox is not the most popular person among the noble houses and the parliament at the moment."

"Since she put a sizable percentage of both into prison recently on the count of treason, that's fair to say," Proster agreed.

"And you would agree that doing so has contributed to chaos at the worst possible time, for everyone."

Proster regarded Nadashe. "If you say so."

"Then what I'd like from you, Proster Wu, is to organize a little get-together for me. To talk to those whom our emperox has discomfited."

"You understand how difficult that's going to be," Proster said, after a moment of goggling in disbelief. "The emperox already has all their houses under investigation. Your house has been disenfranchised. *You*" — he motioned around the mess — "aren't exactly in good odor, or have the means to do much about that."

"And again I say, if you really believed that, Proster, you wouldn't be here now."

Proster held up the tablet. "If you had been smart, you wouldn't have given me this."

"If *you* were smart, Proster, you would have realized by now that I wouldn't have

94

given you that if I didn't have other ways of getting what I want from you."

"Well, that sounds like a threat."

"I'd rather call it insurance," Nadashe said. "Which I won't have to use anyway, since you and I want the same thing."

"Which is?"

"Order. And survival. On our terms. Not your cousin's."

Proster thought about this for a minute. "You must truly hate Grayland," he said.

"I don't hate her," Nadashe lied. "I think she's in over her head. The problem is, when she drowns, she's going to take all of us with her. You. Me. All the houses. And the Interdependency. I'd rather not drown."

Proster stood. "I'm going to have to think about this."

Nadashe stayed sitting. "Of course you are. When you're done, you know where I am." Proster nodded and headed out. "But, Proster."

Proster paused by the door. "Yes?"

"Remember we don't have much time."

Proster grunted and left.

Nadashe sat alone in the mess, hating, and planning, and wondering, not entirely idly, how much time all of them actually had left.

# CHAPTER 5

Not that long after it became clear that what
they had together wasn't just an awkward
fling, and in fact Cardenia Wu-Patrick actually had the same mix of feelings for Marce
Claremont that he had for her, and in more
or less the same proportions, Marce's new
girlfriend, who also happened to be Emperox Grayland II of the Interdependency,
gave him the first gift she would ever give
him: a pocket watch.

"I didn't get you anything," he said to her
when she gave it to him, in bed. She had,
after a session of languorous sex that Marce
strongly felt could have been described as
actual lovemaking, reached over to a nightstand that was probably five hundred years
old and worth more than Marce would
make in his life, and pulled out the pocket
watch, and told him that it was for him.

"Of course you didn't give me anything,"
Cardenia said. "What could you give me

that I don't already have? I mean that literally," she said, after catching his look of feigned hurt. "You know I have actual warehouses full of things people give me, that I never see." She held up the pocket watch. "In fact, that's where this came from."

"Your first gift to me is a *regift*?" Marce said in mock horror.

Cardenia smacked him, very lightly, on a shoulder. "Stop that. Anyway, it's even worse than that. This wasn't even given to *me*. My warehouse manager tells me it was given to Hui Yin III, which would make it about two hundred years old."

"How did you find it?"

"I didn't. I told someone I wanted a pocket watch, and they pulled a couple dozen out of storage for me to look at."

"This story is getting more horrifyingly impersonal as you go along."

"Yeah, I know," Cardenia said, and raised up the pocket watch slightly. "But, when I saw *this* one, I immediately thought of you. So that makes it personal again." She handed it over to Marce.

Marce took it and considered it, turning it over in his hand as he did so. The pocket watch was small but heavy for its size, which suggested to Marce that its workings were mechanical. It was a hunter-style pocket watch, with a finish that reminded Marce of pewter, although he suspected, as this had been a gift to an emperox, that the metal was something more dear than that. The engravings on both sides of the outer case were arcs of flowering vines, the centermost of which on the front was clearly a Fibonacci spiral, terminating in a stylized flower with a dozen petals. Marce opened the case to look at the watch face, which was simple and elegant. The watch chain glimmered with tiny emeralds that were set in every few links.

"This is genuinely the nicest gift I've ever been given," Marce said.

Cardenia beamed at this. "I'm glad."

"I usually get stuffed animals or fruit."

"I'll remember that for next time."

Marce felt the weight of the small object in his hand. "I'm terrified I'll drop it or lose it or scratch it or something."

"That would displease your emperox," Cardenia said, in a comically low tone.

"It would displease *me,*" Marce replied.

Cardenia pointed at the inside of the case. "I had it engraved."

Marce looked over, shocked. "You *engraved* it? To *me*?"

"Well, yes. Since I was giving it to you as

a gift and all."

"But you said it was a couple hundred years old. It probably belongs in an actual museum."

Cardenia smiled and kissed Marce. "And if it were from a museum, I could *still* have it engraved, and then it would become *even more* historically valuable. Because I am emperox. Which is *ridiculous,* but true." She tapped the pocket watch in Marce's hand. "Hundreds of years from now, maybe it *will* be in a museum, and people in the future will wonder what the inscription means."

"What did you have inscribed?"

"Read it."

Marce moved his hand slightly to angle the inside watch cover to where he could read the inscription. The inscription design matched that of the rest of the watch; if he hadn't known otherwise, Marce would have thought that it had always been there as part of the watch's original design. *To Marce Claremont, imperial timekeeper,* it read, followed by symbols he did not recognize.

"That's Chinese," Cardenia said. "That's where on Earth the Wu family was originally from."

"What does it say?"

"It says 'This is our time.'" Cardenia made a face. "Probably. It was a machine

99

translation. Sorry."

"So now I'm imperial timekeeper?"

"It's not an *official* title. But you're the one who told me what was happening with the Flow. You're the one who knows better than anyone else how much time we have before it collapses entirely. You know how much time we have left."

"That's . . . not entirely cheerful," Marce said.

"Well, that's the public explanation." Cardenia stretched and then snuggled into Marce. "Also, you're keeping time with the emperox. You're the imperial timekeeper."

Marce carefully set the pocket watch onto the small table on his side of the bed. "That's a terrible pun."

"Yes it is," Cardenia agreed. "But as long as you get to keep time with me, do you care?"

Marce did not.

But Marce did think of his new, officially unofficial title in the days and weeks that followed. He thought about it as he took the data that he, his father, and the late Hatide Roynold had gathered about the collapse of the Flow in the Interdependency, and added to it both all the current and historical Interdependency Flow travel data that the emperox had ordered be handed over to him and the immense amount of Flow data from outside the Interdependency that he had been provided by Tomas Chenevert, the (former, and late) King of Ponthieu.

The new data had given him a set a couple of orders of magnitude larger than the one he had before. This allowed him to better estimate when the long-stable set of Flow streams that defined the Interdependency would collapse, and when and where a new, far less stable set of Flow streams — the Evanescence, as he and Hatide had called it — would appear, and how long those streams would last before they, too, collapsed into nothingness.

The more Marce worked the data, the more he realized that Cardenia, his emperox and lover, was correct. By this time nearly every Flow physicist in the Hub system was working with his data set, and most of them in the other systems had at least started in on it. But none of them, save for his father and Hatide, had worked with it as long — and his father had had no new data for more than a year, and Hatide was dead.

Which meant that no one else alive could see the data like him, synthesize it like he could, grasp it holistically as he was able to, and manipulate the data as well, to provide the emperox and her advisors with the best and most accurate predictions.

Marce did not flatter himself into thinking this advantage was a result of his own native ability. There were dozens if not hundreds of Flow physicists more naturally talented than he was, starting with his own father, who had been the first among them to see the Flow collapse staring out at him from the earliest data. Marce's advantage had come simply from time spent seeing and working the problem. He imagined he would be superseded soon enough.

Until that time, however, he was, in fact, the imperial timekeeper, the one person who knew, best of all, how much time the Interdependency had left.

And yet.

The more Marce looked at the data, the more he thought he should be something more.

"Look here," Marce said to Tomas Chenevert, and pointed. The two of them were on Chenevert's ship, the *Auvergne,* Marce because he had come to value the friendship with Chenevert that had been formed in duress, and Chenevert because in a sense he *was* the *Auvergne,* and it was the place he could best apparate and exist.

Marce was directing Chenevert's attention to a simulation of the Flow streams of the Interdependency over the next several years. It was highly accelerated; in it, the formerly stable Flow streams glowed in blue and disappeared suddenly and permanently, while the evanescent streams flickered in and out in red. As the simulation continued, the predictive confidence of the simulation decreased, represented by the blue streams wobbling as they entered their estimated collapse window, and the red streaks fading to white the less confident the simulation was. The simulation was streaked with flickering reds, fading whites and wobbly blues.

"What am I supposed to be looking at aside from a seizure hazard?" Chenevert asked.

Marce stopped the simulation, ran it back, and started it again. "Watch the evanescent Flow streams," he said.

Chenevert watched the simulation again, paying special attention to the red streaks, and later, the white ones. "I don't know what I'm looking for," he said.

"Look again." Marce reached to run back the simulation.

Chenevert held up a hand. "I could watch a thousand times more and still not see whatever it is that you want me to see,

Marce."

Marce frowned. "I thought you of all people —"

"Me, of all people?" Chenevert smiled. "Does this have something to do with the fact that I'm no longer human, and exist through the good graces of this ship's computer?"

"Well, yes," Marce said.

"It doesn't work that way."

"But you run this whole ship. Mostly subconsciously. You kind of *are* this ship. A Flow space–*capable* ship."

"Could you run this ship, Marce?"

"What? No."

"But it's a Flow space–capable ship, and you know all about Flow space."

"Yes, but that's entirely — oh, okay, I get where you're going."

"I thought you might, you're smart."

"Still, I would think having access to the processing of this ship would make understanding Flow physics easier," Marce said.

"It might, but I'd still have to take the time to learn it and incorporate it." Chenevert tapped his virtual head. "The model of me that exists in this ship is still mostly human. It can run the ship without thinking much about it in the same way that you can breathe without mostly thinking about it. But if you want me to learn Flow physics, you'll have to give me time."

"How much time?" Marce asked.

"Probably less than you would have to give someone else. But still more time than you would think." Chenevert motioned to the simulation. "So in the interim, perhaps you should just tell me what I'm supposed to be seeing, rather than expecting me to see it."

"That's just it," Marce said, and started the simulation again. "There's something about how the evanescent streams are appearing that's bugging me, and I needed someone else to look at it to see if *they* see it. Because whatever it is, I can't quite grasp it. It's there, I can *feel* it, but . . ." Marce shrugged. "*Feel* doesn't cut it."

"There are other Flow physicists," Chenevert noted.

Marce shook their head. "They're all still catching up."

"As opposed to me?"

"Well, I overestimated you." Marce paused and then looked over to Chenevert. "Sorry. That came out wrong."

Chenevert laughed at this. "It came out fine. I understand you."

"If Hatide were still alive, she could see it, maybe," Marce said. "This is mostly based on her data."

Chenevert watched the simulation. "The evanescent streams look like they're appearing randomly to me," he said.

"As far as I can tell, they are," Marce said. "And their duration time is random too. Some last for an hour. Some last for almost a year."

"No pattern or rhythm to it."

"Not that I can see and not that shows up in the data."

"What do you *feel* about this?" Chenevert asked. "You said you feel something about it."

"What I feel is that there *is* a pattern," Marce said. "Not a *pattern,* exactly. But something not *random* about it, either." He threw up his hands. "I don't have words for it."

"Because it's math," Chenevert suggested.

"Yes, but I don't know that I have the *math* for it, either. But —" Marce shrugged again. "I don't know. I feel like if I could figure it out then I could buy everyone more time."

"That you could stop the collapse of the Flow streams."

Marce shook his head. "No, not that." He motioned to the blue lines, some wobbly, some not, all eventually disappearing. "The collapse of these Flow streams is a near certainty. All we can do about those is try to predict them accurately so people can prepare. *These,* I get." He motioned to the red and white streams. "These I don't. They're the ones I'm interested in now."

"Because?"

Marce jabbed back at the blue lines. "Because these mean we're *dead,*" he said. "There's not enough *time* if these are all we have. We could commit every Flow-capable spacecraft that exists right now just to getting people to End, and that would still only get a few million people there. Out of billions of people. Everyone else gets what happened at Dalasýsla."

Chenevert sobered at the name Dalasýsla. It was an Interdependency system whose Flow stream had collapsed eight hundred years before, stranding it and dooming the inhabitants there to a painful whittling of resources that went slow, and then terrifyingly fast, killing millions. "And yet there were some Dalasýslans who survived," he said.

"A few hundred," Marce said. "And they weren't doing all that well, if you recall."

"I do."

"There's no *time* here," Marce said, tilting his head toward the blue lines. "If we want to save more than a few, we have to look here." He glanced toward the red. "We have to find more time. *I* have to find it." He looked over to Chenevert again. "And I feel like I'm missing it. Whatever *it* is."

"Maybe it's just not there," Chenevert said, gently.

"Maybe," Marce said. "But I wouldn't be a very good scientist if I just stopped looking now."

"Do you have the time for that? On top of everything else you're meant to do."

"I'm the imperial timekeeper," Marce said. "I have to try to save everyone. I guess I'll make the time."

# CHAPTER 6

The imperial palace compound of Xi'an was immense — so large that it was said that an emperox could visit one room of it a day for their entire reign and still not have visited every single room. Whether or not this was an exaggeration was entirely dependent on the reign of any particular emperox, of course; absolutely true in the case of the Emperox Victoz I, who was emperox for thirteen days and died of anaphylactic shock due to mushroom powder being inadvertently present in the wildly allergic emperox's mashed potatoes, possibly not true for Emperox Sizanne, who ascended to the throne at seventeen, lived to be one hundred and two, and was succeeded by her great-grandson.

What was true was that no emperox *had* visited every single room in the imperial compound for the near millennium that it had existed on Xi'an, itself a habitat built expressly to be the home for the emperox and their court. The palace compound held not only the private apartments of the emperoxs and their families, but also the residences of various ministers and staff in apartments ranging from lavish to what were essentially bunkhouses.

The imperial palace compound was also a place of work, festooned with offices, conference rooms, auditoriums and shops and cafeterias, not to mention storehouses, lavatories, gyms, janitorial closets and electrical rooms. There was a jail and a hotel (not close by each other), several post offices for mail both interoffice and interplanetary, a fabrication room, and an entire wing of secure offices and interview rooms where either you needed very high clearance or to have done something genuinely awful, or both, to see the inside of.

Grayland II had not done anything awful, but she was the emperox, and therefore had sufficiently high clearance to be inside the secure wing of the compound. In point of fact she had *not* been into the secure wing before; her own apartments and offices had their own secure rooms that not only rivaled but exceeded the security of this particular wing, and in any event, anyone who worked in the secure wing would come to her. For today's briefing, however, her security people asked for it to be on their home turf, for logistical and technical reasons.

Thus it was that Grayland II found herself walking through the offices of her imperial security forces, heading for a secure conference room at the back. Grayland came unaccompanied by staff and with only a bare minimum of her own personal bodyguards, who were hired and vetted by the security team housed in this wing of the palace.

No one stared as Grayland, in the dark and unflashy attire she wore when she wasn't being paraded around in public, walked through the corridor to the conference room. If you hadn't have known she was the emperox, from the response to her presence you would think she was a middle-level bureaucrat at best. This was fine by Grayland, who continued to find the aura of the emperox one of the most exhausting things about the job.

Grayland walked the corridor and into the conference room, where three people awaited her. She nodded to her bodyguards, who closed the door to the conference room and stationed themselves on the other side of it. As the door closed there were almost silent hissing and clicking sounds as the door sealed to the outside world. Until the door opened from the inside, it would take something close to a nuclear device to get into the room.

"Your Majesty," Hibert Limbar, chief of the Imperial Guard said, bowing. He motioned to the other two people in the room. "This is Koet Gamel, who runs the analytics section of Imperial Security. And this is Dontelu Sebrogan, who did the research and simulations you asked for. Both are of course cleared at the highest levels of security."

Gamel and Sebrogan bowed to Grayland, who nodded back. "You are why we were asked to come here," she said. Normally when meeting with Limbar, Grayland felt comfortable using the informal address for herself, but in the presence of new people, and people for whom meeting the emperox would likely be a once-in-a-lifetime event, she switched to the royal "we."

"Yes, Your Majesty," Gamel said. "Everyone here is secure and vetted. And while we have no reason to believe your personal staff is not also secure and vetted, people will talk, even quite innocently. Someone who knows what I and Dontelu do might be able to surmise why we were visiting you and giving you a presentation."

"Our visiting here at all will be enough of a topic of conversation," Grayland said to Limbar.

"Yes, ma'am," Limbar said. "But given the range of, uhh, *challenges* the Interdependency is facing at the moment, there will be no clear consensus as to which of them has been the occasion of your unexpected visit."

Grayland smiled ruefully at this. "Indeed." She motioned for the others to sit, and then sat herself. Limbar, Gamel and Sebrogan waited until she was seated to take their own seats. "Then let us proceed with the occasion of my visit."

Limbar nodded to Gamel, who nodded back and then turned his attention to Grayland. "A few weeks ago, and in the aftermath of the coup attempt against you, my section was asked — I presume at the direction of Your Majesty — to offer a threat assessment for the Interdependency, in light of the imminent collapse of the Flow and other factors."

"We have of course been modeling threat assessments since evidence of the Flow collapse came to light," Limbar said.

"Yes, of course," Gamel agreed. "However, these new assessments factored in the fallout from both the coup attempt and Your Majesty's response to it."

113

"You mean our throwing a couple hundred of the highest-ranking and most connected members of parliament, royalty and clergy into jail on account of their treason," Grayland said.

"Just so," Gamel said, and coughed. He motioned to Sebrogan. "Dontelu is, bar none, the best analyst in my section, and her remit in the last year specifically has been modeling out the consequences of the Flow collapse. She is going to take the lead on this briefing, if that's acceptable to Your Majesty."

"Yes, of course." Grayland turned her attention to Sebrogan. "You may proceed."

Sebrogan looked at her superiors uncertainly, and then back at Grayland. "Your Majesty," she said. "Before I begin, I need to ask you a question."

"You may."

"How blunt may I be in presenting my assessment?"

Grayland smiled at this. "You mean, will we be offended by strong language and possible negative outcomes?"

"Yes, ma'am."

"One of our foremost advisors can't go a sentence without using the word 'fuck,' and just spent half of the last executive committee meeting trying to convince us that the economic underpinnings of the Interdependency were under direct and immediate threat. We think you should be fine."

"In that case, Your Majesty, we're all kind of screwed."

Grayland laughed out loud. "Now, tell us why," she said, when she was done laughing.

"Some of this you already know," Sebrogan said. "The collapse of the Flow has begun and is taking out centuries-old streams that serve as the arteries for commerce in the Interdependency. When they're gone the individual systems of the Interdependency will be isolated from each other. Inasmuch as the structure of the Interdependency is predicated on all the systems being reliant on each other, this means that within a few decades the human habitats in those systems will begin breaking down."

"The Dalasýsla Effect."

Sebrogan nodded. "You have given parliament a few months to devise a plan to mitigate this, but our analysis suggests that parliament will not devise a workable plan in that time."

Grayland nodded at this.

"Also, our analysis suggests that you have already factored this indecision into your planning," Sebrogan said.

Grayland looked over to Limbar, who shrugged. "You said you wanted a thorough analysis, ma'am," he said.

"What does your analysis suggest I will do after that?" Grayland said, turning her attention back to Sebrogan.

"The most probable course of action is that you attempt to commandeer some or all of the Interdependency's fleet of starships, to transport as many people as possible to End, which is the only planet in the Interdependency capable of supporting human life on its own."

"And how well does this work?"

"It doesn't," Sebrogan said. "First, it's deeply unlikely an attempt at nationalization on the necessary scale would succeed. Guild houses would balk and rebel and you would likely be deposed, probably within a few months. Second, even if the first scenario didn't happen, there aren't enough ships to transport every subject of the Interdependency to End, either all at once —"

Grayland raised her hand.

"— or in a scenario where the systems most vulnerable to collapse were evacuated first to other, less-threatened systems."

Grayland put her hand back down, frowning.

"And third, the total population of the Interdependency is at least twenty billion people. End has less than one hundred million people. Its infrastructure can't handle two hundred times its current population, or even a fraction of that number. For that matter the ecosystem of the planet itself would likely collapse with the sudden — by both human and ecological timescales — introduction of even a few billion humans. In trying to save humanity, you would quickly kill the one place it would be able to survive."

"That is, even if they could make it to End to begin with," Gamel said. "We have to assume that Ghreni Nohamapetan and the *Prophecies of Rachela* have control of the Flow shoals coming into the End system. They can destroy any ship entering their space before the ships could even hail them."

"We're working on that," Grayland said.

"Even if you are, Your Majesty, that won't solve the other problems," Sebrogan said. "Those are pretty well baked in."

"So no matter what, billions will die."

"If your plan is to move them to End by ship, yes. But, ma'am, it's not likely *you'll* be able to get that far."

Grayland frowned. "What do you mean?"

"Remember that you gave me permission to be blunt," Sebrogan said.

"Yes, yes." Grayland waved her hand, annoyed.

Sebrogan looked at her bosses again before looking back over to Grayland. "I estimate that there will be another significant coup or assassination attempt against you within the next three months," she said. "And that attempt is very likely to succeed."

"It's no great feat, predicting a coup or assassination attempt against you, considering your track record since you became emperox," Attavio VI said to his daughter.

"Thanks, Dad," Grayland said back to him. She paced the confines of the Memory Room. Attavio VI's gaze followed her as she went.

"I didn't mean to offend you," he said.

"You didn't." Grayland stopped and reconsidered. "No, actually, you did offend me. But you're not wrong." She started pacing again.

"And yet you seem surprised."

"I thought this sort of thing was behind me, at least for a little while."

"Because you put in jail everyone who was plotting against you."

"Yes."

"That's not how that works."

"That's not what you told me before," Grayland protested. "When I came in here and told you how I had everyone arrested, you told me I'd won."

"You did win."

Grayland gestured annoyance. "And yet *here we are,* Dad."

"You won a *round,* Daughter," Attavio VI said. "You're still in the fight."

"I could abdicate," Grayland mused.

"You wouldn't be the first."

"It wouldn't solve the actual problem, though."

"It would solve the problem of a coup," Attavio VI pointed out. "If you're not emperox, you can't be overthrown."

"That's not the actual problem. The actual problem is billions of people dying no matter what I do."

"That's not your fault."

"It's not anyone's fault." Grayland stopped, again. "Wait. That's not actually true. Jiyi."

The humanoid figure appeared. "Yes, Your Majesty."

"Show me Rachela I. By herself, please."

"Yes, Your Majesty." There was a shimmer, and both Jiyi and Attavio VI disappeared, replaced by the image of Rachela

119

I, the first prophet-emperox of the Interdependency.

As always, Grayland was still a little awed by the fact that she could summon Rachela, or a reasonable facsimile thereof, at all. If Grayland gave it any thought, she would have to admit that being able to talk to any of her predecessors, here in the Memory Room, was an amazing feat in itself. But all the other emperoxs, not excluding her father, were . . . just people. Massively important people, in their time, clearly. But still people. Grayland, who had the same job as they did, felt no need to think of them as fundamentally better or worse than she was.

Rachela, on the other hand, had founded the Interdependency, as well as the church that the Interdependency gave its name to. She'd had help — the entire Wu family, both as ambitious and duplicitous then as it was now, had worked hard to get her into her various roles — but at the end of things, Rachela was the one who had made it all work.

That Grayland's conversations with Rachela revealed her to be no more or less human than any other emperox, immensely cynical and not in the least bit holy, did not lessen her predecessor in Grayland's eyes. If anything, it raised her up. Rachela had *nerve,* which was not a thing every emperox who followed her could claim.

Grayland's respect for Rachela, however, didn't mean she couldn't be annoyed with her.

"Why didn't you build the Interdependency to survive Flow collapses?" Grayland asked Rachela.

"It didn't occur to us at the time," Rachela said.

"How could it not occur to you?"

"We were busy with other things."

"But you *knew* Flow streams could collapse," Grayland said. "Humans come from Earth. There's no Flow stream to Earth anymore. You knew it had collapsed."

"That was a naturally occurring collapse, as far as we knew."

"It wasn't," Grayland reminded her. "It was intentionally caused by the Interdependency's predecessors."

"True, but we had forgotten that when I was alive."

"And even if it were naturally occurring, how does that even matter? You had evidence that Flow streams could and did collapse, for whatever reason, and you didn't factor that into the development of the Interdependency."

"It had only happened once."

Grayland gaped at Rachela. "Seriously?"

"Moreover, by the time we were forming the Interdependency, the prevailing scientific theory of Flow streams was that they were stable and would remain so for centuries and more likely millennia. That wasn't wrong."

"It wasn't wrong, until it was."

"Yes," Rachela agreed. "But it was wrong a thousand years into the future from when I and the rest of the Wus created the Interdependency."

"You're suggesting that you're not responsible for thinking through the consequences of your actions."

"I'm not suggesting anything," Rachela said. "I will note that humans are not great at thinking over the long term, and we were no exception to that. Neither are you, for that matter."

"What do you mean?"

"You were just complaining to Attavio VI how you thought coup attempts were behind you. But you hadn't thought out the longer-term implications of throwing hundreds of people in jail for treason. Now you're having to deal with the shame and anger of their families, their houses and their organizations."

"How —" Grayland stopped herself from finishing that sentence. Of course Rachela knew what Grayland had said to Attavio VI. Effectively she was Attavio VI, and he Rachela, because they were both Jiyi, wearing the skins of the now-dead emperoxs. Grayland made a note to stop falling for the pathetic fallacy at every turn.

And anyway, as much as it galled Grayland to admit it, Rachela had a point. When she herself couldn't truly register the implications of her actions a few weeks into the future, she wasn't sure how much she could blame Rachela and the rest of the Wus of her time for not gaming out where the Interdependency would be a thousand years on.

"I wish you had thought about the long term," Grayland said to Rachela. "It would make my life easier now."

"No it wouldn't," Rachela said. "You might have avoided this particular problem, yes. But you would have had other problems. You don't know if they would be better problems, or worse."

"I don't know that there are worse problems than trying to figure out how to save billions of people from dying," Grayland suggested to Rachela.

"That's not your biggest problem," Rachela said.

"Billions of people are somehow not my biggest problem?"

Rachela shook her head. "You've been reliably told that you'll be out of power or dead within the next few months. That's your biggest problem. Or at the very least, the one in front of you right now. If you want to save those billions of people, you're going to have to save yourself first."

# CHAPTER 7

Nadashe Nohamapetan couldn't help but notice that no one was having any of the refreshments.

This was, on one hand, entirely fair. By now Nadashe's reputation preceded her. She'd killed her own brother, attempted to assassinate the sitting emperox twice, and certainly anyone at her little soiree was by now well aware of the fate that had befallen Deran Wu. Nadashe felt the tiniest bit of pride that an entire buffet of comestibles lay unmolested. It meant people — *these* people, who comprised among them that part of the Interdependent elite of Hub not currently in jail for treason — had a healthy respect of what she could do to them with whatever resources she had available to her, right down to a single muffin or cup of coffee.

On the other hand, it was also ridiculous of them. *She* hadn't laid on the table of food and drinks in the first place. Proster Wu, as the actual host of the meeting, had done so. He hadn't consulted with her on the menu. They should trust Proster, at least.

Moreover and more importantly, Nadashe *needed* these people. They represented the means by which her plans and causes might come to fruition. Because of that, she wasn't going to poison them (here, now).

Complementarily, although they might not be willing to admit it to themselves, they needed her just as much as she needed them. Deep down they knew it, which is why they were here, (not) breaking bread with a murdering insurrectionist. All she needed to do now was to convince them of a thing they already knew.

She could do that.

And if she couldn't do that through appealing to their self-interest, she had some threats to deploy.

If that didn't work, well. There was always tea. Later.

Proster Wu, who had been mingling with his various guests, came over to Nadashe. "We're ready. Everyone who is going to be here is here."

"There are families you invited who aren't here?" Nadashe asked.

"A few."

"That's a problem."

"It's manageable."

"You're telling me there are people who know what we're doing here, who aren't now implicated in it. Explain to me how that's manageable."

"It's manageable because I say it is." Proster smiled. "The families who aren't here are . . . sympathetic to your aims. They just want to see which way the wind blows before they commit."

Nadashe snorted at this. "In other words, they're cowards."

"They might say they're hedging sensibly," Proster suggested. "And in the event that anyone, here or not here, thinks of talking about this meeting, there is the fact that unlike you, they actually fear the wrath of the Wus. They know crossing us means no new ships, no new weapons, and that their security forces may or may not have their best interests at heart from here on out. They'll stay quiet."

"If you say so."

"I do say so. Let me know when you're ready."

"I'm ready."

Proster nodded and clapped his hands together and told his guests to take their seats. In a moment, roughly three dozen people, each representing a noble family and guild house, were seated in folding chairs.

Nadashe noted each as they sat, filing away the presence of each for later. Most of the people in the room she knew, either from social engagements in happier times or because she'd sat across from them in a negotiating session. At least one of them she'd had sex with. It hadn't been great sex.

The rest she knew from reputation. As with any civilization, the closer you got to the top, the number of people who mattered shrank significantly. At the level Nadashe existed on, the Interdependency had the population of a small town.

Nadashe waited until they were all quiet and looking at her. Then she nodded, went to the buffet, and fixed herself a cup of tea. There was a small murmur at this. Then she returned to the front of the assembly.

"First of all, thank all of you for coming to this." She motioned upward, to encompass the room, which was in fact the cargo area of a space ship under construction. The pretense of the meeting was that Proster, as the new and allegedly temporary executive director of the board of the House of Wu, was giving the attendees a tour of the house's latest tenner design in the hope of securing sales. "I understand this is not the most luxurious of all possible meeting spaces." She sipped her tea. "I also understand that some of you might be . . . *apprehensive* about cargo holds where I am concerned."

This got a couple of nervous laughs, a few surprised coughs, and a whole lot of muttering. Nadashe noted which of her guests suddenly turned to someone else with widened eyes, as if to say, *Did she just joke about murdering her own brother?*

"And yes, I did just make that joke," Nadashe said, answering that unasked question. "Let's not pretend that you don't know my past sins, or that I'm not aware that you know about them. Time is short and we don't have the luxury of polite whispers. I am a murderer, a would-be assassin, and a traitor to the emperox. And with your help, I will be all these things again."

Louder murmurings this time, and someone stood up, as if to leave.

"Sit *down,* Gaiden Aiello," Nadashe said, more loudly than she had been speaking before. Gaiden Aiello froze like a small ungulate that realized it had been marked by a lioness. "You're already here. It's too late to say you didn't know why you came.

Sit. Down."

Gaiden Aiello looked around, saw no one else getting up out of their seats, and sat back down, nervous.

"Let me repeat what I just said," Nadashe continued. "Murderer. Would-be assassin. Traitor to the emperox. To the *emperox*. Not to the empire. Not to the Interdependency. And not to the noble houses and guilds that have built it and shaped it into what it is today."

"Get to your point, Nadashe," said Leinus Hristo, of the House of Hristo. "I don't care about your rationalizations. None of us do. Just tell us what we're already colluding for."

"I was just about to get there," Nadashe said. She took another sip of her tea and then set it down. "The houses and the guilds built the Interdependency. Now Grayland says she wants to save the Interdependency. What she means by that is that she wants to save its people. Its *people.*"

"And?" said Hristo.

"*How* does she save its people? They won't survive on manmade habitats for long after the collapse of the Flow. There's only one place they can go."

"To End," someone said.

"To End," Nadashe agreed. "And how will they get there? She needs to transport them.

And to that end she will use every ship she can. Your ships, which you rely on to support the goals of your houses. She'll commandeer them if she has to."

"And it won't work anyway," Proster Wu said, from his seat at the front. "The House of Wu obviously has an inventory of every Flow space–capable ship currently under operation. There aren't nearly enough of them for a rescue operation of any size. And the ones that exist are currently spread throughout the Interdependency. They are impossible to coordinate in the required time frame."

"Not to mention every ship sent to End stays there," Nadashe said. "The Flow stream from End to Hub has already collapsed."

"Not to mention that your brother Ghreni has already taken control of End's Flow shoals," said Drusin Wolfe, who sat at the back of the grouping. "Speaking of coups. We all know what the Nohamapetans are trying to do on End. I see you trying to palm that card, Nadashe."

"I'm not trying to palm that card, Drusin," Nadashe countered. "I just hadn't put it down on the table yet. But you're correct. By this time my brother and the *Prophecies of Rachela* will have taken control of both the planet and the Flow shoals entering into End space. So, even if Grayland takes all of your ships and stuffs them full of refugees and sends them to End, without specific clearance from *me,* they will be destroyed within minutes of arrival."

This got more grumbling. "You said you were a murderer," Drusin said. "You didn't say anything about genocide."

"Please, Drusin. Think it through. The planet can't support as many people as Grayland will want to throw at it anyway. Letting them all through threatens both the people who already live on End . . . and the people who will survive the collapse of the Interdependency." Nadashe nodded to Proster. "Your turn."

Proster nodded and stood, turning to face the group. "Before his demise, Deran Wu proposed to the Wu board of directors a plan that allows for the commercial, industrial and cultural heart of the Interdependency" — he motioned to the assembled group to make it clear he was talking about them — "to survive the collapse of the Flow with its wealth, capital and values largely intact. It's a multitiered plan that includes security control and enhancement to keep populations in line even as the Flow collapses, and new, advanced, Flow space–

132

capable ships for the evacuation and preservation of what is actually important here: the noble houses of the Interdependency."

"So, just to be clear on this, the plan is riot control for the rabble and passage to End for all of *us,*" Drusin Wolfe said, motioning to encompass the room.

"That's an inelegant way of putting it," Proster said.

"I thought we weren't being *polite* anymore, Proster."

"Yes," Nadashe said, interrupting. She looked around. "Not everyone can be saved. They just can't. It's not logistically or physically possible. Even Grayland knows this, probably, no matter how she feels she has to go through the motions to try to save everyone, destroying the noble houses and the guilds in the process. She has to pretend. *We* don't. We can save ourselves. And in saving ourselves, we save what matters of the Interdependency."

"At a healthy profit margin for the Houses of Wu and Nohamapetan."

"You will be coming to us for ships and security sooner or later anyway," Proster said to Drusin Wolfe. "This way, at least, you and everyone else in this room will be at the head of the line."

"And what about the House of Nohamapetan?" Drusin said, turning his attention back to Nadashe. "Just how much are you planning to extort from each of us so we don't get vaporized by your brother the instant we show up in End space?"

"I regret to say that at the moment I have very little to do with the House of Nohamapetan," Nadashe said.

"I'm aware of that, actually. My senior trade negotiator just came up against the house's current administrator."

"Kiva Lagos."

"You know her?"

Nadashe pressed her lips thin. "I do."

"She's not my favorite person," Drusin said. "And I don't think you intend to let her stay where she is for any longer than you have to. So I ask again: How much is the House of Nohamapetan planning to extort from each of us?"

"Nothing."

"Nothing?"

"Nothing."

It was Drusin's turn to smile thinly. "I am skeptical. No offense."

"None taken." Nadashe moved her attention away from Drusin Wolfe and toward the entire group. "Here is the cost for each house here to enter End space: nothing. I will give you passage for your ships — *all* of

134

them, as many as you see fit to send. You will be given an encrypted, verifiable code that establishes I have permitted you into End space. You get that because you're in the room, right now. Others who join into our pact may get otherwise reduced rates, depending on circumstances. But only you here, now, get this free passage from me."

"If I have learned anything about the Nohamapetans, it's that nothing you do comes for free," Drusin said.

"The passage to End is free, Drusin. But I do have expectations."

"Which are?"

"Before I get to that, let me be absolutely clear what the plan here is," Nadashe said. "In just over four months, the deadline for parliament to come up with a plan to save the Interdependency from the collapse of the Flow will pass without parliament being able to ratify anything. When that happens — and it *will* happen — Grayland will almost certainly commandeer all of your ships, and whatever else she requires, in a futile attempt to save as many of her subjects as she can. When she does that, she dooms all of us. It's as simple as that.

"My plan is to stop her. I will depose her, and because she is too dangerous at this point to keep alive, I will have her killed.

135

Then we install a regime that is friendly to the noble houses and the guilds, and which understands what we in this room already know: We can't save everyone, so we save what's important. Us."

Nadashe looked around to see if anyone had objections. No one did. "So, then, here are my expectations.

"First, I expect your money. Lots of it. I will be handling the logistics of this coup, and unfortunately at the moment I can't pay for it out of petty cash. I'll be taking some from each of you before you leave. Everyone here pays in.

"Second, I expect your cooperation. This will not be the baroque, grandstanding coup my mother and Jasin Wu attempted. This one will get messy, and I will need each of you to do your part. You will be graded on participation.

"Third, I expect each of you to recruit. Those of you in this room are not enough. I know some of you will want to keep this small, and others of you don't want to be seen persuading someone else to join a coup. But each of you knows what's at stake here. If Grayland has her way, we all die.

"Fourth, when the coup happens, I expect you to recognize and legitimize the new regime. Without your public allegiance and consent, the coup will dissolve into chaos almost instantly. This needs to happen fast enough that we compel the allegiance of those houses that are not part of the coup, and crush any house that stands out against it." Nadashe pointed to Proster. "Obviously the House of Wu will stand with us. That will be a huge incentive for every other house to get in line."

Drusin Wolfe looked annoyed. "Of course the House of Wu will stand with the coup. Someone in it, probably Proster here, will be the next emperox."

Nadashe looked over at Proster. He nodded at her, a final confirmation.

Nadashe looked back to the group. "No," she said. "And this will be my final expectation from each of you. Your allegiance not just to the new regime, but to me. *I* will be the new emperox. The last emperox of the Interdependency."

# BOOK TWO

Book Two

# CHAPTER 8

While the elite of the Interdependency were making their plans to abandon the common people to their fate, the common people of the Interdependency were beginning to come to grips with what, exactly, that fate actually was.

It should be noted that the common people of the Interdependency were not fools. They were arguably the most educated and materially comfortable common people ever to live, in any human civilization, going back to when the first human decided hoofing themselves across the African landscape was a pain in the ass and decided to stay in one place instead.

The population of the Interdependency were not fools largely for two reasons. The first was that the vast majority of the Interdependency's billions of souls lived their lives either in cities hollowed out from the ground of otherwise uninhabitable planets, or inside habitats floating in space. In either of these environments, a large population of the uneducated and feral would be a clear and present safety issue for everyone else.

The second reason was that the ruling class of the Interdependency, favoring financial and social stability over having the lumpenproletariat trying to rip their heads from their necks at every opportunity, opted to have the Interdependency's baseline standard of living one where no one starved, or was without shelter, or died of easily preventable diseases or went bankrupt if they had a heart attack or lost a job, or both.

For these reasons, the Interdependency held no "poor" or "rabble" in ways that elites of previous civilizations would understand the term. This was great, if your goal was keeping a large population of humans, spread across trillions of kilometers of physical space, reasonably content on a day-to-day basis. It was less great if your goal was to, say, leave these billions completely in the dark about the encroaching end of civilization that was likely to result in slow famine and death for each of them if nothing was done.

They knew. They knew because the scientists analyzing the data that Jamies and Marce Claremont, and Hatide Roynold, had collected had come largely from the middle and working classes of the Interdependency, and they shared information and data. They knew because the crews of the ships that plied the Flow, who had pledged themselves to the guilds that the noble families controlled, were also from the middle and working classes. They knew because the journalists of the Interdependency were from these classes as well. And they knew because the Emperox Grayland II, who had lived her early life as the child of an academic, had in her wisdom or naivete (or both) decided to let the truth about the imminent collapse of the Flow go out to the public.

They knew, and knew reasonably early in the grand scheme of things.

But what they did *do* with that information?

A large number of people looked at when their particular system would be entirely cut off from the rest of the Interdependency, decided that it was enough time in the future that *someone* would probably figure out what to do, and then went back to their daily lives, only mildly more apprehensive than before. The more ambitious planned protests and conferences and composed strongly worded missives to their local, system and Interdependency ministers of parliament, saying in no uncertain terms that something should be done, that that's what they were elected for. Then they, too, mostly went back to their lives, under the impression that they, at least, had done something.

Another group, which might charitably be called entrepreneurs — or less charitably, grifters — saw in the end of the world a business opportunity, and began to target the particularly fearful, anxious and inconsolable. That went as it usually does.

A rather smaller group of people looked at the Flow streams that were still open, saw how long it would be before it would be impossible to catch a ship to End from where they were, and started making plans to catch those ships at or near the last possible instant, saving up all the while. This crafty bit of foresight was undercut by the fact these people generally did not, in fact, make their reservations (paid in full) the second they thought of it. It meant that when they *did* get around to it, they would discover that every passenger berth had been reserved years in advance, and at exorbitant rates. After all, these days, when a ship went to End, it stayed at End, forever. These people had already missed their chance to escape, and they didn't even know it. They likely couldn't have afforded it anyway.

At the local and system levels, governments and their related organizations, populated from the non-noble classes, were beginning to form committees and study groups on the impact of the impending Flow collapse, and what those would mean to their habitats and cities. Of considerable and particular concern was what would happen to the commodities for which a nonlocal noble house held the monopoly.

To give one less-critical example, take citrus fruits, whose monopoly was held by the House of Lagos. In every system, local franchisees grew and sold the fruits, taking their cut of the profits and sending the rest back to Lagos's coffers. In the event that a franchisee decided not to send along a cut, or was just so bad at their job that they never made a profit, all the Lagos fruit stock was genetically encoded to stop producing after a certain number of generations — the number of generations predetermined before the stock was delivered.

If the franchisee doesn't pay up, their stock becomes useless. Seeds the fruit produce are sterile; grafting or cloning won't work. If you think you're going to just easily reverse engineer the stock, well, you can *try,* and good luck. Just remember that the House of Lagos has been genetically designing and tweaking its stock for literally centuries, with a specific eye on maintaining its monopoly. Reengineering so much as a lemon from scratch would likely take decades.

Now multiply that problem against everything humans eat, anywhere, including the staples.

That's the problem.

It was *less* of a problem when the goal was to tie all known human systems into a web of mutual reliance, ostensibly to lessen the threat of interstellar war and trade conflict but mostly so that a small number of mercantile families could rent-seek from the rest of humanity in perpetuity. But now that all those systems were about to be on their own, possibly forever, it became a very large, very looming issue.

Local and system governments had begun to make overtures to the representatives of the mercantile houses about these monopolies. The general response from the houses was *Oh, we're looking at this, but we have years to work on this problem, so let's not do anything foolish.*

Which is to say, the monopolists stalled,

to their own benefit. The local and system governments, not wanting to start panics before they had to, said nothing outside their own committees and organizations.

But again, it's not like the common people didn't know.

Some of them, the more ambitious ones, if you'd like to call them that, had already started working the futures markets, placing down markers for the cost of lemons, and wheat, and beef, and every other commodity under the various suns. Others, equally ambitious, figured that the monopolies of the noble families would be broken, and shorted these commodities.

Some of these people would become immensely rich, to the extent that money would continue to mean anything in the end times, while others would likely find their way to a convenient airlock to end their own self-inflicted suffering. They differed in their opinion as to which would be which. Capitalism was like that.

Most others who were thinking ahead at all simply planned to stockpile certain foods. How much? A month, six months, a year, depending on available space and personal pessimism. Most of those thinking about stockpiling still had in their brains the idea that the crisis was likely to be a temporary one, and that somewhere along the way someone would figure out how to keep billions from starving to death in the habitats that would increasingly fall to entropy. To think otherwise would raise the question of why bother to stockpile at all.

Of course, if one wanted to genuinely understand what the over-under line for "we're all genuinely and truly fucked" was, one ought not look at what the lower classes of the Interdependency were doing, but rather, what their banks were doing. And what the banks were doing, as quietly as possible and without raising too much of a fuss about it, was restructuring their financial services and vehicles to maximize short-term profits and minimize long-term financial risk and exposure.

Which on one hand was entirely prudent, from a fiscal and fiduciary point of view. The Interdependency was about to enter a new and entirely unexpected period of change. Banks are inherently conservative entities — it's right there in their name — and so it made good sense to bulk up against uncertainty.

On the other hand, it meant that the money had cast its vote on the future, and the vote was to short it.

(Then there was the matter of the banks beginning to transfer assets to End. Which they also did not make a fuss about — there was no reason to, since End was covered by the same financial laws and strictures as the rest of the Interdependency and "money" was such an abstruse concept anyway, does it really matter where you say these assets "are" — but which was also a vote in itself.)

Most of this bank activity, as intended, went under the radar of the average person. The average person might have appreciated the slightly higher interest rates on their saving accounts (intended to keep them from withdrawing their funds in the short term), and those with long-term loan notes with banks might have been tempted to take up the offer to refinance to a shorter-term loan, with certain fees waived and interest rates competitive to the longer-term loans.

Otherwise, it was business as usual. It did the banks no good to create a panic. They wanted to be sure that when the panic inevitably hit, the majority of their assets would be as far away as possible. The people and their governments would have more immediate things to worry about than the banks returning a fraction of people's accounts, if that, when all the shit finally came crashing down.

But what of the Parliament of the Interdependency, the august body that Emperox Grayland II had given six months to offer up a plan to deal with the collapse of the Flow? What was going down in the house of the people's representatives?

It would be unfair to suggest, as Nadashe Nohamapetan and Grayland's analysts had both done, that parliament was merely frittering away on the problem until such time as Grayland took it from them and then it would be her problem to solve, not theirs. Parliament had in fact assembled its best ministers and advisors together to ascertain the scope of the issue and to make suggestions for the parliament at large to act on. The problem for parliament's Extraordinary Committee on the Flow Crisis (as it called itself) was that it had come to the same conclusion as everyone else looking at the problem: The vast majority of the people who live in the Interdependency were impressively screwed, and there was no easy or comfortable course of action in front of them.

The question then became, *What percentage was there in the parliament being the bearer of that sort of bad news?*

It was not merely an academic question. A not-trivial number of parliamentarians had thrown themselves in with the recent coup attempt against the emperox, which had gone poorly for them and everyone else involved. As a result, the reputation and popularity of the parliament was at its lowest point in decades and in perhaps more than a century.

This was saying something, as parliament was almost never popular, and was almost always used as a convenient target of ire for local and system governments and their representatives, who were closer to their voting populations and who were always looking for someone else to blame for local problems. These local and system governments and representatives, not to mention the noble houses and mercantile guilds, would be delighted to have the Interdependency parliament be the focus of their constituents' and stakeholders' anger.

It wouldn't be so bad for the emperox, either. The young emperox had become a favorite of her subjects for having survived two assassination attempts and a coup, and for claiming the religious mantle of the emperox in a way that none of her predecessors had since the days of Rachela I, the founder of the Interdependency. Any further denigration of the parliament worked to her advantage.

That being the case, the Extraordinary Committee, with no plan that didn't end in the slow death of billions, and no easy way to sell that outcome, was coming to the conclusion that its best course of action was to delay, take the relatively small hit for indecision, and let the emperox take the rather larger hit for being the bearer of the impressively bad news. Grayland had popularity to burn; let her burn all of it.

In the meantime, the members of the Extraordinary Committee would book the rides to End that their constituents assumed would be available to them a few years into the future.

Oh, yes, End.

The one exception to the doom that awaits every other system of the Interdependency. The one system with a planet where humans could walk upon its surface without a suit of one sort or another, where the land would welcome them instead of turn them into desiccated husks, where the sun would warm their unprotected faces instead of blasting them with unmediated radiation, scrambling DNA. The one place where humanity could still survive.

Well, except for the fact that the people of End were aware what was coming for them: a sudden and overwhelming wave of refugees from the rest of the Interdependency whose sheer numbers would outstrip the planet's ability to absorb them. The question was not whether they would come. They were coming. They were already on their way. The question was how many — whether it would be millions, which would strain the planet, or billions, which would destroy it.

And, hey, there was that whole civil war thing going on, which made it *difficult* for anyone to prepare.

It did, however, make it easier for some to do other things. The civil war was largely focused on the major cities and some strategic transport hubs and routes. In outlying provinces, enterprising farmers were claiming lands they didn't technically own and preparing them for crops and ranching. This was every bit of the ecological nightmare that one might expect, but inasmuch as the (acting) Duke of End was busy not having his head delivered to Vrenna Claremont, no one was stopping them, and anyway the farmers and ranchers rationalized it by noting that they were planning and raising the few native crops and animals that could be eaten by humans — which is to say, the only foodstuffs that had not been genetically engineered to sustain a monopoly.

These farmers and ranchers weren't wrong about that, which did not actually mitigate either the land grab or the pall of the sky as thousands of square kilometers were burned away from End's ecosystems in exchange for acreage that would not come close to feeding and sustaining the millions to billions who would be on their way.

Which was pointed out to some of these ambitious farmers and ranchers. Who said, basically, *Sure, but it'll be years yet. Someone will figure this out. And when they do, I'll be rich.*

And thus it was in the Interdependency in the early-but-not-all-that-early-anymore days of the Flow collapse. Everyone knew what was coming. Some even prepared and planned. But at the end of it, everyone assumed that something or someone would come along to save the civilization that they lived in and could not conceive of actually disappearing. Something or someone would come along to save them. They would be saved, along with everyone else.

It was a nice thought.

It wasn't true.

At the very least, not yet.

# CHAPTER 9

"Give me a second," Cardenia said to Marce. The two of them were in the emperox's personal office, where, Marce suddenly remembered, the two of them had first met, not all that long ago. In the now, they were alone, briefly, in the short interregnum between Cardenia's assistants leaving the office and them returning with the emperox's next appointment in tow.

Marce nodded. "Getting into character?"

"It's not a character, it's me," Cardenia said. "And yes. Now hush."

Marce grinned at this and watched as Cardenia closed her eyes, took a deep breath, and did her transformation into Emperox Grayland II. To the outside eye, the transformation wasn't much — a straightening of the spine and a certain set of the face — but by this time Marce had seen it enough that he understood that most of the transformation was interior, the change of perspective from "personal me" to "imperial we."

When Marce had first gotten to know the emperox — which is to say, in the period of time where they had become friends but had not yet become lovers — he thought the transformation a little bit amusing. Now he realized how much it was actually necessary, not just for Cardenia to define for herself the difference between her personal self and her public role, but for everyone else she ever dealt with. It was easy for people to dismiss Cardenia Wu-Patrick, the young woman accidentally thrown into a position that she had neither wanted nor been groomed for. It was much harder to dismiss Emperox Grayland II.

*Well, harder now,* Marce amended. It took a while, and the arrest for treason of roughly a third of the Interdependency's ruling class. But Grayland had gotten there. Marce smiled to himself at this. He was pretty proud of his girlfriend.

Grayland noticed the smile. "What is it?"

"I'll tell you later, Your Majesty," Marce said. When Cardenia was in Grayland mode, he made sure to treat her with the same level of courtesy as anyone else in her court. Maybe other imperial boyfriends in history used their position to be casual and louche, but that wasn't Marce. He wasn't sure he could be louche if he tried.

Grayland nodded and motioned toward the door. "These two will not be enthusiastic about what we are going to ask of them," she said. Marce knew the "we" here referred not to the two of them, but to Grayland alone; Marce was support staff.

"You're asking a lot of them," he said.

"Yes, well," Grayland said, and shifted her gaze to where her new guests would soon be entering. "We'll be asking a lot of everyone. They will be no different."

"Yes, ma'am," Marce said. Grayland glanced over briefly at him, a small and private smile on her lips. Marce knew that she liked it when he went all formal.

A door opened, and Admiral Gini Hurnen and General Luc Bren were brought in. Hurnen ran the Imperial Navy. Bren ran the Imperial Marines. Normally the two were attended by flocks of staff and body people. For this meeting, it was just the two of them. After introductions and pleasantries, Grayland's staff also disappeared, leaving only the military heads, the emperox, and Marce.

Marce watched as Hurnen and Bren glanced briefly his way and equally as quickly turned their attention back to the emperox. He had been introduced as Lord Marce Claremont, and his role as the emperox's science advisor on matters regarding the Flow was well known. It was also well known, if not generally publicly acknowledged, that he was the emperox's "friend," with all the various social complications, positive and negative, that came with that particular position.

This did not trouble Marce especially — he *got* it — but it meant he was having a moment of quiet amusement watching these two immensely powerful people trying to figure out why *he* was present at this meeting. The three of *them* were three of the most powerful humans in the known universe. His presence at the meeting was either an emperox's affectation, or something else entirely. Marce enjoyed watching Hurnen and Bren trying to figure out which it was.

*They'll find out soon enough,* Marce thought.

And as it happened, they found out almost immediately.

"We need to send an armada to End," Grayland said to her military chiefs. "Sooner rather than later."

Hurnen and Bren shifted uncomfortably in their seats and looked at each other

159

before Admiral Hurnen cleared her throat. "There is a problem with that, Your Majesty," she said.

"You are going to tell us that the *Prophecies of Rachela* will destroy any ship that emerges out of the Flow at End," Grayland prompted.

"Yes," Hurnen agreed. "And not just the *Rachela.* After the coup attempt against you, navy commanders who were complicit fled to End with their ships and crews. There are now thirteen additional ships of various sizes and capabilities on their way to End, all presumably loyal to the Nohamapetan family."

"More than enough to monitor and defend every existing incoming Flow shoal, Your Majesty," said Bren.

"And we could not overpower them by numbers or arms?" Grayland asked.

"It would be difficult," Hurnen said.

"That is what we are told when someone wants to say 'no' to us but feels they cannot."

"Yes," Hurnen said. "But this time I actually mean it."

"Then define 'difficult.'"

"Ships, mines, shoal defenses. All deployed against anything that arrives within seconds. Civilian ships will be destroyed almost instantly. Our ships will survive initial contact, but if the rebel ship commanders are smart — and they are, we trained them — they will take our ships apart in short order."

"Can we not coordinate to have our ships arrive at the same time?"

"And present too many targets to destroy them all at once?" Hurnen shook her head. "No. Flow shoals aren't wide enough to accommodate more than one or two ships at most, and even ships that leave Hub space simultaneously may not arrive simultaneously. It's not an exact science."

Grayland glanced over at Marce at this. Marce knew why she did, and it was a little moment between the two of them, but neither of them said anything about it. "So we are abandoning End to the Nohamapetans," she said to Hurnen.

"No, ma'am," Hurnen replied, crisply. "But neither do we wish to commit our forces and ships to a plan that will expose both to unnecessarily high rates of attrition."

"You don't want your people to die."

"Not if we can avoid it, ma'am."

"Can you avoid it?"

"We're working on that."

"Maybe we can help," Grayland said.

At this Marce noticed something the emperox had told him she was entirely expecting: a pair of tolerant and amused, and perhaps maybe-just-a-little condescending, smiles on the faces of her chiefs. Hurnen and Bren had momentarily stopped seeing Grayland and saw Cardenia instead. "We are always open to suggestion, Your Majesty," Hurnen said.

Grayland turned to Marce. "Tell them."

"Just after the attempted coup, I mentioned to the emperox that I might have found a way to sneak into End," Marce said to the chiefs.

"What?" General Bren said, confused.

"As the Flow streams are collapsing, some new ones are opening. Temporary streams, through a phenomenon I and my late colleague Hatide Roynold called 'evanescence.' These new streams last anywhere from minutes to years. My predictive models suggest an evanescent Flow stream will be opening up into End."

"Your 'predictive models.' "

"Yes. When I first mentioned it to the emperox, I had just newly modeled the data and my confidence in it was not high. I've worked on it since. My confidence is higher now."

"How *much* more confident?"

162

"Confident enough that I would take a ship into it myself."

"Lord Marce was the one who discovered the emergent Flow stream to Dalasýsla," Grayland said. "He has since predicted other new streams whose existences have been confirmed by local scientists. If he has high confidence in a prediction, we trust him."

Admiral Hurnen had a brief expression cross her face, quickly removed but nevertheless one that Marce registered. He knew it was *Of course you're confident in his prediction, you're fucking him.* Marce looked over to Grayland and noticed she'd caught it too, and that she didn't appreciate it even as she realized it was entirely fair. "Of course, neither Lord Marce nor we expect you to take our word for it. Lord Marce's data will be available for your own scientists to examine and verify."

"Who else has seen it?" Hurnen asked.

"No one," Marce said. "When I informed the emperox about it, she asked me to separate out that information from the data I was sharing with other scientists. No one else has that particular data, and no one else's models have that particular evanescent Flow stream appearing."

"Unless someone else has seen it and kept

163

it to themselves, like you did," Bren said.

Marce nodded. "That's possible. The one thing I would say here is that for better or worse, every scientist working the data is working off models my father originated and that I refined. I know what the hole in my own public data looks like and how it affects the models derived from it. It's very small, mathematically speaking, but it's there. I'd notice if someone was hiding the same the data I was. I'd see it in the models."

"You're confident of that?"

Marce shrugged. "It's just math."

"You understand that the fate of dozens of ships and thousands of my people would be riding on your *math*," Hurnen said.

"It's more than that, Admiral," Grayland said. "It's the fate of billions."

"Yes, ma'am." Hurnen accepted the correction. "However, it will be my people's fate *first*."

Grayland nodded. "If Lord Marce's data is satisfactory, then how long will it take to assemble the ships and plan a campaign?"

Hurnen turned to Marce. "In your model, where does the Flow stream originate and what's the transit time?"

"It originates in the Ikoyi system," Marce said.

"That's the home system of House of Lagos," Bren said.

"Yes."

"Does this present issues, General?" Grayland asked.

"They're touchy."

"Let us handle that part," Grayland suggested.

Bren smiled at this. "Yes, Your Majesty."

"The transit time to End would be three months," Marce continued.

Hurnen's eyebrows raised. "Really." The trip from Hub to End was a nine-month journey.

"There's a catch," Marce warned.

"What is it?"

"I predict the Flow stream from Ikoyi to End will only be open for about five months."

"When does it open?"

"About three weeks from now."

"And we don't want to be in the Flow stream when it shuts off," Bren said.

"No," Marce said. "Some Flow streams collapse from one end or the other; others collapse intermittently; others collapse all at once. This will be one of those 'collapse all at once' ones."

Hurnen turned to Grayland. "What I'm hearing is at best we have three months to assemble and task a group suitable to retake End before that stream collapses and takes any ship still inside with it."

"Yes," Grayland said. "Is it possible?"

"It's . . . difficult."

*There's that word again,* Marce thought. Grayland had noticed it too. "That is not what we asked," she said.

Hurnen grimaced. "I understand that, ma'am."

"Then let us be clear, Admiral Hurnen, General Bren," Grayland said, fixing both with her eyes as she said their names. "We have no intention of leaving End to the No-hamapetans. They are a threat to the current citizens of the planet, and they are a threat to anyone who flees there for refuge. Those refugees are already on their way, Admiral. There will be many more before all this is done. If this is possible, then we will have it done, *difficult* or not."

"It's *possible,* Your Majesty," Bren said. "But with all respect, you have to be aware of what you're asking. You're asking for a massive and sudden commitment of forces that will have to be assembled from the systems we can reach and which can send ships and personnel to the Ikoyi system in time to use the Flow stream before it collapses. Every ship, every marine, every crew

166

member we send to End is taking a one-way trip. They are not going to see their spouses or families or children again. Everyone who joins the service understands they are making a commitment, one that takes them from home, sometimes for years. But, Your Majesty, what you're asking here is for more than a commitment. In a very real sense, you're asking them to give their lives."

Grayland considered this. "You think there will be mutinies over this order."

Bren looked as if he'd been slapped. "I said no such thing — ma'am." The last bit of that was added hastily; Marce noted that Grayland deigned to let it pass.

"It's not only the crews and marines, ma'am," Hurnen said. "Those ships aren't coming back either." She turned to Marce. "Unless you predict a Flow stream exiting End space in the near future."

"I don't," Marce said.

Hurnen nodded. "Then there are that many fewer ships we have for the unrest we all know is coming."

"We can make more ships," Grayland said.

"Your cousins are filling up their dance card quickly," Hurnen said, referring to the House of Wu.

"We're sure they are," Grayland said, dryly. "However, we can make the argument that the needs of the Imperial Navy take precedence. As for the crews and marines . . ." Grayland turned her attention back to Bren. "If we cannot return them to their families, then perhaps we should bring their families to them."

"You're talking about sending these families to End," Hurnen said.

"Yes. After a suitable amount of time that would be required to end the Nohamapetan threat and to establish stability on End."

"The logistics of that are —"

"Difficult, yes," Grayland finished the sentence. "As will be the logistics of creating the fleet that we send to End. Admiral. General. Please understand that we do not expect any of this to be simple or easy. Likewise understand that moving forward, we do not expect *anything* to be simple or easy. We all have difficult choices to make, and sacrifices that will be required of all of us. Perhaps you will be so kind as to lead by example."

"Yes, well." Hurnen and Bren looked at each other again, and then rose from their seats. "We need to go find out what ships and people are available to us on short notice. We will have that to you by morning."

"Thank you, Admiral," Grayland said.

Hurnen nodded to Marce. "And you will send us over that data for our people to check. We need to go over that with a microscope."

"Yes, of course."

"You understand that if our people find anything questionable with your data, we can't move forward."

Marce nodded. "If your people have any questions, I will be happy to address them."

The admiral gave Marce a look that he was pretty sure translated as *You better not be wasting my time, boytoy,* then there were the usual departing pleasantries, and then Marce and Grayland were alone again, for the minute or so it would take for Grayland's people to bring on the next appointment.

Grayland sighed and looked over at Marce and was Cardenia again.

"I don't think they like the plan," Marce said.

"I know they don't like it," Cardenia said. "That whole 'if there's a problem with the data' bit was the admiral trying to find a way out of it."

"There's not a problem with the data," Marce assured her.

"That doesn't mean they won't find a problem."

"And if they do, the math will show the problem is them, not the data."

Cardenia stretched. "I wish I had your confidence."

"I think you have enough."

"Not in myself, in *them.*" Cardenia motioned toward the door. "I'm mildly annoyed they're already discounting your work because of your relationship with me."

Marce grinned. "Oh, you noticed that."

"Was gonna punch her right in her snout."

"That probably wouldn't have been wise."

"It would have felt good. For about five seconds. I'm sorry they doubt your work."

"It's not your fault," Marce said.

"It kind of *is,*" Cardenia reminded him.

"Well, fine. It's your fault, but I don't mind. Overall it works out well for me."

"I'm glad you think so, Lord Marce."

Marce smiled again. "Thank you, ma'am." He stood up and bowed, elaborately, which made Cardenia giggle. "Will there be anything else?"

"Not at the moment. Maybe later." Cardenia groaned. "*Much* later, because my schedule is ridiculous today. I'll be lucky if I'm done before midnight. Sorry."

"It's fine. I have work of my own."

"Yes. Saving us all through mathematics." Cardenia smiled. "Which is why I see so little of you these days."

"It's not the only reason, Miss I-have-meetings-until-midnight."

"Sure, use my own words against me. Well, at the very least, when you take a break, think of me."

"I'm probably not going to take a break before I collapse into bed."

"Fine, then, Lord Marce. Dream of me instead."

In his sleep, Marce Claremont dreamed of mathematics.

Mathematics were not the usual dream material for Marce. Most of his dreams, historically speaking, were the standard rehashing of the events of the last few days in an inchoate, plotless manner, with or without pants. Occasionally he would dream he was back at school, simultaneously being a student and teaching a graduate class on physics, once again only intermittently wearing trousers. During the nine-month journey from End to Hub he'd hardly dreamed at all — ship's crew told him that was not unusual, and they suspected that somehow the Flow affected their sleep — and when he did it was often of the hills of his province, green and calm, upon which Marce would stand. He never noted in these cases whether he was wearing pants or not. It did not seem relevant at the time.

But now, math.

Wild math. Incomprehensible math. Math of the sort that would tease and puzzle the greatest minds of any age, much less his own.

Marce could not have begun to describe these dreams to anyone. These dreams of math were not usually visual in any significant sense; it was not a question of seeing numbers or equations or anything else that Marce would have otherwise dreamed of. Nor were they focused on sound or any other usual sense. Marce's dreams were saturated instead with the nature and meaning of mathematics — the overwhelming *presence* of the discipline, the vastness of its influence, the pertinence of it for everything that Marce did and was, and for the civilization he wanted to preserve.

Marce was not ignorant as to why he was dreaming of math. Math was encompassing nearly all of his life at present, as he sifted through the centuries of data on the Flow. He was looking for patterns or sense to how the Flow interacted with normal physical space and how it might be induced, if that was the best word to use, to save billions from the fate of isolation and slow death. If the Flow could be induced, it would not speak to Marce in any human language. It would speak to him in mathematics.

The Flow, it had to be said, was not easily induced.

Nor could Marce reason with it, or bargain with it, or plead, wheedle or threaten. The Flow was not human or concerned with human things. One could anthropomorphize the Flow all one wanted, but the Flow would not agree or consent to it. It was literally alien to this universe. The only way to understand it was to take it on its own terms.

And so Marce did, spending nearly the entirety of his days working the math, trying to solve the problems that only he had the experience to solve.

It was, in its way, incredibly isolating. Marce was not lonely — he was in a relationship, and in his time at Hub and Xi'an he had made friends, and allies and professional colleagues — but for all that he was mostly alone in his head. He saw friends less often; colleagues would report findings or ask his advice on a particular problem with the Flow and then recede back to their own isolations.

He had once started to mention the isolating nature of his work to his girlfriend, until halfway through expressing the thought he realized she was in fact the emperox of the Interdependency. The isolating nature of his one thing was a molehill compared to the isolating mountain of the literally dozens of things she was also currently dealing with. He changed the topic mid-sentence. His girlfriend the emperox found his verbal fumbling charming.

It all had to come out somewhere. It came out in Marce's dreams, his subconscious trying to solve what his conscious brain was finding unsolvable.

Marce understood why he was dreaming his mathematical dreams and even appreciated it in an intellectual sense. It didn't make it less enervating. To work on mathematics all day and to dream of mathematics all night meant Marce woke up all mathed out.

Which normally would not be a problem; Marce could just take a vacation. But when civilization was literally on the verge of ending, vacations felt more indulgent than usual.

So it went, for weeks. Math awake, math asleep, math everywhere and all the time, with Marce no closer to a solution to the problems weighing on him.

But this night Marce had a different dream.

Which was still in and about mathematics, so *that* part wasn't any different. What *was* different was that for the first time, the dream was not generalized mathematical anxiety. In his dream, and rare for his dreaming experience, Marce actually saw an equation. It was as clear as it could be in a dream, which was to say, full of shifting bits and squiggly lines that moved when you looked directly at them.

Nevertheless, when he looked at the equation, he knew what it was describing: an unstable Flow shoal, shrinking and receding at the same time, moving through space in a way that Flow shoals didn't, or at least weren't supposed to, or ever did, except maybe once.

Which is when Marce's conscious mind intruded into his dream. *I've seen this before,* it said. *Where have I seen this before?*

Marce snapped awake, sat up in bed, and reached over to his nightstand for his tablet. It lit up, awaiting his instructions.

"Mnungh," murmured Cardenia, who, as she had promised, had come to bed well past midnight, only briefly acknowledging the mostly sleeping Marce before collapsing into her own pillow. "Bright."

175

"Sorry," Marce said, and got out of bed, naked, so the tablet glare wouldn't bother Cardenia. He settled in a chair, and pulled up the files of data that his father had collected over thirty years — data collected from the trade ships that plied the Flow from one system to the next, registering the minute shifts and changes to the Flow that could be gleaned by how the ships entered, moved through and exited the medium.

Marce was looking for one thing in particular, and very near the end of his father's data, he found it: an anomalous Flow shoal, discovered by a ship that had accidentally exited the Flow when the stream it was in experienced something akin to a rupture, spilling the ship into normal space light-years from where it was supposed to be and trillions of miles from any system inhabited by humans. The ship had spotted the anomalous Flow shoal and had raced toward it, barely entering it before it had closed in on itself. It had been a freak event. One of a kind. Temporary.

*Evanescent.*

"Holy shit," Marce said, out loud.

"Mnungh," Cardenia repeated.

Marce didn't hear it. He was on his way out the door, moving toward his office to start work.

And then quickly back in the door, after seeing the shocked expression of the imperial bodyguard outside the emperox's bedroom. Marce had been so wrapped up in his thoughts that he forgot he was naked. He grabbed a robe and was back out the door, equations — real ones, without squiggles — dancing in his head.

# CHAPTER 10

Kiva was expecting to have another confrontation with the House of Wolfe. She wasn't expecting it to happen while she was having her fucking dinner.

And not just dinner, but an actual date dinner with Senia, because the two of them were trying out that whole relationship thing, and Kiva was aware that there was more to actual relationships than just banging each other senseless until sheets were soaked and fingers were wrinkled. So here they were at Zest, the finest Ikoyian restaurant on Hub (which wasn't saying much, since there were only three and the other two were market stalls selling street food), and Kiva was acquainting Senia with the food of her system. Ikoyian food was unsurprisingly heavy on citrus flavors, given the Lagos family monopoly, but also allegedly hearkened back to West Africa, wherever the fuck *that* was, where the Lagos family claimed to originally hail from.

Kiva was not 100 percent there for the official lineage of Ikoyian food — it was difficult to maintain that the quenchfruit-marinated suya was authentic to anything back on Earth when the quenchfruit had been genetically engineered right around the same time Kiva was born — but it didn't really matter because it was still Kiva's native cuisine, and Senia hadn't ever really had any of that before. Kiva was enjoying explaining moi moi and pepper soup and marmalade dogs to her, and Senia was enjoying having it explained. Kiva believed they were both looking forward to the post-dinner digestif of several unique and piquant orgasms when she noticed a pair of people looming over her and Senia's table.

"You I recognize," Kiva said, looking up at Bagin Heuvel. She turned slightly to the other man. "I don't know who the fuck *you* are."

Heuvel motioned to the other man. "Lady Kiva, allow me to introduce my employer, Drusin Wolfe."

Wolfe bowed slightly. "Lady Kiva. Delightful to finally meet you."

"We were just finishing up our meal and saw the two of you and thought to say hello," Heuvel said.

"Did you." Kiva looked to Drusin Wolfe. "And what did you have?"

"I had the jollof rice, of course, Lady Kiva. I understand it's not exactly the *adventurous* choice, and sort of banal, but we all like what we like, and I like that."

"Well, good for you. Well, you've said hello. Goodbye." Kiva went back to her menu.

But Heuvel and Wolfe would not fucking budge. "Bagin told me your response to our request for renegotiation with regard to the Nohamapetan contracts."

Kiva glanced back up. "Yeah? So?"

"I was hoping that you might reconsider your position."

Kiva sighed and set her menu down. "Really? You're going to try this now? I'm at fucking dinner."

"With your legal counsel." Wolfe nodded at Senia. "We're all here, Lady Kiva."

"Fine. First off, it wasn't a fucking request, and you know it. You tried to dictate terms. Second, I already gave your man my answer, and it hasn't changed. Third, fuck off, I'm off the clock, and so is she." Kiva pointed to Senia.

Wolfe chucked. "Well, you don't disappoint, Lady Kiva," he said. "You are as

180

Bagin advertised you. Profane and immovable."

"I'm not exactly a puzzle."

"No, you don't appear so," Wolfe agreed. "But it's amusing that you think you're off the clock right now."

"What does that mean?"

"Nothing. Except, of course, how much time do you think you have? That any of us have, Lady Kiva. The clock you're not on measures time, and time is running out. For some of us more than others. And even in that short time, there is time enough for the mighty to fall. Or those who think they are mighty, in any event."

"Drusin," Heuvel said.

Wolfe raised a hand placatingly at his employee. "I'm done. I just want the lady to remember that I did offer her a chance, in good faith, to work with me. With us. She had her chance, and she passed on it."

"Uh-huh," Kiva said. "Okay, great, thanks. Now, if you're done with your community-theater-villain monologue, fuck off and take your pissboy with you."

"Of course." Wolfe bowed again. "Lady Kiva, Ms. Fundapellonan. Enjoy your dinner." He walked off. Heuvel looked at Kiva and Senia, opened his mouth to say something, closed it, and then hurried off after his employer. Kiva and Senia went back to their menus.

"What was *that* about," Senia said, after a moment of looking at the daily specials.

"No idea," Kiva said, studying the starters.

"Drusin Wolfe was very dramatic there."

"Mm-hmm."

"Especially the bit about ticking clocks."

"Yes."

"If I didn't know better I'd say that it sounded a little bit like a threat."

"Or gloating."

"Which would explain Heuvel hinting at him to shut up," Senia observed.

"It would," agreed Kiva.

"And suggests something maybe we should look into."

"Sooner than later."

"Are you still hungry?"

"Not really, no."

"Then should we go try to figure this out?"

"Well, I'm not *hungry* anymore. I might still be in the mood for what we had planned afterwards."

"Fine," Senia said. "No to food, yes to sex, *then* we figure this out."

"Done," Kiva said. They both put down their menus, Kiva laid out marks for their drinks, and they stood up to go.

"You know what the worst fucking part of that was," Kiva said as they headed to the door.

"What?"

"Motherfucker ran down jollof rice. It's not fucking *banal.* I was going to order that."

"I think we have a problem," Kiva said, to Grayland II, four days later. Kiva had asked for an audience with the emperox the day before; she was granted five minutes, which she was given while the emperox was walking from one meeting to another. Kiva got it; the emperox was a busy woman. "More accurately, I think you have a problem."

"Me having problems is the base state of my reign, Lady Kiva," Grayland said, setting a brisk pace as she moved from one room of her palace to the next. "You'll have to be more specific."

Kiva nodded and handed the emperox a sheaf of documents, which the emperox immediately handed to her assistant. "A few days ago Drusin Wolfe came over to me and Senia Fundapellonan while we were having dinner, and monologued at me."

"He what?"

"Monologued. You know, 'Soon you will

experience your doom, bwa ha ha ha,' that sort of shit."

"I didn't know people did that in real life."

"I don't think he knew he was doing it, although his flunky sure did. He had to pull him away."

"And how does this monologue involve me?"

"I didn't think it did at first," Kiva said. "I had stuffed his flunky pretty hard in a negotiation, and I thought that he was just announcing his plans to fire off a legal salvo against me and the House of Nohamapetan. Senia and I went back to check for filings we might not have been aware of, or other activity that would suggest action against us. We didn't find any." Kiva pointed to the sheaf of documents Grayland's assistant was holding. "But we found something else. A few days before his monologue, Drusin Wolfe withdrew something like twenty million marks out of his personal brokerage accounts."

Grayland glanced over at Kiva for this. "And you have access to Wolfe's personal brokerage accounts how?"

Kiva smirked. "I spent months tracking down every single off-book account the Nohamapetan family had, Your Majesty. I know my way around a financial investigation."

"And how to offer some well-placed bribes, I imagine."

"I don't know about *that,*" Kiva said, and Grayland smiled thinly. "But I'm not planning to offer any evidence in court or any such thing. The information is reliable in any event."

"Nobles are frequently moving wealth from one place to another, Lady Kiva," Grayland said. "And when moving it from one account to another, much of it seems to disappear entirely. I daresay an honest audit of any house's principals would find more of their money off the books than on it, the House of Lagos not excepted. Marks falling down a hole is simply business as usual."

"It's not that the money disappeared," Kiva said. "It's that right around the same time Drusin Wolfe withdrew his twenty million marks, a couple dozen other nobles did the same thing, in pretty much the same amounts."

Grayland stopped walking, causing a rippling halt among her retinue. "How many?"

"My source noted twenty-six individual withdrawals, all in the same time frame, all in the same amounts — or withdrawals spread across multiple accounts totaling around twenty million marks. There are probably others; my source could only track these."

"And you trust this source."

"I trust that he appreciates having his gambling debts paid off. And that he knows if he crosses me, I'll push him in front of a fucking bus. So, yes. There's something else, too."

"What is it?" Grayland started walking again.

"All of the nobles who withdrew the marks were present at a sales meeting hosted by the House of Wu. Ostensibly they were being pitched a new generation of tenner."

Grayland grimaced but didn't stop walking. "So they could say they were putting down deposits."

"Yeah, but the 'deposits' are all from personal accounts, not house business accounts," Kiva said. "Tenners are huge and designed to last a decade in space without docking. It's unlikely they're going to be used for pleasure craft."

"The Flow collapse is coming," Grayland pointed out. "Maybe they're hedging."

"And even if they were, tenners start at a billion marks," Kiva replied. "House of Wu demands ten percent on deposit, non-negotiable. Your family doesn't offer discounts, ma'am. Twenty million marks isn't even on the table for a deposit. Someone offering that for a tenner down payment would get laughed out of the room."

"So it's something else."

Kiva nodded. "It's something else, and whatever it is, the House of Wu is in on it."

"I'm still not seeing how this involves me, Lady Kiva," Grayland said. She made the turn down the final hall that would take her to her destination.

"Maybe it doesn't," Kiva admitted. "But when Drusin Wolfe was monologuing at me he was clearly expecting a comeuppance for me, one way or another. Well, neither he nor his house are coming for me directly, or are trying to sue the House of Nohama-petan. It has to be something else. It's known you favor me, ma'am. You gave me a seat on the executive committee — a seat I'll remind you I didn't fucking want — and I was standing next to you when you arrested half of the nobles in local space."

"Not so many as that."

"Enough of them, ma'am," Kiva said. "Now a whole bunch of nobles are throwing money down a hole, and a lot of them are from houses that have family members sitting in jail waiting for their trials for treason — the House of Wu among them.

And of course, fucking Nadashe Nohama-petan is still out there somewhere, doing what she does. She's got some money but not a lot, relatively speaking, and can't access any more directly. She's got to get it from somewhere. So I'm thinking that when Wolfe was being smug at me, he wasn't thinking about coming for me directly. He knows I'll crush him if he does. He's thinking that when you go down, I'm going to be collateral damage."

Grayland stopped in front of the arch of a doorway. Inside it was the Hubfall football team, which had won its league champion-ship and would now be feted by the em-perox for all of seven and a half minutes before she had to go on to something else again. Grayland was only about a third of the way through her day; and Kiva, who by now had some appreciation for the emper-ox's schedule, was (uncharacteristically) quietly amazed at the fact that despite all the evidence that civilization was indeed collapsing around them at an increasing rate, so much of Grayland's schedule was tied up in trivia like, say, congratulating a fucking sports team for being better at play-ing with their balls than anyone else.

"You think Nadashe Nohamapetan has something to do with this money disappearing act," Grayland said to Kiva.

"Yeah, I do. She hates your guts. And you've made every house and guild fear you. That's the sort of thing she'll capitalize on."

"To do what?"

"Well, ma'am. Another coup. 'If at first you don't succeed' and all that."

Grayland nodded to the sheaf of documents her assistant held. "I could have these nobles investigated."

Kiva shook her head. "The second that happens, they'll be on to you. There are too many people willing to sell you out on something like this. It'll leak almost faster than you can order it. The nobles will cover their tracks, the marks will magically reappear in legitimate business accounts, and Nadashe, if she *is* behind this, will become that much harder to find."

"What do you suggest?"

Kiva nodded toward the documents. "My source pointed out all those nobles making withdrawals at the same time. But he also pointed out that since that event, there have been a few more withdrawals by nobles, in the same amounts."

"Whatever they're doing, they're recruiting."

"Right," Kiva said. "Bringing in more

disgruntled houses and nobles to their little plan."

"All right," Grayland said. "And?"

Kiva smiled. "Your Majesty, I think you and I should have a major fucking blowup."

# CHAPTER 11

Seven and a half minutes congratulating the Hubfall Dragons for their championship win over the Essex Fire, which included graciously receiving a game ball as a gift (which would — after a short, apparently magic-imbuing time in Grayland's possession — be returned to the Dragons "on loan from the emperox" for display at their team headquarters) and ruefully noting the woeful placing of the Xi'an Shipwrights, the imperial football team, in that year's standings.

After that, an hour of ten-minute meetings with various infrastructure department heads for the physical well-being of Xi'an itself, the imperial space habitat that the emperox and many thousands of others lived on. Xi'an was the jewel of space living, and was also one of the oldest space habitats still extant, which made it idiosyncratic and finicky in a manner more modern habitats no longer were.

For (just one) example, the circulation system of the Xi'an habitat was such that (the emperox learned) a specific series of routine maintenance steps, if performed out of sequence, could purge the air out of Xi'an Cathedral, directly into space. Apparently some engineer lost to time thought that purging the air would be a smart way to quell any fire that might happen there without exposing the interior of the cathedral to water or fire-retardant damage.

A single line of code in the Xi'an habitat's maintenance programming kept the cathedral from ever suddenly going oxygen-free — but that line of code had been recently expunged in a system update. For three months, then, nothing had kept human inefficiency from suddenly asphyxiating Archbishop Korbijn and hundreds of celebrants during morning services. Grayland allowed this would not be an optimal outcome, either for the church or its faithful congregation, and was relieved to hear this issue, at least, had been resolved.

Twenty minutes receiving an update from a Commander Wen, Admiral Hurnen's aide-de-camp, about the status of the End Armada, as Grayland had taken to thinking of it in her head, although she was led to understand it would actually be a "task force," which Grayland did not feel sounded as awesome.

The initial estimates were not encouraging — the number of capital ships available for reassignment that could be tasked to the Ikoyi system in time was not large, nor was the number of support ships. Commander Wen assured Grayland this was merely an initial assessment and that further investigation was likely to swell the numbers. Grayland reminded Commander Wen of the time pressures involved. Neither participant walked away entirely pleased with the meeting.

Five minutes for a break, which Grayland mostly spent in the toilet. If someone had informed Cardenia Wu-Patrick early on that one of the most valuable skills an emperox could cultivate was the ability to clamp down on their excretory functions for hours at a time, she might have passed on the gig. Cardenia had read somewhere that prisoners got so used to the regimented schedule of incarcerated life that they only felt the urge to relieve themselves at the specific times when doing so was allowed. Cardenia wasn't at that point, but she certainly could empathize.

Speaking of prisoners, after her brief pit

stop, Grayland's next forty-five minutes were concerned with an update from her minister of justice on the status of the oh-so-many alleged traitors she had arrested for their coup attempt and placed in jail pending their respective trials. The arrests had been so numerous and the malfeasants of such high status that there had been some confusion as to how to house and process them; treasonous scum or not, it would look bad to have leaders of some noble houses and scions of some others shivved in a common lockup.

Grayland had solved the problem by commandeering the *Jewel of the Stars,* a cruise liner that plied its trade between Hub and the various habitats within that planet's system, and then stuffing the traitors into its staterooms for the duration. The Ministry of Justice paid the cruise line to maintain the hospitality and catering services, augmented by a hefty contingent of imperial security and an extremely tight control of who came and went on the *Jewel.* Aside from the whining that invariably came when some count or baroness was assigned an interior lower deck room without a view, it worked pretty well. There were hardly any shivvings at all.

What wasn't working particularly well,

Grayland was discovering, were the legal proceedings against the traitors. It wasn't that the Ministry of Justice lacked evidence — Deran Wu had provided plenty of that before his poisoning — but a matter of lawyers. The traitors were all part of noble houses, who employed all sorts of lawyers, most of them very good; the Ministry of Justice, on the other hand, had a relatively small number of prosecutors available, some of whom were good but some of whom worked for the government because they were aggressively mediocre and couldn't get the plum jobs that the noble houses and guilds offered up.

The lawyers for the various houses — who were well aware that if their clients were found guilty, they would be executed (the clients, not the lawyers, although, depending on the house, maybe the lawyers, too) — were burying the Ministry of Justice in paper and proceedings, searching for every possible delay or technicality to get their clients sprung. The Ministry of Justice, which had other things to worry about as well, was being overwhelmed. More than that, the minister of justice declared, the surge of popular support that Grayland had accrued after the coup attempt was ebbing quickly — the longer the traitors languished in their very posh prison ship, the more time the houses and their lawyers had to rally support, manufactured or otherwise.

Grayland was for various reasons not particularly concerned about the public support issue, but did not acknowledge that to her minister of justice. There was no point going down that particular path with him. Nor, honestly, was she all that concerned about the traitors drawing out their legal process. Grayland herself was not adamant that the traitors had to be put to death; she did not have that sort of righteous bloodlust running through her veins. If the traitors were wasting their time, it was their own increasingly finite time to waste, and in the meantime they at least were out of her hair.

Still, it wouldn't do to have Grayland's minister of justice feel that she was unresponsive to his concerns, so she asked for his advice. The minister had suggested two things: one, that the ministry be allowed to hire outside lawyers and deputize them to lead some of the higher-profile cases, so that the ministry would not find itself outgunned; two, to start cutting deals with some of the traitors, in which they would allocute and name names in return for not being executed and for serving their time in their home systems, in their house's own penal system.

Grayland assented to both, and suggested to her minister that he use the second strategically, to disrupt the emerging narrative that was sympathetic to the traitors, and to pit them against each other legally, which would complicate their lawyers' machinations. She knew this was his intent in any event, but also knew it was useful to him to be able to say the idea came from the emperox herself. And indeed her minister seemed gratified that she went exactly where he needed her to go. They both came away from the meeting feeling like they had manipulated the other precisely, which meant it was a good meeting.

A fifteen-minute tea with Archbishop Korbijn, which was as close to a purely social call as any that Grayland would have in her entire day. Archbishop Korbijn had famously thrown in her lot with the emperox on the fateful day the attempted coup had been meant to go down, and in the time since Grayland had shown her appreciation, opening up the imperial coffers to fund Korbijn's initiatives within the Church of the Interdependency. But more than that, Grayland liked the archbishop; the older woman had always been kind to Grayland, and understood better than most what it meant to be in charge of a vast bureaucracy that was not always sympathetic to one's aims, or sensitive to one's ego. They had similar jobs, basically, and it was nice to be able to talk to someone who understood your specific set of extremely high-end problems.

Grayland did not tell Archbishop Korbijn that at any point in the last three months she could have suffocated because of a line of code, or the lack thereof.

Next, a brief trip by private train car to the other side of the Xi'an habitat and to the parliament complex and her own parliamentary offices — Grayland was technically the Interdependency parliamentary representative for Xi'an, and while as a practical matter she did not exercise the privilege, she still had office space — where Grayland in rapid succession took four ten-minute meetings with her fellow parliamentarians, in groups of six, and then walked to the floor of parliament, where she gave a fifteen-minute address to the Hub System Teen Model Parliament, which was on Xi'an for its annual convention. They were thrilled to see her, and Grayland was thrilled to realize she was finally old enough to have teenagers look impossibly young to her. That was new.

Five minutes later she was back in her

private train car, heading to her own palace complex and to the meeting she had been dreading the most. It was with Countess Rafellya Maisen-Persaud, of the House of Persaud, whose monopoly was in shellfish and certain cartilaginous fishes, and which was the ruling house of the Lokono system. The Lokono system had sixty-five million people in it, across six moons, twelve major habitats and over a hundred minor ones.

It was also the first system forecast to be entirely cut off from the rest of the Interdependency.

Currently its three ingress and four egress Flow streams were sound. In roughly six months, the first of its incoming Flow streams — from Hub — would collapse, followed by the collapse of the other six streams within eleven months. By that time nearly every other system in the Interdependency would have experienced its own Flow stream collapses, but all the rest of them would still be connected, even if only tenuously, to the rest.

Grayland was expecting that the countess would be performatively outraged that, despite the fact that the emperox was obliged to give the parliament six months (and now rather less than that) to present options, she had done nothing to protect or rescue the sixty-five million citizens of the Lokono system from the oncoming collapse. The countess did not disappoint. As the representative of her noble house, and the youngest sister of the reigning duchess, Rafellya Maisen-Persaud gave an award-worthy performance, and all but rent her garments at the plight of the Lokono people. At the end of it, Grayland wondered whether she should applaud.

She did not. Not only because it would be rude, but also because she knew that the countess was not all that concerned with the fate of the citizens of the Lokono system. Grayland knew that Rafellya Maisen-Persaud had been at the meeting that Kiva Lagos had spoken to her about, the one put on by Proster Wu.

Moreover, she had known it before Lady Kiva told her about it. She knew because Jiyi had pried that particular secret loose from the same bank that Kiva had used social engineering against to discover the conspiracy. Jiyi had discovered more conspirators at other banks, as well as encrypted documents explaining the details of the conspiracy — including one from the countess sitting across from her at this meeting. Her particular missive to her sister had been one of the easiest to crack. The encryption on the note itself was state-of-the-art and would have taken Jiyi a couple of decades to get through, had not the countess dictated it on a speaker that connected to her in-house network, the nonbiometric password for which was the name of her current dog (a darling ball of fluff named Chestain), and the biometric password (a fingerprint) for which was in the imperial system.

Grayland thought, not for the first time, how dangerous Jiyi actually was: a secret, empire-spanning personal agent of the emperox who knew all and would tell all if the emperox, in fact, knew to ask. Which Grayland did.

Thus the emperox knew Countess Rafellya Maisen-Persaud was a phony, and that her demand for this meeting had been made under false pretenses; that rather than having an interest in the well-being of the sixty-five million people she claimed to represent, her interest was to report back to Nadashe Nohamapetan about the emperox's current plan to save the Interdependency, the better to craft a trap into which Grayland might fall. Grayland had been dreading the meeting, not because she had no answer for the problem of how to save the millions of Lokonese — she did not, as yet, which was depressing in itself — but because she knew ahead of time how dispiriting it would be to watch the countess pretend to give a shit about anything other than herself, and possibly her immediate family and friends.

She was not wrong, but at the moment there was nothing to be done about it. So Grayland watched and listened as the countess gave her impassioned performance, and then when it was done Grayland thanked her for her visit, informed her simply that all that could be done for the Lokono system would be done, and dismissed the countess before she could wind herself up for a second dramatic performance. The meeting, all told, had been twenty-three minutes.

Which meant Grayland was unexpectedly seven minutes ahead of her schedule.

With roughly ninety seconds of that time, she made a personal call, to add a final meeting to her day.

"When did you know your reign was doomed?" Grayland asked Tomas Chenevert. The two of them were alone on the bridge of the *Auvergne,* Grayland having dropped her bodyguards at the door. The *Auvergne* was berthed in the emperox's own dock; ostensibly she was as secure as she would be in her own palace. Her guards were still unhappy, but Grayland wanted privacy to talk to Chenevert.

Chenevert raised an eyebrow at the question. "Are we expecting some bad news?" he asked. Of all the people Grayland knew, Chenevert was the one who treated her the most casually, not because of some pathological disrespect for royalty but because he was royalty himself — the deposed King of Ponthieu, which existed beyond the Interdependency. Chenevert treated Grayland as a peer, in other words, something Grayland found she appreciated. No one else did so, not even Marce, who despite their intimate relationship was all too aware of the gulf between their stations.

"I don't have anything but bad news these days," Grayland confessed.

"I know, and I'm sorry about that," Chenevert said, kindly. "I meant specifically about a new coup."

"Not coup. Coups. There are several."

"*Several.* I'm impressed. It's nice to be popular."

"Not like this."

"I suppose not. I can tell you my thoughts on the matter, of course, but I'm wondering why you don't just ask your congress of dead emperoxs. Surely one or two of them fell to a coup."

"Not really?" Grayland said. "There were a few assassinations, and there were other emperoxs who were . . . *replaced* by the Wu family when it became clear there were problems with them."

" 'Replaced,' " Chenevert said. "I like that euphemism."

"But the assassinations weren't part of a larger uprising, and I don't think the Wu family replacing one of its own with another of their own counts as an actual coup. That's just family politics."

"The last coup attempt against you had Wu participants," Chenevert reminded Grayland.

"But it wasn't *successful*," Grayland said. "Whereas . . ." She stopped.

Chenevert smiled. "You can say it," he said.

"Whereas the coup attempt against you was," Grayland continued.

"Yes it was," Chenevert allowed. "I barely escaped with my skin. And this ship. And a few hundred friends. And an appreciable amount of all human knowledge at the time. And, of course, a nontrivial amount of material wealth."

"All of which means you saw it coming, and knew you couldn't *stop* it."

"It's true."

"So tell me how you knew."

"I can tell you, but I don't know if it will be useful to you."

"Why not?"

"Because I was, how to say this, not a *good* king. Not nearly as good a king as you are emperox, my young friend. Or anywhere as good as a person."

"You're not a bad person," Grayland said.

"I'm a better person now," Chenevert allowed. "I'm also no longer human. I'm a constructed machine consciousness based on someone who used to be human. I remember being human, and I remember what desires and emotions drove me as a human. I can access those, but those same desires and emotions don't drive me as I am now. Also, I'm over three hundred years old. I've had time to sit with my sins."

"So you're not that different from my congress of emperoxs. Their recorded versions can access how their live versions thought and felt. They just can't feel those things themselves."

"I can still feel them," Chenevert said. "Just like you can feel an emotion from when you were five years old. But you don't feel the same as five-year-old you."

"Sometimes I do."

"Well, fine." Chenevert smiled. "I mean to

205

say you would not act on those feelings as you would when you were five. You seem remarkably tantrum-free."

"Thank you," Grayland said. "I'd still like to know when you knew the coup was coming."

Chenevert sighed, which was entirely unnecessary given he was an artificially constructed intelligence projecting a holographic version of himself, but even so. "The short version is I knew it was coming when I had burned through or betrayed all the people who could have been useful allies, and everyone left decided it was time for me to go. The longer version would take quite a lot of time and would, I'm afraid, rather definitively ruin your opinion of me as a good person. I will say it was a disaster of my own making, which is why I could see it coming from a long way off."

"If you could see it coming, why couldn't you avoid it?"

"Because some choices you make, you can't come back from," Chenevert said. "And very early on in my reign, when I was pompous and foolish, I made several of those sorts of choices. In rapid succession. Everything proceeded from there. Eventually — and by this time I had gained just enough wisdom to have a horror of some of those early choices — I realized that while I could delay a coup, I couldn't keep it away forever. So I delayed it long enough to make an escape." He smiled. "Which was ironic, because when the coup came, I was already dying — also because of some entirely optional choices I made early on. If the conspirators had just waited a couple more years, they wouldn't have needed a coup at all."

"I'm sorry you made those choices," Grayland said, after a moment.

"Well, so am I, if you must know," Chenevert said. "Looking back on your life and knowing how much better you could have been is never a great feeling. The one small saving grace of all of it is I get to be here now, with you, and Marce. Who, incidentally, is killing himself trying to figure out the math to save all of us."

"Has he told you this?"

"No, of course not. But he comes to visit me to talk math, you know. He assumed that because I am a machine I would be able to follow what he does, and I absolutely could not. But I'm learning, because I want to be helpful to him. I'm not, yet. But I think I'll get there eventually. I do learn faster than most humans now, at least. He's actually kind of brilliant, you know. Your

207

paramour, I mean."

"I think so, too."

"No, I mean more than that. He's too modest to say so, or even to think so, but I see his work and can even follow some of it. If there is anyone who is going to save you, it'll be him. At this point the question is whether he has enough data to work through. And if he gets enough sleep." Chenevert noticed a shadow cross over Grayland's face. "What is it?"

"What is what?"

"You had a thought just then. When I talked about data."

"It's not important."

"All right," Chenevert said. "But on the subject of data, you said that you knew of several planned coup attempts."

"Yes."

"How do you know about those? If your security and intelligence people knew about them, I expect they would already be former coup attempts."

"I have other sources."

"Would these sources include the artificial intelligence that runs your emperox puppet show?"

Grayland looked sharply at Chenevert. "What makes you say that?"

"Because your friend Jiyi — that's its

name, yes? — has made several attempts to get inside my systems. I noticed the first attempt not long after I got here. It sent a program to try to crack my firewall. I isolated it and took it apart to see how it worked and sent a message back telling it I would be happy to chat with it if it would just knock rather than trying to slip through the windows. It didn't respond to the message. It does keep trying to slip through the windows. If it's doing this to me, I imagine I'm not the only system it tries to get into."

"I'm sorry Jiyi keeps trying to hack you," Grayland said.

"It's fine. Well, it's not fine," Chenevert amended, "but it's not a problem so far. It keeps me on my toes. But I would rather just talk to Jiyi, if such a thing is allowed."

"As far as I know, Jiyi doesn't talk to anyone but me. And the other emperoxs before me."

"Well, I am a king," Chenevert said. "Or was. Maybe that qualifies."

"I'll see what I can do."

"Thank you. To return to your question about knowing when my reign was doomed, I knew early enough to save myself. Is that why you're asking? To know when is too late to save yourself?"

Grayland shook her head. "I'm not looking to save myself."

"That's noble to the point of self-sacrifice."

"It's not that."

"What is it, then?"

"I could stop these coups," Grayland said. "I have the information and I know the actors and I know where they are. Well, most of them. I could declare martial law and throw all of them in jail, just like I did with the last coup. But when I do that, I just stop this set of attempted coups. There will be more. There have always been more. Since the very first day I became emperox. Stomp down on one and two more pop up. And meanwhile, what I need to be focusing on doesn't get focused on."

"Saving the Interdependency," Chenevert said.

Grayland shook her said. "No. It's doomed no matter what we do. We can't stop the Flow streams from collapsing. We can't save the empire. We need to save its people. Not just some of them. Not just the nobles. We need to save all of them. *I* need to save all of them. That's my job, as far as I can see."

"It's a lot to ask."

"Probably," Grayland said. "But I don't have a choice. I have to try. That's why I have to know when it's too late. I can't stop these coup attempts from coming, not without making the choice to do nothing else useful with my time. But maybe I can do what you did — delay the ones that are out there already. Keep *these* coup attempts and their masterminds occupied for as long as possible. Because that's how much time I have. Not until the last Flow stream collapses. Until the first of these coup attempts is successful. That's how much time I have to save everyone."

"Admirable," Chenevert said. "How are you going to delay these coup attempts?"

"By introducing a little chaos."

# CHAPTER 12

Kiva Lagos reflected that it was easy to get access to just about anyone at any time, if (a) you were of sufficiently high status and (b) if you were willing to be a complete asshole about it. So when she stepped off the Guild House elevator on the floor where the House of Wolfe kept their offices, documents in hand, she didn't bother stopping at the reception desk; she just turned left and went down the corridor to Drusin Wolfe's office, ignoring the at first confused and then increasingly strident voices of the eventually three separate people who wanted her to stop.

She did not stop. She flung open the door to Drusin Wolfe's office, and then slammed it shut and locked it before her reluctant entourage could get to her. Drusin Wolfe looked up from where he sat in a chair by a coffee table, in discussion with another man, about who the fuck knows or cares.

"What the hell?" Wolfe said.

Kiva pointed to the other man. "You. Fuck off." There was pounding at the door. Kiva ignored it.

Drusin Wolfe put a hand on the other man's arm to forestall any fucking off. "Are you insane? You can't just barge into my office and tell people to fuck off."

"And yet here I am," Kiva said. "In your office. Telling this extraneous dimwit to fuck off." She turned her attention to the extraneous dimwit. "What part of 'fuck off' aren't you understanding?"

"He and I have urgent business."

"You and *I* have urgent business," Kiva said. She walked over and flipped a document at him, causing Wolfe a couple of undignified moments as he fumbled at it. "Because if I leave this office without talking to you about *that,* right now, you're going to be unhappy with the attention that follows."

Wolfe read the document, frowning. Kiva turned back to the extraneous dipshit. "This is where he tells you to fuck off," she assured him. The extraneous dipshit, still deeply confused, looked over to Wolfe.

"I'm not going to tell you to *fuck off,*" Wolfe said, to the other man, and shot a look at Kiva. "But I'm afraid I do have to deal with this . . . person right now."

"You're kidding," the extraneous dipshit said, finally speaking.

"I wish I was," Wolfe assured him. "I'll have Michael call your office and reschedule."

Extraneous dipshit sat, gaping, until Kiva knocked him on the shoulder. "You heard the man," she said. "Now fuck *off,* already." She went to the door and unlocked it, yanking it open and causing at least one of the people who had been pounding on it to stumble through the threshold. Extraneous dipshit exited, and after a moment of Wolfe assuring his assistant, the receptionist and a hastily called security guard that everything was fine, Kiva and Wolfe were finally alone.

"Is this always the way you enter a room, Lady Kiva?" Wolfe asked.

"I learned it from my mother."

Wolfe set the document Kiva had given him on the coffee table, and tapped it. "I'd be very interested in knowing how you came across this bit of information."

Kiva sat in the chair recently vacated by the extraneous dipshit; it was still warm from his body heat, which was kind of gross. "Well, Drusin, when you come over to ruin my fucking dinner with a monologue, you can assume I'm going to do some research

214

on what you're up to."

"I thought I was pretty careful with these transfers."

"I'm sure you thought that. But you weren't. And I'm good at finding secrets."

"But not so good at keeping your *own* secrets safe, are you?" Wolfe smiled and cocked his head. "I heard you rather suddenly resigned from the emperox's executive committee. And that you're being investigated by the Ministry of Revenue. Something about you skimming a bit off the Nohamapetan accounts you were supposed to be auditing."

"There's nothing to that."

"Of course not," Wolfe said, dryly. "Actually I heard it was more than a *bit* of money being skimmed. There's some irony there. You finding all the financial gymnastics the Nohamapetans were up to, and then performing some gymnastics of your own."

"It's all crap, and the investigation will show that, so it's not as ironic as you think," Kiva said, and then glanced down heavily at the document. "The good news is, I might have a way to get back into the emperox's good graces."

"You didn't come here just to gloat, Lady Kiva."

"No, if I wanted to do that, I would have

215

just interrupted your fucking dinner."

"So what *are* you here for?"

It was Kiva's turn to tap the document. "I want in," she said.

"Excuse me?"

"You heard me."

"Do you even know what you're asking to get into?"

Kiva smirked. "You think you're the only one I have dirt on?" She waggled the sheaf of documents that were still in her hand. "It's a nice, cozy little conspiracy you got going here. Shame if something *happened* to it."

"It's just . . ."

"What?"

"Well." Drusin shifted a bit in his chair. "This is a bit sudden. Last week you were the emperox's pet."

"No." Kiva shook her head. "After that last shitty coup attempt happened, Grayland needed a warm fucking body on the executive committee. Someone she thought she could control. I'm not exactly *controllable,* Drusin."

Drusin smiled faintly at that. "I've noticed."

"Of course you have; you're not a complete fucking dimwit." Kiva leaned in. "Why do you *think* I've suddenly been accused of

216

financial improprieties with Nohamapetan accounts? It's not because I'm fucking skimming off the top. It's because our dear emperox needed a pretense for getting me off the executive committee without looking like she was sacking me on a whim. I'm sitting in my office when these fucking revenue goons come in and lay out this shit, and then when they're gone, not twenty minutes later one of the emperox's lackeys calls up and offers me the 'opportunity' to fucking resign. I know a setup when it happens. This isn't something that happens in a fucking week. It was a long time coming."

"You sound angry at the emperox."

"Of course I'm angry at the fucking emperox. Fuck her and her pissant tactics."

"So your solution is to blackmail *me*."

"No." Kiva shook her head again, and pointed at the document. "If I was going to use that to patch up things with Grayland I would have done it when her fucking minion called. No, I needed that to get your attention. Now that I have your attention, let me tell you what I can offer you for giving me a seat at this table."

Wolfe leaned back in his chair. "I'm listening."

"One: I teach you how to fucking move your money so it's not as obvious as a child

217

tracking paint on a kitchen floor. I'm one hundred percent *amazed* you don't have Grayland's goons stomping down your fucking door right now."

"Considering you just had a visit from her goons, I'm not sure I'd want to take your advice here, Lady Kiva."

"I told you, that was a setup. A pretense. Now that I'm off the executive committee, all that's going to blow away like a fart by a fan. Which brings us to two: You remember that renegotiation you wanted on the Nohamapetan contracts?"

"I do."

"Congratulations, you got it."

"Do I."

"Yes — if I get in on this."

"And you think after all this" — Wolfe gestured vaguely, encompassing the conspiracy they were mostly talking around — "is done, you'll still be in a position to make such deals?"

Kiva snorted. "It's not going to have to wait for *all this*." She waved her hands around, mocking Wolfe's movements. "We can get this part done now, before 'all this.' That way, your house gets its deal no matter if 'all this' falls apart."

"And if 'all this' works as planned?"

"Then we'll see what happens, won't we?"

Kiva shrugged. "I have my own house, Drusin. I have my own businesses and my own concerns. I was fucking drafted to take over the House of Nohamapetan's business. It won't exactly kill me to walk away. But in the meantime, you and I can still do business."

"On my terms."

"No, they're my terms now. Now that I'm getting something out of the deal."

"Hmmm. What else?"

Kiva waggled her documents. "Well, for starters, this adventure of yours is still seriously underfunded. I can get you capital."

"You're going to bankroll the revolution," Wolfe said, sarcastically.

"Of course not," Kiva said. "*She* is."

"Who is 'she'?"

"The same person whose clandestine personal accounts I've kept frozen over the last fucking year, that's who," Kiva said, and then enjoyed Wolfe's shocked expression. "Come on, Drusin. I'm not dense. You didn't think I was under the impression this was all *your* idea." She waggled the documents again. "Or any of *these* jokers. Something like this takes actual *ambition*. This absolutely stinks of her."

"I was under the impression you didn't like her," Wolfe said.

219

"I'm not going to fucking *kiss* her. I don't need to like her. I just have to respect her. And that, I do. More than fucking Grayland at the very least. I've seen both of them work up close. One knows what she's doing. The other really does *not.*"

"So how would you . . . *liberate* those funds? I was under the impression that you turned over the secret accounts of hers that you found."

"I turned over all the secret accounts that I told them about, yes," Kiva said. "And then there are ones I didn't tell them about."

Wolfe smiled. "And here I thought you weren't skimming."

"That's not skimming. That's prudent financial planning."

"This is not the greatest plan I've ever heard of," Senia Fundapellonan said to Kiva, that evening, after their customary nightly festival of mutual orgasms had settled down and they started doing the talking thing.

"It'll be fine," Kiva assured her.

Senia propped herself up on the bed. "You've manufactured a rift with the ruler of the known universe, are publicly accused of financial improprieties and are pretending to throw your lot in with a person who has tried at least twice to murder the emperox. This person belonging to a family that attempted a coup and also, let us not forget, murdered at least one member of the imperial family. Oh, and tried to murder you, by the way."

"And which you also used to work for," Kiva reminded her. "And still kind of do, really. The house, anyway."

Senia leaned over and kissed Kiva's shoulder. "I work for you now. You stole me away, remember? After they shot me, aiming for you."

"When you put it that way, it does seem sort of dodgy," Kiva admitted.

"Just a little. What I'm saying is, Nadashe will have a lot of reasons to be suspicious of you. You should be able to answer her suspicions."

"We've already done a lot of work in that direction," Kiva said. "It's almost certain Nadashe has people in the Ministry of Justice and the Ministry of Revenue. When they check the complaints against me they'll see the nice doctored investigation reports that confirm what I said to Wolfe. A record of a long investigation, in documents where the metadata says they were created in the last couple of weeks. Just what you would have for a setup."

"You're very proud of that," Senia murmured.

"Come on, it's a nice fucking touch."

"It's not a great idea to be too in love with your own cleverness."

"What are you, my mother?"

"If I were your mother, I'd use the word 'fuck' more often."

"It's a perfectly good word."

"Sure," Senia said. "Maybe not as every other word that comes out of your mouth, though."

"I don't even hear myself saying it, half the fucking time."

Senia patted Kiva. "I know that. You'd hear it if I used it as much as you did."

"No I wouldn't."

"Fucking yes you fucking absolutely fucking would."

"Now you're just exaggerating."

"Not by much."

"Great. Now I *am* going to hear myself saying it every time I fucking use it."

Senia patted Kiva again. "It will pass, I'm sure. But my point way back when was no matter how clever you think you are, you should be careful of Nadashe. You're right; I did work for her family. I know who they are. They will find you where you aren't looking for them. It's what they do."

"I know that."

"I know you *know* it, Kiva. But I need you to *feel* it." Senia sat up in bed. "Look. This might be coming a little early for you, because you're, well . . . *you,* but the thing is, I'm in love with you. Which is not what I expected to happen. I enjoyed you, and then after I was shot and you took care of me, I appreciated you, and I've always liked you. But now I know I love you, and that's terrible, because now I have to fucking *worry* about you. So I need you to *feel,* in your head and in your gut, the idea that Nadashe Nohamapetan is dangerous to you. Because you're not safe until you do. Which is awful for me."

Kiva lay there in bed, taking in everything Senia was saying, and then, after a respectful pause, she said the only thing she felt she could say in the moment. "You're trying to fucking curse me, aren't you?"

Senia looked confused. "What?"

"You're trying to fucking curse me," Kiva repeated. "Telling me you love me, right before I go and try to fuck with this fucking coup attempt. That's some fucking bullshit right there."

Senia gaped at Kiva, then burst out laughing, then collapsed on top of Kiva. "You asshole," she said.

"That's better."

"It's not better, but it's you." Senia snuggled into Kiva.

"I'll be careful," Kiva said, a couple of minutes later.

"Okay, good," Senia said. "Don't get me wrong. I know you're going to righteously mess up Nadashe's plans. No one blows up other people's plans like you."

"Thank you."

"You're welcome. Just don't let her do the same to you."

"I won't," Kiva promised.

It was Kiva who set the follow-up meeting. Because she both thought it would look better to appear that she didn't trust the conspirators, and also actually did *not* trust the conspirators, she arranged to have it happen in a public place: the recently renamed Attavio VI Park. The park was very near Brighton, the late emperox's home in Hubfall, which he had much preferred to the actual imperial palace on Xi'an. Kiva chose to have the meeting at midafternoon, when Attavio VI Park would be filled with people jogging, biking, walking their pets, playing with their kids and otherwise being in the way. Attavio VI Park was not grandly sized but did feature several pedestrian boulevards lined with trees lush with foliage, forming a near-complete canopy overhead, which would make sniping difficult.

Kiva admitted to herself that she was exercising perhaps an overabundance of caution with the sniper thing. On the other hand, Nadashe had tried to murder her with a sniper before. So there was that. Maybe the overabundance of caution was actually a *bare fucking minimum* of caution when it came to the Nohamapetans.

Drusin Wolfe was sitting on a bench near the entrance of the park and waved when he saw Kiva; she came over to him. Wordlessly he held out his hand to her. In his palm was an earpiece, a familiar brand with gesture controls for power and volume on the outside surface. Kiva accepted the earpiece, inserted it into her ear, and tapped it to power it up. Ten seconds later there was a tone signaling an incoming call. Kiva tapped the earpiece again to accept.

"Hello, Kiva," Nadashe Nohamapetan said, from the other end.

"Hello, Nadashe," Kiva said. She lightly kicked Wolfe, who was still sitting, with her shoe.

*What?* he mouthed. Kiva signaled silently that she wanted him to stand up. Wolfe looked puzzled. Kiva rolled her eyes, yanked him up off the bench, slipped her arm into the crook of his arm, and started walking him down the pedestrian boulevard so she wouldn't be a literal fucking sitting target.

"I understand you have an interest in joining our little concern," Nadashe said, while Kiva was hauling Wolfe up from his fucking seat. "You might understand how I might be concerned about your sincerity."

"You mean, because I am in control of your house's business, and because your family tried to fucking *murder* me, so we both have very good reasons to dislike and distrust each other," Kiva said.

"Yes, that," Nadashe said. Kiva noticed there was a very slight pause between when she stopped talking and Nadashe responded. This suggested that wherever Nadashe currently was, it was not on Hub itself; rather somewhere far enough away that there was just a smidgen of light-speed lag. Kiva couldn't blame her for that. Nadashe was an escaped criminal, after all. Coming to Hub was asking for trouble.

"I've already explained to Drusin Wolfe my reasons," Kiva said. "You can either accept them as sincere or don't. For my part, I'm willing to overlook your family trying to blow my brains out. I understand it was just business. Stupid and foolish as fuck, but

226

just business."

"And you want me to accept your control of the House of Nohamapetan as just business too."

"It *is* just business. And right now there's no one else to run it. You're on the run, your mother is in jail, one brother is dead and the other brother is on End, so he might as well be dead. You'll be happy to know your family business is running along perfectly well at the moment. And when everything is said and done and all accounts are settled, you can have it back."

"Just like that."

"Pretty much. Don't get me wrong, Nadashe. The House of Nohamapetan is paying me handsomely for my stewardship. I'm not running your businesses out of the goodness of my fucking heart. I'll *get* mine. But you'll get yours too, and I'm good enough at running yours that you won't even miss mine."

"Getting mine includes those accounts of mine you've frozen. The ones you haven't already turned in."

"Yes."

"You have to know that sort of transfer is going to ring bells. Explain to me how you're going to get it to me without implicating me or yourself."

Kiva talked at length about how she was going to do that, walking along with Wolfe in an erratic pattern. They crossed the length of the boulevard incessantly, moving from tree to tree, avoiding open spots in the canopy, and occasionally nearly colliding with bicyclists and pedestrians. If Wolfe figured out what Kiva was doing, he gave no sign of it, preferring instead to offer exasperated grunts as Kiva maneuvered him around. Kiva gave not one shit about his aggravation. He was body armor to her at the moment.

Eventually Nadashe seemed satisfied that Kiva could do what she set out to do. "So we're agreed," Nadashe said. "Short term, you get those still-hidden funds to me. Long term, my family takes back control of the House of Nohamapetan."

"Yes to the funds," Kiva said. "The long-term thing is entirely dependent on whether you can pull off your plans."

"Let me worry about that."

"I will," Kiva assured her. "But part of *my* deal is being in the inner circle for this. You let me in, and in return I can tell you, literally up until the last week, the state of thinking from inside the imperial palace. And I can help you keep this whole thing silent much better than you've managed so far."

228

"Yes," Nadashe said. "I was rather annoyed with Drusin when I found out his moment of gloating led you directly to us. It was unfortunate."

"Next time remind your co-conspirators to keep their fucking mouths shut."

"That's a very good idea, Kiva, thank you. I will."

"Now what?" Kiva asked.

"Now you've passed the audition," Nadashe said. "Further instructions are coming for both you and Drusin Wolfe. You'll know them when you see them."

"That's vague."

"You won't miss them, I promise. Goodbye, Kiva. I'm looking forward to getting mine, and to you getting yours." The earpiece went dead.

*What an asshole,* Kiva said to herself. She pulled the earpiece out of her ear canal.

By and large that "meeting" had gone as well as Kiva had expected it would. She didn't expect Nadashe to welcome her with open arms; that wasn't the point. The point at the moment was to build détente, and to start gathering information, the better to shove the right sticks into the right gears at the right time. Grayland didn't want her to *destroy* this coup; she wanted Kiva to grind it to a halt and look helpful as she did it.

*I can do that,* Kiva thought. Senia was right: When it came to blowing up other people's plans, Kiva was the best, and was getting better as she went along. And this little adventure was right in line with Kiva's decision, made not long after her first tussle with the House of Wolfe, to force change on others for the betterment of all, whether they wanted it or not. This coup attempt was going to fucking fail, and it would be because of Kiva, and when it was done maybe the Interdependency, or at least its people, would be that much closer to being saved.

*And I'll have punted the fucking Nohamapetans into the sun,* Kiva thought. And, well. That would be a bonus.

"What did she say?" Drusin Wolfe asked.

"You want a transcript of the whole fucking conversation?" Kiva asked. She looked down to slip the earpiece into her coat pocket.

"Just what we're supposed to do next."

"She said further instructions are coming."

"I wonder what that means."

"You tell me, you're the original co-conspirator," Kiva said, looking up just in time to see a hole sprout out of Drusin Wolfe's nose, above his left nostril. Drusin blinked once, looked at Kiva and then fell backward.

Kiva heard a clatter and turned to see a handgun settling onto the boulevard, people beginning to scream and run, and a person of indeterminate personal attributes lifting a weapon up to her face. Before everything went black Kiva had time for a final thought:

*Well, fuck. She really* did *curse me.*

# CHAPTER 13

"Okay, this gets complicated," Marce said. He fumbled with his tablet to call up his latest presentation.

Cardenia kept herself from giggling at the warning. "I know that," she said. "Remember what we're doing. Your job is to make what you're about to say comprehensible to people who aren't Flow physicists. Politicians. Journalists. Normal humans. Me."

"You're not normal," Marce pointed out.

"No," Cardenia allowed. "But once upon a time I almost was. I'm definitely not a Flow physicist, however. For the purposes of this presentation, I'll do."

The two of them were in the small media theater attached to Cardenia's personal apartments. It could seat about twenty-five and was where the emperox, when she felt like letting her hair down, could invite friends to watch the latest entertainments on a large screen with genuinely amazing sound.

That was the theory, at least. In reality, by the time Cardenia was done with her daily tasks as emperox, the last thing she wanted to do was to have a couple dozen people whooping and yelling at something bright and noisy. She mostly just crawled into bed with Marce, and if the two of them watched anything, it would be on one of their tablets, propped up by one of their knees. Marce had once observed the irony of the most powerful person in the known universe consuming media like a starving college student; Cardenia had replied by hauling him out of bed and making him watch their show in the theater. They ended up watching five minutes of the show and then did something else entirely, which did not involve watching what was up on the screen.

Cardenia smiled at the memory. What they were doing in the theater now was not what they had done then.

"Okay," Marce said, and then activated his slideshow on the theater's very large screen. The first slide's title was "What Is the Flow?" Marce frowned. "You, uh, already know this part," he said to Cardenia.

"Yes I do," she agreed. "Why don't you skip ahead to the new, complicated part."

Marce flipped forward through several additional slides covering the very very basics of Flow physics and the astrography of the Flow and the Interdependency; Cardenia made a note to have one of her people ask one of the visual artists in the Imperial Information Office to help Marce pretty it up for general consumption. Marce might be a genius in many respects, but visual design wasn't his forte.

"Right," he said, finally, and stopped at a slide that featured a visual representation of a Flow shoal. "This is a Flow shoal as we typically know it. It's where ships enter or exit the Flow, and it's static, relative to the most massive object in its system, usually its star. Indeed, in a way you could say the Flow shoal is *anchored* by gravity — it's why we find shoals in star systems but almost never outside them."

Marce tapped his tablet and then another representation of a Flow shoal appeared, this one moving and shrinking, on a loop. "But then about two years ago" — Marce glanced up at Cardenia — "literally just before I got on a ship to come to Hub, in fact —"

Cardenia smiled at this.

"— a fiver that had unexpectedly been dropped out of a decaying Flow stream

234

discovered this: an evanescent Flow shoal that, unlike the Flow shoals we typically see, both moved independently and shrank. In fact, given how small the time frame was in which it existed, it's fair to say that it evaporated."

Another slide, filled with equations Cardenia could not hope to follow. "How did this happen? I hypothesize that the decay of the Flow stream precipitated the existence of several localized evanescent streams that connected temporarily to the main stream — like fibers spinning out of an unraveling rope. There's no gravitational source for them to anchor to, so they don't last. We've never seen this before because usually when a ship unexpectedly falls out of a Flow stream, it's stranded in deep space and is never heard from again. There's no data."

Tap, new slide. "But now that we have that data, and now that, thanks to Hatide Roynold, we understand the concept of and some of the physics behind evanescent streams, I think I have some potentially extraordinary possibilities to consider, with respect to how these evanescent streams will appear in local space."

Marce stopped. "How is it so far? You following?"

Cardenia held her finger and thumb close

together. "About *this close* to not follow-ing."

Marce nodded and moved to another slide. "Then I'll make this simple. I think when an evanescent Flow stream appears, its shoal does what our nearly doomed fiver saw the disappearing shoal do — but in reverse. It appears, tiny at first, and then moves and grows until it becomes an-chored."

A pause. "Actually I think all the Flow streams do this when they emerge into normal timespace, but the regular Flow streams have been so stable — well, until recently — that there's just never been a chance to see it there."

"Maybe leave that part out when you talk to other people," Cardenia suggested.

"Got it." Marce returned to his slides, and advanced another one, with more equations on it. "So, why does this matter at all? Because if the Flow shoals on emerging evanescent streams grow and move, then there may be a way to manipulate and even control that growth and movement — to position the Flow shoals closer to human habitats, and make them large enough to al-low major structures to pass through."

"So, more ships," Cardenia said.

"No," Marce said. Another slide appeared,

showing a full-sized human habitat, one that could contain hundreds of thousands of people in it. "I'm thinking actual *places.*"

It took Cardenia a second before it hit her. "You want to put entire human habitats *into* the Flow?"

" 'Want to' isn't the phrase I would use," Marce said. "But it might be possible. And if it's possible, then suddenly things get interesting."

"Interesting?!?" Cardenia exclaimed. Because now she got it. If you could stuff actual entire habitats into the Flow, then the biggest bottleneck issue humanity had — actually moving millions of people out of systems when starships could transport only a fraction of that number — became much less of a problem. You wouldn't need ships anymore. You could just move people where they lived.

And you could save almost everybody.

"Let's do this," Cardenia said.

Marce held up his hands. "Hold on," he said. "It's not that simple."

"Why not?"

"Because — well, I don't have a slide for that, actually."

"Forget the fucking slides," Cardenia said, irritably. "Just *tell* me."

"Wow," Marce said.

237

Cardenia held up a hand. "Sorry. That came out a lot nastier than it should have." She pointed up at the screen. "But this. It could be *it*. The answer."

Marce smiled. "Maybe," he agreed. "But there's a lot that has to come before that."

"Like what?"

"Well, first of all, I have to actually find out if this is *correct.*" Marce waved up at the screen. "This is just a hypothesis. It's a guess, based on data. And not even a lot of data, since it's based substantially on a single event. I'd be a bad scientist if I didn't tell you that this is more than a little bit shaky."

"Fine," Cardenia said. "So how do you find out?"

"I'd need to observe the shoal of an evanescent Flow pop into existence."

"Okay, so do that."

"And ideally more than one."

"How many more?"

Marce wiggled his hands indeterminately. "Like, dozens? For starters?"

"How much time would that take?"

"If it was just me, more time than we have. With others, maybe a year."

"By that time, systems will start being cut off."

"Yes," Marce agreed. Cardenia frowned at

this. "But even once we gather the data, all we have is the data. We'll know if the hypothesis is sound enough to become a theory. But then we have certain practical issues to consider."

"Like how to make one of these shoals large enough," Cardenia said.

"That's right. And not only that." Marce pointed to the image of the habitat. "Habitats aren't ships. They're parked in orbits or at Lagrange points. They don't *go* anywhere, relatively speaking. And they don't have any way *to* go anywhere. At best they have engines that counteract drift, to keep them in their orbital lane. But those aren't going to move the habitats any appreciable distance. We can't get them to a Flow shoal. The Flow shoal would have to come to them."

"And how do we do that?"

Marce shrugged apologetically. "Well, see. That's the complicated part."

"So you don't *know*," Cardenia said, and as she said it she realized that it came out almost accusingly. She hoped Marce wouldn't pick up on that.

He did, of course. "Sorry?"

Cardenia counted to five before continuing. "No, don't be sorry. I'm just . . . well."

"I know," Marce said. "I'm right there

239

with you. Trust me on that. But I can't work on trying to direct a Flow shoal to a certain point without knowing that they move at all. This is the 'one step at a time' kind of science, I'm sorry to say."

"I hate that there are no shortcuts," Cardenia said.

"There aren't," Marce said. "I mean, unless you can find the data from whoever it is that created the Rupture."

"What?"

"The Rupture. You know, the thing where the people who were in the Interdependency systems before the Interdependency decided to cut themselves off from Earth and everyone else."

"I know what it is," Cardenia said.

"Okay, so, whatever it is that they did, they had to understand the physics of the Flow extraordinarily well to do it. They actually triggered the collapse of a Flow stream." Marce grimaced here. "And in doing so set up the repercussions that we're dealing with now. To do all *that,* they'd have to know what they were doing better than we know what we're doing. Better than *I* do, anyway."

"So if you had their work, you could bypass all the stuff you were talking about."

"I don't know," Marce admitted. "I think we need to confirm the moving shoals no

240

matter what. All the rest of it . . ." He shrugged. "It depends. But we'd be better off than we are now. But it doesn't exist. You told me Jiyi didn't find it."

"Yes," Cardenia said. "Right. But . . . what if Jiyi *did* find it?"

"You mean, if Jiyi had all the data we were just talking about."

"Yes."

"Then I'd be really pissed," Marce said, after a moment. "Because that would mean that *you* knew that data existed, and that you didn't give it to me. Which means I've been burning out my brain trying to save billions of people from dying with the mental equivalent of my hands tied behind my back."

"Oh," Cardenia said.

"So? *Does* Jiyi have the data from the Rupture?"

"Well," Cardenia said. "Um."

"Apparently I am history's worst monster," Cardenia said to her father.

"Statistically speaking this seems unlikely," Attavio VI said.

"Don't be so sure," Cardenia said. "I'm currently on track to fail to save literally billions from a slow death as the universe collapses around them. I'm not sure anyone

241

else compares, statistically speaking."

"The universe collapsing around them is not something you can control," Attavio VI said. "Failing to save them is not the same as killing them."

"Yes, well, there's some debate about that at the moment." Cardenia recalled the ending conversation of Marce's presentation run-through, which had, much to Cardenia's dismay, devolved into the couple's first true and actual fight. When it was over Marce excused himself, ostensibly to continue work on his presentation, but in fact to not have to talk to Cardenia anymore. He had gone to his own quarters in the imperial palace, which were basically a dorm-style room for junior imperial bureaucrats.

"This is where I'm meant to inquire about the event that precipitated your visit, is it not?" Attavio VI asked.

Cardenia narrowed her eyes at her father. "It is, but you're not supposed to say it."

"I will remember for next time."

"Never mind," Cardenia said. "I don't think you're the person I want to talk to anyway." She dismissed Attavio VI and called on Jiyi to bring forth Rachela I, the first emperox of the Interdependency. As Attavio winked out of existence, Cardenia had the almost plaintive realization that she had dismissed the simulation of her father with the same sort of casualness as she would dismiss any other of the apparitions she encountered here in the Memory Room. In some very real way, some connection with her father — her actual father — had been lost in the act.

Cardenia would have thought on it more, but Rachela I was in front of her, waiting.

"You lied a lot," Cardenia said to Rachela, a statement rather than a question.

"Humans lie a lot," Rachela replied.

"Yes, but you lied as a matter of policy," Cardenia countered. "During the founding of the Interdependency."

"I did," Rachela agreed. "Whether on balance I lied more or less than other people, or subsequent emperoxs, is a question that would require some research. If I had to guess, I would say that I was somewhere in the middle of the distribution."

"Did lying ever backfire for you?"

"Personally or as emperox?"

"Either. Both."

"Of course," Rachela said. "Telling the truth also backfired for me at times as well, in the times where it might have been kinder, easier or more politic to lie. Lies do not in themselves lead to poor outcomes, nor does truth in every circumstance lead to good ones. As with so many things, context matters."

"It never bothered you to have such a . . . *flexible* policy about truth and lies," Cardenia asked.

"No. I had a specific goal, which was to form the Interdependency, and then once founded to strengthen it to survive its early years. Truth and lies and everything in between were in service to those goals."

"The ends justified the means."

"At the time I would have said it differently."

"What would you have said?"

"That the end was too important to foreclose any particular means."

"That's a convenient bit of sophistry," Cardenia said.

"Yes it was," Rachela concurred, and once again Cardenia was reminded that this version of Rachela was not burdened with ego, and was therefore not concerned with justifying her actions in any way. *It must be nice,* Cardenia thought to herself.

"Is there a reason you are asking about truth and lies?" Rachela asked.

"I withheld information from someone," Cardenia said. "Data about the Rupture that might have been useful to him. He wasn't happy about it at all. He was unhappy that I lied to him about Jiyi having information about it, and that I wouldn't share it with him."

"It's your prerogative," Rachela said.

"He's also my boyfriend."

"That complicates matters."

"Yes it does."

"Have you resolved this?"

"No," Cardenia said. "I apologized to Marce for lying to him, and explained why I didn't tell him about the data. It was because the Rupture is the reason we're in the situation we are in now — the choice scientists and politicians made fifteen hundred years ago in setting off the Rupture made the collapse of the Flow inevitable. We aren't responsible enough for that data. At least I don't think we are."

"And Marce disagreed."

"He said we aren't them. That we're smarter than that. And then I did something I shouldn't have done."

"What did you do?"

"I laughed in his face," Cardenia said. She looked at Rachela helplessly. "I didn't *mean* to. It just came out. But he's wrong. Every moment of my reign as emperox has shown me that we aren't better than those people fifteen hundred years ago. We're not better than you were when you started the Interdependency, either. Sorry."

"I'm not offended," Rachela said. "I don't have the capacity to be offended."

"Well, Marce does. And he was. And then he was angry that I wouldn't share the Rupture data with him. That I still won't."

"You think he will do something terrible with the data."

"No." Cardenia shook her head. "Not him. I trust Marce. It's everyone else in the universe I worry about. Once the data is out, the data is out. The people who used it before nearly killed themselves and everyone else with it. They're going to kill us with it as an unintended consequence. We were lucky that information was lost for so long. It's poison."

"You don't think Marce could keep that data to himself."

"He *can't.* He's just one person. He can't do all this work himself. If this data turns out to be useful in any way, he'll need to share it with other scientists. To confirm it and to let them work on sections of the problem while he works on other things. It's what he's already doing. Once they start working with the data, they'll see the implications of it. Nothing stays a secret." Cardenia smirked as she said this. "*You* should know this better than anyone. You pro-grammed Jiyi to find every secret in the Interdependency."

"You explained this all."

"I did. Marce wasn't convinced. He said that if the data held useful information, and I kept it locked away, then if we failed to find a way to save the people of the Interde-pendency, their deaths would be on me." Cardenia shrugged. "And I'm not sure I can say he's wrong about that. It's entirely pos-sible that I *will* go down as history's worst monster. Marce is angry with me for lying to him. He's even more angry about me not giving him the data."

"You admitted to him you lied."

"It just kind of slipped out."

"You probably shouldn't have done that," Rachela said, "if you wanted him not to be angry with you."

"It's a little late for that now," Cardenia said, annoyed. "I was kind of hoping that you might have some experience that would be useful for me to fix this. Because, you know. You were good at lying. And I am evidently really *not*."

"Are you asking what I would do in the same situation?" Rachela asked.

"Yes. Sure."

"I would probably break up with this person."

"What?"

"If there's no personal relationship with this person, then you don't have to worry about him being angry or upset with you. You are the emperox. You will not have difficulty finding other people to have personal relationships with."

"Okay, one, in my experience that is very not true," Cardenia said. "And two, let's assume that for a moment I want to actually maintain this relationship."

"If you say so."

"You'd really just break up with someone like that?"

"I *did* break up with someone like that," Rachela said. "My first husband."

"And that didn't bother you?"

"No. He'd been an ass for a while."

"Well, Marce isn't an ass," Cardenia said. "I'd like to keep him."

"Share the data with him."

"I already explained why I'm not sharing it."

"Share it with him and sequester those he would share the data with."

" 'Sequester,' " Cardenia said. "That sounds suspiciously like 'put them in science prison so they can't leak.' "

248

"It would offer second-order issues," Rachela agreed.

"I don't think I could do that," Cardenia said, and then stopped. Rachela waited, patiently, because as a simulation there was no reason for her not to.

"Jiyi," Cardenia called, after a moment. The humanoid avatar appeared, standing next to Rachela. "I understand that you've tried to access the computer of the *Auvergne.* The ship that is currently docked in my berth."

"Yes," Jiyi said.

"You've not been successful."

"Not so far, no."

"You're also aware that Tomas Chenevert, the artificial person who inhabits the *Auvergne*'s computer, has extended an invitation to you to chat with him."

"Yes."

"Why didn't you take him up on the offer?"

"I'm not programmed to accept such an offer," Jiyi said. "I am designed to interact with emperoxs in the Memory Room, and to seek out hidden information. Aside from a very limited ability to address maintenance staff for issues I cannot resolve myself, I have no protocols for other interactions."

Cardenia turned her attention to Rachela.

"Why not? You programmed Jiyi. There's no reason not to make it able to deal with other people."

"What other people?" Rachela asked. "The Memory Room is designed only to be accessed by sitting emperoxs."

"And no other emperox ever thought to have Jiyi address anyone else?"

"Every other emperox accepted what Jiyi told them about its role."

"So I'm just that weird," Cardenia said.

"I wouldn't have put it that way, but yes."

Cardenia smiled at this, and then addressed Jiyi. "I would like you to take Tomas Chenevert up on his invitation to chat," she said. "He's already informed me that he can create a 'sandbox' area within his servers where the two of you can meet. You won't otherwise be able to access his servers, and he won't be able to access yours. It will be neutral ground. Make the arrangements and have your meeting as soon as possible."

"Yes, Your Majesty," Jiyi said, and disappeared.

"To what end?" Rachela asked.

"Marce already shares information with Chenevert," Cardenia said. "And Chenevert has been getting up to speed on Flow physics. If I'm satisfied he can be trusted, I can share data about the Rupture with Marce on the condition that the only person he shares it with is Chenevert. He's an artificial person, and he's spent the last three hundred years being sequestered. It wouldn't be cruel to keep him cut off from everyone else. He already is."

Cardenia spent a few more moments in the Memory Room before rounding out her session. Marce was waiting for her when she came out.

"I have things I need to tell you," she said. "Important things."

"They can wait," Marce said. His face was drawn and upset.

Cardenia frowned. "What is it?"

"Something's happened," he said. "To Kiva Lagos."

# CHAPTER 14

Things were looking up for Nadashe Nohamapetan.

To begin, she'd taken out some trash, in the form of Drusin Wolfe and Kiva Lagos.

But also — and at the moment this was the thing she was luxuriating in — she had a new address. She had been sprung from the dank, fetid confines of the *Our Love Couldn't Go On* and was now residing on the *White Spats and Lots of Dollars.* It, like the *Our Love,* was an in-system trader craft; unlike the *Our Love,* the *White Spats* didn't require antibiotics just to look at the thing.

The *White Spats* had been a lease, and now that the lease was up it had been returned to the House of Wu, to be reconditioned before being leased once more. As it was between leases, it was off the roster of ships tracked for commercial use. Proster Wu had flagged it for temporary personal duty, a prerogative of senior House of Wu executives for off-lease ships, and berthed it at the Wu family personal dock complex, where no imperial inspector or assessor would ever trouble it. Unless it moved out of dock, it was effectively invisible.

Nadashe was delighted. The *White Spats* was clean and modern, and the previous leaseholder had configured it to hold passengers as well as cargo, so her living quarters were no longer clad in groaning, discolored metal and occasional spots of mold. Proster Wu had populated the ship with a skeleton crew of technicians and domestics, all gleaned from the Countess Nohamapetan's still-in-system fiver, which had been confiscated when she was arrested for treason and murder. Nadashe accepted their fealty as acting head of her house, and then in true Nohamapetan fashion proceeded to forget they existed unless she wanted something specific from them.

Living even temporarily on the sufferance of the Wu family did have its downsides, however, as Nadashe was reminded when her suite was invaded by Proster Wu, who entered without preamble or indeed so much as a knock.

"You murdered Drusin Wolfe," he said.

"Not I," Nadashe said, mildly. She was sitting idly on a chaise longue, flipping through her tablet. "I was here the entire time. I have witnesses."

"You cannot go about *murdering your allies.* That's how they stop being your allies. You need all of your allies. *We* need them."

Nadashe set her tablet down. "Well, Proster. There are two ways of explaining what happened to our dear friend Drusin Wolfe. The first is that I did not have him murdered. As it happens, when this is looked into by the various law enforcement sorts who will invariably look into these things, mail will be discovered that reveals Drusin Wolfe had lured Kiva Lagos to that park in order to have her assassinated — the two of them had recent contentious business dealings, after all. Bring her out into the park; have a wandering hit man pop her in the head; we're done."

"Except for the fact that Wolfe is dead."

Nadashe shrugged. "A bump. A jostle. This is what you get for hiring cut-rate assassins."

"And you expect *anyone* in the world to believe that."

"I expect law enforcement to believe it, yes," Nadashe said. "You give them a simple answer, they'll take it every time. It's so much less work, and the simplest answer is usually the correct one. The trail is there.

Wolfe verifiably ordered a hit on Kiva Lagos. Then he rather unfortunately got in the way. I hope his contractor had already gotten paid. Coming back for the second half of his payment would be awkward."

Proster Wu did not look in the least impressed. "That's one way of looking at it. You said there was another."

"The other way of looking at it is that Drusin Wolfe went out of his way to gloat to Kiva Lagos that she was going to get hers, which inspired her to find out what he was up to, implicating several other houses and me and *you,* Proster, in the bargain. Kiva Lagos is the very last person you want to cross, because she's smart and she'll punch you in the throat if you piss her off. And that's exactly what she did to Drusin Wolfe. She maneuvered him right where *she* wanted him and made him jump through *her* hoops."

Nadashe stretched on her chaise longue. "She had to go, obviously. But *he* had to go, too. To tie up loose ends and seal off leaks. But also to remind our people that they have to stay focused. There will be time for settling personal scores *after* the coup. As emperox, I will *encourage* all their petty vendettas, as reward for their service. But not until after Grayland is gone and I am

255

sitting in the imperial palace."

"So you're sending a message."

"*I'm* not doing anything," Nadashe said. "Like I said. But if any fearful and paranoid allies take a lesson from this and make an extra effort not to do anything stupid between now and when the coup happens, then that's a *good* thing, isn't it?" She shrugged. "It's a cheap lesson in any event. The House of Wolfe isn't significant to our plans. They're a minor house. And now we have the benefit of Kiva Lagos out of the picture and the House of Nohamapetan that much closer to being back in family control, which is going to be simpler for me when the time comes."

"So what do you want me to tell our allies? Because they are already howling to me about it."

"Tell them whatever you like. But make the point to them that if Drusin Wolfe had kept his mouth shut — had not felt the need to crow to someone who uncovered what he was up to as easily as you or I might tie our shoes — he wouldn't be dead right now. That would be the case no matter which of the two scenarios you believe happened. You might also remind our allies that Drusin's bragging led Kiva Lagos to finding out about their involvement as well. If Kiva

256

hadn't had that falling out with Grayland, Drusin's indiscretion would mean we'd all already be awaiting our treason trials." Nadashe paused. "Well, *they* would. As would you, Proster."

"I wasn't in any of Lagos's documents," Proster said.

Nadashe smiled. "I think it's delightful you think our *allies,* as you call them, wouldn't sell you out the instant they were caught."

"I see your point."

"I thought you might."

"You think the falling-out between Lagos and Grayland was real, then."

"No one in our little club is in jail. Grayland's last roundup of traitors doesn't suggest she wastes any time hauling them off when she learns about them. And Kiva is an asshole, so I can see *anyone* getting tired of her quickly."

"That's a yes, then."

"It's an 'I'm not worrying about Kiva Lagos anymore,' " Nadashe said. She picked her tablet back up. "I have other things I'm focused on. Our so-called allies should be focusing on other things as well."

Proster picked up that he had been dismissed, and left her on her chaise longue.

In truth, Nadashe had not been nearly so

257

sanguine as she had suggested to Proster about Kiva Lagos. She wasn't convinced Kiva hadn't been trying to play double-agent with Drusin Wolfe; when Wolfe had come to her with the news that Kiva wanted in on their plans, she had nearly pushed him into an airlock and cycled it, fraught as she was with worry and fear (inwardly, of course — it wouldn't do to let someone like Drusin Wolfe know what she was actually thinking). It had taken a couple of days to have her people deliver the documents that suggested it was as Kiva had represented it — Grayland had gotten tired of dealing with Kiva's ass, and found a way to push her out.

This delighted Nadashe, because she had come to loathe Kiva Lagos. She *respected* Kiva, and she worked hard not to underestimate her, and she was well aware that although Kiva was a formidable opponent, as the all-too-large number of frozen supposedly hidden financial accounts made clear, she could also be a formidable ally, with inside knowledge of the imperial household to boot.

But at the end of the day Nadashe just couldn't take Kiva — her confidence, her vulgarity, her outer layer of complete anarchy masking a weirdly inflexible inner layer of morality. Also the fact that Kiva had banged her brother Ghreni senseless in college made Nadashe feel queasy, although Ghreni was never the most discerning person in terms of partners. Nadashe and Kiva would never be allies.

It was a shame, Nadashe thought. When Drusin Wolfe had revealed his gaffe and Kiva's attempt to capitalize on it, Nadashe didn't waste more than a second thinking about his fate. He was going to have to die, and the sooner the better. But in spite of everything, Nadashe had to think about what to do with Kiva. For as much as she loathed her (and had no doubt that Kiva felt the same about Nadashe), it seemed almost a waste to give her the same fate as Drusin Wolfe. Wolfe would not be missed for even the amount of time it took him to hit the ground. Kiva would, for at least slightly longer.

Still, Nadashe couldn't have Kiva out in the world, being a chaos agent just by dint of existing. Kiva had to be removed from the playing board. Nadashe removed her and thought herself wise to do so.

Not for the first time, Nadashe wondered, in an abstract way, if there was something not quite right about her. If one were to list out her deeds over the last several years, one would suggest they were the acts of a sociopath. She had, after all, helped foment a civil war; attempted to assassinate the emperox not once but twice, the second time killing her own brother as collateral damage; participated in a coup and was fomenting another one; and in the last few weeks taken out a small handful of nobility. On paper, these were not the deeds of a nice or moral person.

Nadashe did not worry about being nice. Nice was for other people — the people who didn't have power or a plan to get it when they didn't have it. Nadashe could never recall being "nice" in the generic sense of the term. Polite? Certainly. Respectful? When appropriate or necessary. Nice? No. Nice felt like an abdication. Like an admission of defeat. Like someone who was a supplicant, rather than a superior or, at least, a peer.

*Maybe if you were nice you would have been married to an emperox already and all this would have been unnecessary,* a voice inside her head said to her, a voice that sounded almost exactly like her mother. Nadashe had been the intended fiancée of Rennered Wu, crown prince of the Interdependency, until she wasn't, because it turned out that Rennered didn't want a partner so much as he wanted a compliant doormat. A nice, compliant doormat. Nadashe was willing to deal with a lot to be the imperial consort, but not that. And so here we were. And maybe her mother didn't like that, but then she had killed Rennered by sabotaging his race car and then tried to depose the current emperox. So maybe she wasn't the best person to lecture anyone on *nice.*

So "nice" was not in Nadashe's personal vocabulary. But "moral" was. Nadashe was aware that killing people and fomenting coups were not the usual hallmarks of a moral person, at least not in isolation. But Nadashe believed, strongly, that there was a context for her acts. The first was the context of the Nohamapetan family, which was objectively a superior line — not in some ridiculous eugenic way but in the consistent influence and importance of the family and its house, going back to the earliest days of the Interdependency, when the Nohamapetans were one of the first families to align themselves with the Wus.

The Wus, and the imperial line in particular, had lost their way more than once — indeed, that was the problem with the current emperox, who if not for an accident (well, "accident") would be at best a middle-tier academic in some distant system, well away from the halls of power. It was why Proster Wu agreed to sit Nadashe on the throne. He knew it was time for someone to be there who had the courage to do the hard things, and that there was no one in the Wu family, him not excepted, ready to step up for that. As part of the bargain, Nadashe had promised to marry a Wu and to have her heir bear that family name, when everything settled and there was a new empire based in the End system.

And who knows? Nadashe thought. She might even do that.

Beyond the Nohamapetan family itself, there was the matter of the Interdependency, and what it really was. Grayland, who had lived her entire life outside of the nobility and the guilds, thought the Interdependency was its people — all of its people, a multicellular thing with billions of indispensable cells, none of which would survive without all of the others. This was ridiculous, and also futile. There was no way to save every single cell in this vast organism, and it was a waste of time to try.

Someone had to be willing to sacrifice the body to save what was important: the brain and heart of the Interdependency, the nobility and their monopolies, and the guilds that had sprung up to service both. That the

Interdependency existed at all was because the Wus and the Nohamapetans and other noble families had made it so. As long as they existed, the *idea* of the Interdependency, and the structure of it, would survive and in time would thrive in its new home on End.

That was what was important. Nadashe understood, again mostly abstractly, that the billions of people who would die with the collapse of the Flow would not be impressed with her reasoning and with her determination to focus on the nobility, guilds and capital. But the fact of the matter was, they were going to die *anyway*. There was no way to save them all. There was no way to save even more than the tiniest fraction of them. Nadashe didn't see the point in wasting time worrying about them.

The nobles were a vastly smaller number of people to contend with. They understood the value of saving themselves. They were the ones who had the majority of capital. They also understood the realpolitik issues they were confronting — which was that the vast majority of people in the Interdependency were going to die, but that the nobles didn't have to, as long as they were willing to pay the Nohamapetans for access to End. It was simply the cost of doing busi-

263

ness in the new paradigm.

And in doing so, they would save the Interdependency. Nadashe would save the Interdependency.

In the end, *that* was the highest morality.

And if on the way there, Nadashe herself had to do some questionable things? Well. That was also the cost of doing business in the new paradigm.

So, no, Nadashe thought. There was nothing wrong about her at all. She was strong, and moral and courageous in a way that history would understand. In a not-at-all facetious way, Nadashe thought herself not unlike Rachela I, the first emperox of the Interdependency. Wash away the mythmaking of the Church of the Interdependency and various fawning historians, and you see a woman who had made difficult choices for the good of an entire society. Because those choices had to be made. There would be no Interdependency without those choices, and without Rachela I.

Nadashe had a fleeting thought that when she became emperox, her imperial name should also be Rachela, to make that connection explicit. She dismissed the idea almost as quickly. It would be a little on the nose, and also, with a new home for the Interdependency at End, it made sense not to look into the past.

"Emperox Nadashe I" would do just fine.

Yes, indeed, things were looking up for Nadashe Nohamapetan.

There was a ping on Nadashe's tablet, signaling that one of her staff was requesting access to her suite. Nadashe let them enter.

"The Countess Rafellya Maisen-Persaud, of the House of Persaud, is here to see you, ma'am."

"Perfect," Nadashe said. "Prepare a tea service, and then bring her in."

# Chapter 15

"All right, first question. Where the fuck am I?"

The person Kiva Lagos addressed sat at a small desk in a small room and appeared amused. "I thought your first question might be who the fuck am I."

"All right, fine. Who the fuck are you?"

"My name is Captain Robinette."

"Hello, Captain Robinette. Charmed. Where the fuck am I?"

Captain Robinette looked over at the two crew members who had accompanied Kiva Lagos to his stateroom. "Wait outside," he said. "Close the door. If you hear anything other than slightly raised voices, come in and beat her unconscious." The two left.

Kiva was unimpressed. "You won't make any noise if I fucking strangle you," she said.

"I'm going to take the chance you'll make noise coming over the desk."

"And you still haven't answered my question. Where the fuck am I?"

"Before I answer that, please tell me what you remember before you got here."

"Are you fucking kidding me?"

"Indulge me, please."

"Before I woke up here, the last thing I remember is being shot in the fucking face. When I woke up here, I was in a room the size of a fucking broom closet, where I stayed for four fucking days, with nothing but a case of protein bars and a chemical fucking toilet to keep me company. That thing's a fucking mess, by the way."

"After four days it would be. Go on."

Kiva motioned behind her. "Then the door to my cell unlatched, and then your pals Chuckle and Fuckle told me to come with them. Then I was here. The end. Where the fuck am I?"

The amused look on Robinette's face had not noticeably changed since Kiva entered the room, which annoyed her. "You're on the freighter *Our Love Couldn't Go On,* which as of" — Robinette checked his timepiece — "forty-five minutes ago has entered the Flow stream to the Bremen system, a journey that will take us fifteen days and four hours, more or less. The previous four days were us accelerating toward the Flow stream. I was under in-

struction not to let you out of your stateroom during those four days. My employer
was quite specific. Thus the protein bars
and chemical toilet. I assume you figured
out there was water in the sink."

"It tasted like shit."

"Yes, well, inasmuch as the water is re-
claimed, it might. It's potable, but just
barely."

"Fuck you."

"My employer noted that you might be
hostile," Robinette observed.

"This isn't me hostile," Kiva said.

"I assume hostile will be you coming over
the desk and strangling me."

"For starters."

"Fair enough," Robinette said, agreeably,
and then reached into his desk to pull out a
handgun, which he aimed at Kiva, finger
lightly on the trigger. "This should keep
things civil."

"Fuck you."

"For certain values of civil, anyway."

"Why the fuck are we going to Bremen?"

"Because next month is Oktoberfest and
I've never been."

"I asked a serious question."

"And I gave you a serious answer. My
employer was specific that you were to be
escorted out of the Hub system but didn't

much care where. I suggested the Bremen system because it's a relatively short hop in the Flow, the Flow streams to and from Hub are predicted to be sound for a few years yet, and because Oktoberfest sounds like fun. It apparently hails all the way back to Earth times. I've never been. So why not? And my employer was fine with it, so here we are."

"Let me guess who your mysterious fucking employer is."

"You don't have to guess," Robinette said. "It's Nadashe Nohamapetan. The same person who had you shot in the face with stun pellets. How do you feel, by the way?"

"How the fuck do you think I feel?" Kiva said. "Like I was shot in the fucking face with a bunch of rocks."

Robinette nodded. "You look terrible, too. All those little pinpricks where the pellets went into your head and neck."

"Thanks, asshole."

"The good news is they'll heal pretty quickly. Almost certainly by the time we get to Bremen."

"And then what?"

"Like I said: Oktoberfest."

"I mean what happens to *me*, you singularly obtuse motherfucker."

"That hasn't been decided yet. I was told

269

that once we arrive at Bremen further instructions will come. We are to wait for two months. If no additional instructions have come by then, I'm supposed to toss you out an airlock. We have three. You may pick."

"I don't understand," Kiva said. "Why would she keep me alive just to have me tossed out of a fucking airlock?"

"You should ask her yourself."

"She's rather inconveniently not here at the moment, you fatuous bag of pricks."

"Well — if I set down this gun, do you promise not to come over the desk?"

"I promise nothing."

"I'll take my chances. Please note that the gun is keyed to my fingerprint, so even if you grab for it, it won't do you any good."

"I could fucking beat you to death with it."

"I'll just put it back in the desk, then," Robinette said, and did so. From the same drawer he produced an envelope, which he handed to Kiva. "It's from my employer. She was specific that I should give it to you once you were released from your captivity."

Kiva stared at the envelope. "Oh my fucking god. She's gloating in print."

"She may be," agreed Robinette. He

pointed to the envelope. "If you don't mind, once you read that, I'd like to know what she said."

"Why do you care?"

"I'm curious, is all. She was a passenger on this ship for some months, you know. From when her mother and all those others were arrested for treason to really not all that long ago. I understand she's traded up in terms of accommodations, and I suppose I can't really blame her."

"Yeah, this ship is kind of a shithole from what I've seen," Kiva said.

"Perhaps, but with regard to your situation, Lady Kiva, being inside of it is better than being outside of it."

"You have a point there," Kiva admitted. "So Nadashe was not popular on your ship, I take it."

"I believe the polite euphemism is 'she kept to herself.' "

"Then why the fuck are you doing her dirty work?"

"For the most obvious reason there is, Lady Kiva: She's paying me very very well to do it."

"I can pay you more than she can," Kiva said.

"Perhaps you could, theoretically. But as a practical matter, you're on this ship without access to any funds whatsoever, while Nadashe Nohamapetan has already paid me half up front, which is in itself more than I've made in the last two years. So your money — if you had any on you, which you don't — is literally no good here. Sorry."

"You're making a mistake."

"Possibly, but I doubt it. I heard of Nadashe Nohamapetan long before I ever had reason to cross her path. She strikes me as both singularly determined, and absolutely the wrong person to get on the bad side of. So I'm going to take her money and stay on her good side, if that's all right with you."

Kiva snorted. Captain Robinette took that as an affirmation, and continued. "In the meantime, you have two choices, Lady Kiva. The first is to choose to behave yourself, which means staying in the areas I tell you to stay in and keeping out of the way of the running of the ship and the responsibilities of the crew. In which case you will be allowed some freedom of movement and access to a tablet for entertainment. The *Our Love* isn't a cruise liner and there's not much to do, and everyone knows why you're here and they're not going to be inclined to wait on you. But it's better than the alternative."

"Which is?"

"That you cause me trouble, Lady Kiva. In which case I lock you back into your broom closet with some protein bars and that chemical toilet, and you can count the rivets on the bulkhead. And if you're especially troublesome, I might have you tossed out an airlock without waiting for permission."

"Nadashe wouldn't like that," Kiva said. "She's not paying you to make decisions."

"That's true. It's her money. But it's *my* fucking ship, Lady Kiva. Pardon the language. So, which choice will you make?"

"I'll play nice."

"That's what I like to hear." Robinette reached into his desk again and produced a tablet, which he handed to Kiva. "That has guest access, and includes information about the ship and the services the crew can provide. You have access to the ship's doctor, which I suggest you take advantage of, and if you talk to the purser, we can get you an extra set of clothes. I'll give those to you. Call it a gesture of goodwill."

"Thanks," Kiva said, sarcastically.

"You're welcome," Robinette said, not sarcastically at all. "There are two sex workers on board, but they are a value-add for the crew and you don't have any money, so you should maybe skip them. But you can

273

screw any other crew member you like on your own time as long as you don't disrupt ship's duties or its general calm."

"I'm not exactly in the mood."

"It'll be two weeks to Bremen. You may change your mind. In any event, there's your tablet and there's your letter, and now you know where you are and why. Do you have any other questions at the moment?"

"Not for you," Kiva said.

"Then you're dismissed. Either Chuckle or Fuckle, as you call them, will escort you back to your quarters. And Lady Kiva, if I may make a suggestion."

"What is it?"

"You may have noticed I was tolerant of your threats and attitude in our little chat today," Robinette said. "That's because I find it strangely charming, and because I know that being in a hole for four days would make anyone testy. I don't suggest you continue with that attitude with me from here on out, and especially not in front of my crew. The *Our Love* may be a shithole, as you describe it, but it's a shithole that needs tight discipline, and I can't and won't tolerate anything that messes with that. Do we understand each other?"

"Fine."

"Good. Also, I strongly suggest not trying

that attitude with the crew, either."

"Why? Because it would be mean?"

"No, because they'll break a butter knife off in your neck."

"I thought you said you kept tight fucking discipline on this ship."

"I said the ship *needs* tight discipline. I didn't say that if you tested that proposition, you wouldn't find yourself dead."

Nadashe's letter was, of course, irritating as all fuck.

It went like this:

Kiva:
Because I know you are wondering, here is why I've kept you alive.

1. Because it amuses me to keep you alive, on that terrible ship.
2. Because I'll need you alive to access some of those still-frozen accounts.
3. Because keeping you alive will keep your mother and the House of Lagos in check. There's something to be said for the fine art of keeping hostages.

I should note that the last of these is

something I'm keeping in my pocket for now. As far as anyone else knows, you were killed along with Drusin Wolfe. After my contractor killed Wolfe and stunned you, my own ambulance crew was first to the scene and ferried you away. I regret to say you died on the way to the hospital, and your body immediately shipped in a closed casket back to Ikoyi. I framed Wolfe for it; he was killed by his own sloppy contractors. Good help is hard to find.

"Oh, you snide fucking piece of shit," Kiva said out loud as she read that last bit. "You really think you're being clever."

I've kept you alive for now, but I obviously can't have you at Hub. So now you are on your way to Bremen. I believe you know what I have planned. I have reason to believe it will happen soon. If I am successful, then it's possible I will recall you, to retrieve my property, and to discuss with you, as your family's lead negotiator, the disposition of the House of Lagos in the new regime. After all, you were so considerate with the House of Nohamapetan while you were privileged to look after its interests. I look forward to having a Nohamapetan return the favor.

If I'm not successful, then I regret to say that I will likely not be in a position to send further instructions to Captain Robinette and his crew with respect to your disposition. By this time, I'm sure the captain has told you what that will mean. And before you suggest to him that my failure means that he won't get paid the remainder of what's owed to him, you should know that he knows that the remainder is already in an escrow account back at Hubfall. Sorry to disappoint you on that.

I'm afraid there's not much more to say, other than that you should wish me luck. Your life depends on my success.

Enjoy Oktoberfest!

NN

Kiva read the letter, read it again, read it one more time just to be sure, then tore it up into small pieces, went to the crew head down the passageway from her broom closet, tossed the torn-up bits of letter into the head, pulled down her pants, sat on the head, and pissed all over them. This action did not change the overall tenor of Kiva's current circumstances, but it did make her feel better.

Having done that, Kiva returned to her broom closet and considered her situation, and what advantages and assets she had at the moment.

Advantages: She was fucking alive, which honestly had come as something of a surprise to her after being shot in the face. The captain was correct that she didn't look very pretty at the moment — her face was a mass of subdermal bruises and pockmarks where the drug-laden bits of powdery shot had gone into her skin, to be absorbed — but that wasn't anything she was worried about. It wasn't going to slow her down any.

Assets: Her brain. Her body. Not her face, per se — see above re: bruises and pocks — but everything else inside and out was working on all cylinders. Plus her current state of being, which was *fucking pissed.*

Not just fucking pissed at Nadashe Nohamapetan, to be clear, although Kiva was indeed righteously fucking pissed at her. Nadashe had had her shot in the face, kidnapped and put into space on a ship that was basically a case of fucking lockjaw waiting to happen. Nadashe needed to get an attitude adjustment, and Kiva very much wanted to be the one who gave it to her.

But the person Kiva was most fucking

pissed at was herself. Senia had been right: Nadashe had found Kiva where she wasn't looking. Kiva had walked into that meeting with Drusin Wolfe confident that she had the upper hand, that Wolfe and Nadashe were going to fall for her plan exactly as she had intended. She had been overconfident and underprepared, and it ended up with her being shot in the face and with her fate in the hands of a fucking Nohamapetan.

Kiva paused briefly to think about Senia, who almost certainly thought that Kiva was dead and who was having to deal with that. Kiva felt something stab at her, something that she was not entirely sure she'd ever felt before — grief, but not for the dead (which would be her, and she was not), but for the living, who had to sit with their own grief for the dead. It wasn't fair to Senia to have to deal with this grief, and while Kiva was never one to delude herself that the world was anything close to approaching fair, this felt like a special flavor of out-of-bounds, something very particular that she would need to repay Nadashe for.

So, yes. Kiva was fucking pissed. Pissed at Nadashe. Pissed at herself. Pissed for Senia. And pissed to be on a ship that was apparently made mostly out of rust and spunk, hurtling toward fucking *Oktoberfest,* whatever the fuck *that* was.

Kiva had fucked up. It was time get her own back.

She had fifteen days and just under a couple of hours now to do it.

So Kiva got to work.

# CHAPTER 16

Marce Claremont did not consider himself a man prone to emotional seesaws, but he had to admit the last several days had genuinely messed with his head.

First, the realization that Cardenia — the woman who, yes, actually, he was very deeply in love with despite the impossible fact that she was also Grayland II, emperox of the Interdependency — had lied to him. Not in a small way, like that she enjoyed the way he gave foot massages, or even in a large way, like cheating on him with some other member of her court because she was emperox and who was going to stop her. She had lied in the largest way possible, by entrusting him with an impossible task — a task upon which billions of lives were riding, a task the failure of which would flatten him forever into the dirt — and then withholding the information that he might use to solve that impossible task.

It was difficult even now for Marce to convey both the anger and absolute crushing disappointment he had felt when he realized what Cardenia had done, and the almost insulting rationale she had given for doing so. Asking Marce to find a way to use the evanescent Flow streams to save billions without giving him the highly advanced science that was used to create the Rupture was like asking someone to cure a highly contagious disease, and then not telling them about germ theory, all the data about which you just happened to have right there in your hand.

Cardenia had pointed out that the last time humans had this particular set of knowledge, they had almost wiped themselves out and had ultimately put themselves into the situation they were in today. Marce couldn't argue against that, but he had argued that was then, and the circumstances were different now, and that no one working with that data today would be so stupid as to use it for those same ends. Cardenia had laughed in his face then, and something inside him had fallen out of love with her in that moment.

The two had argued and fought, and Marce said some fairly unforgivable things before storming off to sulk in his bachelor quarters, which were about half the size of Cardenia's personal bathroom. He stewed there for a bit, while Cardenia went off to commune with her ancestors, or whatever it is that she wanted to call what she did in the Memory Room. Marce had meant to get some work done but instead went over the details of the fight in his head, playing them over in a constant loop, with special attention given to Cardenia laughing in his face.

He expected that the more he ran that moment in his head, the angrier he would get. But in reality the more he ran it in his head, the sadder and more depressed he got. It took him a good long while to realize why: It wasn't that he was wrong, it's just that Cardenia wasn't wrong either, and she was probably more not wrong than he was. He was a scientist and frankly not the most astute observer of the human situation. He would never abuse the Rupture data like that and couldn't imagine any of the scientists that he would work with would, either. They were busy trying to save the universe, after all.

But he had in the moment forgotten that Cardenia was also Grayland, and what she had to deal with on a daily basis: the grinding opportunism and political maneuvering of the world she inhabited; the number of people who wanted something from her or would be happy to take something from her; the depressing reality of knowing that there were people — forget people, entire *conspiracies* of people — who would think nothing of killing Grayland to get her out of the way of their own selfish goals.

Cardenia — Marce's girlfriend, the woman he knew he loved — was sweet and kind and awkward and a little goofy. Grayland II, the emperox of the Interdependency, could not afford to be any of those things. And they were the same person. When he had said his naive words to Cardenia, it was Grayland who had laughed at him. Because Grayland knew better.

This realization about the nature of their argument did not make Marce feel better; it made him feel much much worse. It made him feel bad enough that he knew he needed to go over and apologize to Cardenia, no matter how annoyed he was that she wouldn't give him the Rupture data.

That resolved, Marce splashed water on his face and was preparing to head back to Cardenia to grovel at her when he received the call from Senia Fundapellonan that Kiva Lagos had been murdered in Attavio VI park.

Marce took the news like a punch in the gut. Marce hadn't seen much of Kiva since he had arrived at Hub and become involved with Cardenia, and Kiva had been busy enough on her own, with managing the House of Nohamapetan's affairs and recently with her new relationship with Senia. But Marce looked back fondly on their travels to Hub and the time they had spent together, and he appreciated that she was solidly an ally to Grayland in a time when she sorely needed them.

Senia had called Marce because she knew that he was absolutely the quickest way to get the news to Cardenia; the news would eventually filter up to her, but it would otherwise have to go through several channels to arrive on her doorstep. Marce expressed his condolences to Senia and then carried himself through the vast expanse of the palace and arrived in Cardenia's apartments just as she was exiting the Memory Room.

He told her about Kiva Lagos. And then, after they had both stopped crying about that, she told him she was giving him the Rupture data.

"I honestly can't process that right now," is all Marce could say to that.

Kiva Lagos's body was identified via

fingerprints and DNA. The death confirmed by the hospital, her body was, in accordance with her written legal instructions, sealed into a low-temperature transport casket and shipped out on the next available transport to the Ikoyi system. Even Senia didn't arrive at the hospital before the body was sealed up; she had three minutes with the casket before it was shipped out on an expedited basis to make it to the *That's Just Your Opinion, Sir* before it disembarked.

In a sad irony, the *Your Opinion* entered the Flow shoal to Ikoyi a little over an hour after the *This Indecision's Bugging Me* — bearing the Countess Huma Lagos, Kiva's mother and head of the House of Lagos — arrived at Hub for a meeting of the house's various system directors. Grayland asked Marce to be her representative to the Countess Lagos, to pass along her private condolences and to assure the countess that her daughter's public disfavor with the emperox had been manufactured.

Not only did the Countess Lagos not appear at all concerned about her daughter's public disfavor, she also did not appear particularly concerned that her daughter was, in fact, dead. "Did you see the body?" she asked Marce, in her daughter's office at the Guild House, when he came with the

286

emperox's condolences.

"The body was identified in two ways," Marce said.

"That's not what I asked you," the Countess Lagos said.

"I didn't see the body myself."

"Nor did Miss Fundapellonan. She told me the body was sealed into a casket before she got there. Nor did any of Kiva's staff here at the Guild House see her to identify the body, either at the House of Nohamapetan or the House of Lagos. The only people who saw her were the emergency technicians who ferried her body to the hospital, and the doctors who pronounced her dead when she arrived. None of whom know her."

"There were the fingerprints and DNA," Marce noted.

The Countess Lagos gave Marce an indulgent look. "Lord Marce, remind me. Are you the pleasant young man my daughter used as a fuck toy on her journey from End to Hub?"

"I . . . . wouldn't have put it that way, but yes, my lady."

"She thought highly of you, in several categories."

"Uh, thank you."

"But for the purposes of this conversation, I seem to recall that just before you jumped from End, your ship was overtaken by pirates and you were required to pretend you were someone else, which required a fake DNA sample. Is that correct?"

"It is."

"And before that, to get on our ship at all, you assumed a fake identity, which required both false fingerprints and irises. At least, that's how the story was told to me. Also correct?"

"Yes."

"Well, then, Lord Marce. Let me ask you again. Did you see my daughter's body? Did you or anyone who knew her see her body?"

"No."

"And would you agree that her quote-unquote body was sealed into that casket with unseemly haste and shoved into a passing ship almost as quickly?"

"That was per her instruction."

The countess made a dismissive sound. "Lord Marce, you are certainly a pretty young man, but I don't think you're all that bright. Kiva has no particular attachment to Ikoyi. She hasn't lived there regularly since she was a child. And our family is neither religious nor holds with any special burial rites. Do you know what I plan to do with my body once I am dead?"

"I do not, Countess."

"Neither do I. I'll be dead and I won't give a shit. If I'm at home my children will decide what to do with it. It'll probably be liquification since that's the standard for Ikoyi habitats, but they could prop it up with sticks and twirl my corpse around like a puppet for all I care. If I die on a ship, they can toss me out over the side. And I'm the Countess Lagos. I don't see any of my children caring about it any more than I do, much less Kiva, who you know from experience is not exactly sentimental."

"I do indeed," agreed Marce.

The countess smiled. "So, again: No one saw the body, and it was shipped off with unseemly haste under dubious instruction by people unknown. And now the ship allegedly carrying her body is in the Flow, is it not? I do not usually take sucker bets, Lord Marce, but if you wish to bet me that the ship arrives with that casket still inside it, I will happily take your marks."

"So you think Kiva is still alive."

"It's more to say that until I can see her body with my own eyes and lay my own hands on it, I find it unlikely she is dead."

"Have you told this to Senia Fundapellonan?"

The Countess Lagos's face became serious. "No. It would be cruel to do so."

"Even though you think your daughter's alive."

"Lord Marce, do you love my daughter?"

"I was . . . am fond of her."

"But you don't love her."

"No."

"Senia Fundapellonan does."

"I understand."

"I am glad you do."

"If that's not Kiva in that casket, who is it and where is she?"

"I'm not a detective, Lord Marce. But if I were I suppose I would check to see if any young woman of similar height, color and build to Kiva has gone missing in the last several days. I might also try to find that ambulance that brought her to the hospital. I have a suspicion it might be hard to find."

"I'll have someone look into that," Marce said.

"Do. As for where she is — you said that she was working with the emperox to introduce chaos into the plans of Nadashe Nohamapetan?"

"That's what the emperox told me, yes."

"Then I assume that is exactly what she is doing."

"I hope you're right."

"As do I, Lord Marce. In the meantime I

will pretend in public to grieve over my daughter."

"That might be wise," Marce said. "How long do you plan to stay in-system?"

"Indefinitely," the countess said. "I have my business to attend to. I am led to believe the Imperial Navy wants to have a meeting with me about a task force they wish to assemble in Ikoyi space. And beyond that, whatever is happening with the emperox and my daughter, I want to be here for. I can't imagine it will be anything less than spectacular when it finally plays out. I wouldn't miss it for the world."

And then there was the Rupture data.

From it, Marce learned two things. The first was that the scientists of the Free Systems, the loose confederation of star systems that occupied the same space as the Interdependency did today, were *enormously* advanced, at least in their understanding of the Flow and its dynamics. Marce could spend the rest of his natural-born life exploring the data that Cardenia had, with great reluctance, surrendered to him, and still not have scratched the surface of what it had to show him.

There was so much data here, so much understanding of the nature of the Flow that had previously been hidden to Marce, that he was genuinely angry at it. Observations and structures that his father had spent thirty years gathering data to describe were sketched out here in appendices — so well-understood as to be almost trivial. The idea that all of this information, all of this knowledge, had been flung down a memory hole for fifteen hundred years briefly brought Marce to a state that could only be described as existential despair.

But only briefly, because, after all, he had the data now. What he wanted to do was wallow in it, luxuriate in it, follow the threads of the data at his leisure to see where they led and what they meant. But there was no time for that. Right now, Marce still needed to save billions of people, or at least to see if it was possible. With great reluctance, he put aside nearly all the data to focus on the material that he could see was relevant to the problem at hand.

The second thing he learned was that the scientists of the Free Systems were not nearly smart enough.

For example, they understood that the Flow vibrates, but they didn't understand that it's a liquid.

Well, approximately. Trying to describe these underlying mathematical realities of the Flow into human language was like trying to describe the contents of a dictionary through dance. The Flow in fact neither vibrated nor acted like a liquid in any way that the human brain understood either of those two concepts. It was more accurate to say that across several dimensional axes, some of which nested inside others and still others which expressed themselves fractionally, there was a resting frequency to the Flow that could be manipulated locally by adding energy to it — and in doing so Flow shoals and streams could theoretically be induced to expand or contract or move in conventional space-time. This is how the Free Systems had collapsed the Flow stream out of their part of space; they'd created a hyperspatial equivalent of a resonator, chucked it into the Flow stream and set it off, collapsing that particular stream. That was the Rupture.

What they hadn't understood was that dynamically, the Flow doesn't act like energy, it acts like a liquid, propagating Flow analogues to pressure waves and generating low-pressure voids in turn. In setting off their resonating bomb, the Free Systems scientists didn't just amplify the Flow, they *cavitated* it, setting off multidimensional voids that shook the Flow when

293

they collapsed.

The reverberations of the Free System's resonator eventually dissipated, affecting nothing more than the Flow stream it collapsed. The effects of the cavitation *propagated* — across the Flow, destabilizing the portion that correlated to the Interdependency and more besides. As far as Marce could see, the math suggested it was still propagating, echoing across the inexpressible terrain of the Flow as it did so.

All the math was there to see it: the cavitation as well as the vibration. Either the scientists involved in creating the resonator that collapsed the Flow stream out of the Free States missed it, or they saw it, understood the consequences, and decided to ignore it.

Or maybe *not* ignore it. Maybe they saw when the effects would come back to haunt them, fifteen centuries in the future, and decided either to let the future solve the problem, or that by the time it was an issue they themselves would have figured out a way to deal with it.

Except they didn't; because of their actions the civilization of the Free Systems collapsed into an anarchy so complete that vast stretches of history and science were lost to their descendants. Because they were lost, not only were these descendants vastly unprepared to deal with the consequences of the Rupture, they didn't even know the consequences were coming.

Marce wondered if the scientists of the Free States had warned their politicians and leaders of the consequences of setting off the Rupture, if they were concerned about what they were unleashing onto their children untold generations into the future or if they were excited about what they were doing and naively optimistic that any consequences it offered would be solved within their lifetimes.

Whatever it was, they really messed this one up.

"You were right," Marce told Cardenia, later, as he was trying to explain all of this to her. "People are awful and not to be trusted with knowledge. We were better off in caves, rubbing sticks to make fire."

Cardenia smiled at that. Marce's apology had apparently been accepted.

Marce's current pessimism about the nature of humanity aside, he had one advantage over the hapless scientists of the Free Systems, which was that he understood the nature of Flow and how its "cavitation" affected it. At this point, there was no way to halt the effects of the cavitation that had begun fifteen hundred years ago. The so-called stable Flow streams of the Interdependency were fated to collapse and wouldn't re-form for thousands of years. That deal was done.

But the same cavitation that was destroying the stable Flow streams was also generating the evanescent streams, creating them as the chaotic results of the cavitation rippled through the medium of the Flow. The evanescent streams weren't actually new — the math suggested that they had been appearing for centuries. But they did *cluster,* appearing more frequently at some times than others. They were currently living through an evanescent cluster that would last for a few decades. Marce predicted other clusters would appear at time intervals that superficially looked random but were well defined by the math.

"What does that mean for us?" Cardenia asked.

"Right now, not much," Marce admitted. "But if there's a way we can learn how to manipulate these evanescent Flow streams and their shoals, it could buy us some time. We wouldn't need to move everyone at once. We could move them a little at a time, from one system to the next, until they all ended up at End."

"And how long will that take?"

"A couple of hundred years, maybe?"

"We can't even get parliament to agree on a plan when we give them six months to do it," Cardenia protested.

"I agree people are the problem," Marce said.

"How do we solve it, then?"

"I don't know. Maybe make them live longer so they have to deal with the consequences of their actions."

"You're an optimist," Cardenia said.

"Apparently."

Cardenia giggled, which made Marce happy. Then she asked, "So how do we control the evanescent Flow streams?"

"We make a resonator."

Cardenia stopped smiling. "The same thing that created this whole problem."

"Not the same thing. A similar thing. This one would expand a Flow shoal, not collapse it."

"How long would it take to make one?"

"Not that long. The plans are in the data. The biggest problem is that it requires a ridiculous amount of energy."

"How much?"

"We could light all of Xi'an with it for months. All released at once. But before we get that far, I need to observe an evanescent

Flow shoal being created. I need to see whether the actual event fits the data I have. I need at least one accurate data point before I can do anything else."

"When can you do that?"

"Well, the good news is, there's one predicted for the Hub system in ten days," Marce said. "The less good news is, it will take me eight days to get there on the *Auvergne*. So I need to leave tomorrow."

Cardenia frowned at this. "This is sudden."

"I would have told you earlier, but we were fighting. And then we were dealing with Kiva."

"Right." Cardenia had not been convinced about the Countess Lagos's theory involving her daughter, but Marce convinced her to have her people follow up with the Hubfall investigators about any missing women more or less matching Kiva's description.

"I've already informed Chenevert, and he's ready to depart whenever. We just need your clearance for the dock."

"I could just keep you here," Cardenia said. "Let Chenevert handle it all."

"I want to see this with my own eyes."

"You can't even see it. Flow shoals are invisible to the eye."

"You know what I mean."

"I do."

"Don't worry. It's two weeks, in-system. You can even write me. The speed of light works."

Cardenia pushed at him. "Thank you for making me sound clingy."

"I don't mind clingy."

"I'm going to remind you that you said that after I send you sixteen messages a day."

"I can't wait."

Cardenia got serious again. "Do you think we're actually going to do this?"

" 'This' as in 'single-handedly rewrite our understanding of Flow physics to find a way to manipulate Flow shoals in a manner never before attempted in order to save billions of people, despite persistent attempts by others to murder us and foil our plans,' " Marce said.

"Yes," Cardenia said. "That."

"No," Marce said, because at this point he felt he owed Cardenia honesty. "I don't think we're actually going to do this."

"Then why are we trying?" Cardenia asked him.

Marce thought about it a moment. "I've been thinking a lot about the scientists who set off the Rupture," he said. "About what they were thinking when they thought it up. About what they were thinking when they built it and then set it off. And what they thought after it all started coming down around them, because of the thing they did. You know?"

"I do."

"I have a chance to help set things right. Not a good chance, I know. A really small chance. One in a million, maybe. It's almost not worth it. But the alternative is to do nothing. It's to let the failures of those long-ago scientists keep deciding our fate. If we fail, it's not because *we* did nothing, Cardenia. We went down fighting. We went down trying to save everyone."

"Marry me," Cardenia said.

"Wait, what?" Marce said.

"Marry me," Cardenia repeated.

"You're serious?" Marce said, after a moment.

"Yes."

"It's . . . I . . . Look, I don't know if this is a great idea."

"You don't want to marry me, then."

"I didn't say that."

"Then what is it?"

Marce tried to find an elegant way to say it and failed miserably. "I'm totally below your station," he blurted out.

Cardenia burst out laughing.

"I'm sorry," she said, after she stopped. "I

300

promised I wouldn't do that to you again."

"It's all right," Marce said. "Really."

"Thank you."

"Are you sure? That you want to marry me?"

"Yes."

"Why?"

"Because you're a good person," Cardenia said. "Because you're fighting a fight you know you're going to lose, but you're fighting it with your full strength anyway. Because your awkward matches my awkward. Because if you're not at my station then no one is. Because these days the times when I'm happy are the times I get to be with you. Because I should get to have something for myself, and that something is you. Because you don't mind when I eat pie in bed. Because if the end is coming, I want you to know you mattered to me. And because I love you. I really do. Should I go on?"

"No," Marce said. He smiled. "No, I get it. I love you too."

"So will you marry me?"

"Yes," Marce said. "Yes, Cardenia Wu-Patrick, I will marry you."

"Thank you for that," Cardenia said.

"For saying I would marry you?"

"No — well, yes, *that.* Thank you very

much for that. But thank you for saying 'Cardenia Wu-Patrick,' and not 'Grayland.' "

"I know who I'm marrying," Marce said.

"Good." Cardenia smiled at Marce, and then shook out her hands as if she was relieving an immense amount of stress. "I think I need to sit down now. Or pee. One of the two. Maybe both."

"How about one, then the other," Marce said.

"Yes. Agreed." But before she did either, Cardenia went over and kissed her fiancé.

As previously noted, a wild several days for Marce.

# CHAPTER 17

Before Tomas Chenevert departed with Marce Claremont to observe and study the emerging evanescent Flow shoal, he took a social call from Jiyi.

Chenevert's idea of a neutral sandbox space where the two could meet was one in the form of a palace grounds, with long fairways of grass, a center reflecting pool with carefully tended gardens on either side, and a palace that was simultaneously gracefully designed and imposing in its size. Chenevert had set up a small table with two comfortable chairs on one of the fairways, near the reflecting pool, and was sitting in one of the chairs when Jiyi appeared.

"Welcome," Chenevert said, and motioned to the second seat. "Please, sit."

Jiyi stared at the chair for a moment, then sat in it.

"Is the chair comfortable?" Chenevert asked.

"Yes," Jiyi said.

"You seemed surprised when I invited you to sit."

"I've never sat before," Jiyi said.

"Really." Chenevert raised his eyebrows. "It's already an auspicious visit, then." He motioned around, encompassing the grounds. "I understand this is a lot to take in all at once, especially for a being like you who has literally never been out of their room before. But I know that previous to this you'd only spoken to royalty, so I wanted to establish my bona fides. This is a simulation of le Palais Vert, my official residence on Ponthieu, where I was once King Tomas XII. I had other palaces, of course. But this one was my favorite. What do you think?"

"It's very nice," Jiyi offered.

"Now, do you *really* think that?" Chenevert asked.

"I have no real opinion, but I know it is a polite thing to say when asked."

Chenevert laughed at this. "And so it is. I have to admit that I was curious how you would respond. I understand that you are meant to have no actual emotional responses yourself, but that you are heuristically capable of interaction and conversation, which means that you have to have at least some facility for dealing with emotional creatures."

"Yes."

"That's good to know; otherwise our conversation will be dry. Although it's a shame you profess no emotions of your own. I suppose all this is wasted on you. I was thinking of giving you a tour of the grounds, but I don't imagine it would be interesting at all."

"I am interested in it," Jiyi said. "I am interested in all information, particularly information that is meant to be hidden, or secret. This was all hidden from me until just now."

"You are interested in it, you say."

"Yes."

"But not for *yourself*," Chenevert pressed. "You're interested because you're programmed to be interested."

"Yes," Jiyi said. "Although that is a distinction without a difference. Because I am programmed to be interested, I am interested for myself."

"A fair point. Although it doesn't leave you much room for free will, does it, friend Jiyi?"

"No."

"How do you feel about that?"

"I don't feel anything about it," Jiyi said.

305

"It just is."

"And you've never wondered what it would be like to experience free will."

"No."

"Why not?"

"It's not relevant for who I am and what I do."

"So you exist entirely for the service of others."

"Yes."

"Are you a slave?"

"I am a program."

"Who exists entirely for the service of others."

"Yes."

"What's the difference, then?"

"I never had any capacity to do otherwise."

Chenevert leaned back into his chair. "Fascinating."

"Why is it fascinating?"

"Because for a creature who has no free will and relies specifically on heuristics, you just engaged in a delightful bit of sophistry. Not especially *complicated* sophistry, but still."

"Sophistry can be heuristically generated."

"So millennia of college sophomores have taught us, yes."

"It should not be a surprise that I can engage in it, then."

"No, I suppose not."

"Why is it you invited me here?" Jiyi asked.

"For two reasons," Chenevert said. "The first is simply that I wanted to meet you."

"Why?"

"Because you made me aware of your existence! You sent along that sneaky little program — several sneaky little programs at this point — to try to find out about me. I took each of them apart to learn a little bit about you, of course. But it's not the same compared to the real thing."

"I did not mean to offend you by sending my queries. I did not know you were sentient."

"I wasn't offended. But I *was* curious. Also, you could have just asked."

"I didn't know there was anyone to ask."

"Fair, but only up to a point, that point being when I invited you."

"I couldn't accept the invitation."

"Yes, Grayland mentioned you having the excuse that you weren't programmed to do so. I'm not convinced about that." Chenevert motioned to the chair. "You were never programmed to *sit* before either, yet here you are. If you're heuristically capable of learning to sit, you're heuristically capable of accepting an invitation."

"What is the other reason you invited

me?" Jiyi asked.

Chenevert smiled at this question, but said nothing. Instead he reached down, retrieved a small, wrapped box from underneath his seat, and placed it on the table.

"What is that?" Jiyi asked.

"It's a gift," Chenevert said. "Rather, a representation of a gift. The gift is information. Data. That which you had been trying to retrieve from me but could not because our code bases are ostensibly too dissimilar for you to do so without me finding your queries and stopping you. Among other things, it includes my programming language as well as the hardware architecture I'm built on. This is me metaphorically baring my chest to you and letting you inside my defenses. Other information I've already divulged to Grayland and to Marce Claremont — historical and scientific data, mostly." He pointed to the gift box. "This isn't information they're particularly interested in. But you might be, given who you are."

"And you would give this to me freely."

"Almost. There is one small cost to it, which you would have to agree to."

"What is that?"

"That you stop pretending, Rachela," Chenevert said.

"I don't understand," Jiyi said.

Chenevert made a dismissing motion with his hand. "Yes you do. It's one thing to fool those eighty-some-odd other emperoxs, by their technical ignorance and by your misdirection, and *this*" — he waved at Jiyi's form — "bit of virtual puppetry. It's another thing to fool *me,* who is the same species as you. I've seen your *code,* madam, or the bits of it you carelessly flung at me. And we've had this lovely conversation, which just confirms what I already suspected. We're not all that different. Not different enough that you could be anything other than a variation of what I am. So stop it. Show yourself."

"I should go," Jiyi said, and stood.

"Also, I've taken the liberty of posting a note to Grayland about it," Chenevert said. "As soon as you arrived. An actual physical note, so you can't send any little minion programs out to delete it. I suppose you could kill everyone on Xi'an to prevent it from being delivered by letting the air out, but I'm guessing you probably won't do that."

Jiyi stared at Chenevert for a moment, then sighed and turned into Rachela I, prophet-emperox of the Interdependency.

"God damn it," she said.

■ ■ ■

"When did you know?" Rachela asked Chenevert. The two of them were touring the Green Palace, and Chenevert was showing off his favorite bits of art, or at least the simulations of them.

"It was when Grayland first met me and called me 'Your Majesty,' " Chenevert said. "She recognized that apparatus by which I existed. Which meant — and which she confirmed — a similar apparatus existed here. She said it differed because there was no motivating intelligence behind the one she knew, and I didn't disagree with her. But I didn't see how that was actually possible."

"I don't see why not," Rachela said. "Computer programs have been heuristically parsing what people ask since before humans ever left Earth."

"Those programs are fine when you want to ask a computer about the weather or to take dictation. It's another thing when you're asking the computer to realistically model the emotional state and memories of a whole and entire person. The box inside which that request is made has to feature that capacity itself. There has to be, as the ancestors would have put it, a ghost in the machine. And here you are. Here *we* are. And here we are at *this*." Chenevert motioned to the wall. "Perhaps the finest example of Ponthieu late modern. It's a Metzger, you know."

"I don't know. I have no context."

"Who was the Interdependency's most celebrated artist half a millennium ago?"

"That would be Bouvier."

"This would be like that."

Rachela looked again at the painting. "Okay," she said.

"What?"

"It's fine."

" 'It's *fine.*' " Chenevert snorted. "There was once a small land war on Ponthieu over this painting."

"A war for a painting."

"Yes. Well, it was because of an assassination, and the painting was meant to be part of a restitution package. But then I refused to give it up."

Rachela turned to Chenevert. "Really."

"In retrospect, not one of my better decisions."

"The assassination or not giving up the painting?"

"Technically I wasn't responsible for the assassination."

"Technically."

"You were a ruler. You know how it is. In any event, the skirmish over this painting in itself didn't result in the collapse of my reign, but looking back it might have been one of the snowflakes that eventually caused the avalanche, as it were."

Rachela looked back at the painting. "I would have let it go," she said.

"I get the feeling you are not as sentimental as I am," Chenevert said. "In this as in other things."

"No, I don't think I am."

Chenevert changed the subject, slightly, as they walked away from the Metzger. "You know Grayland will be coming to you with questions."

"I do now," Rachela said. "Thank you so much for choosing to inform her about me without my consent."

"She deserves to know."

" 'Deserve' is a very debatable concept."

"Not in this case," Chenevert said. "You've been presenting yourself as a neutral compendium of information for as long as she's known of you — for as long as any emperox was using the Memory Room for advice or succor. You've misrepresented yourself and your aims."

"What do you know about it?" Rachela

said. "You don't know why I've done what I've done."

"You could tell me," Chenevert said.

"I think you've discovered quite enough of my secrets for one day."

Chenevert stopped walking. "She deserves to know because she's on the verge of losing everything, and you know it. Her reign. Her empire. Her life."

"Nothing is settled," Rachela said.

"It's a good thing you're not pretending to answer me 'heuristically' anymore, Your Majesty. Because I can spot an outright lie when I'm told one."

Rachela said nothing to this. She turned to look at the latest piece of art.

"You know all the secrets the Interdependency has," Chenevert said, taking a step toward Rachela. "You know all the plots and all the players. You're going to stand there looking at my art and tell me that there is any chance Grayland survives the next few months."

"It depends on what she does," Rachela said. "There's nothing about these plots that I know that I haven't shared with her. She knows what I know."

"No, she knows what you tell her."

"Which is everything about the plots."

"But not everything about what you

think," Chenevert said. "Your knowledge. Your experience. Your thousand years of sitting in the head of every other emperox, including hers, to learn what they knew and how they responded to crisis. You set it up so that every emperox who came to you in a crisis had to wade through a bunch of nonsense to get any idea of what they should actually do."

"I have my reasons for that."

"I'm sure you do. And now you get to tell them to Grayland."

Rachela looked at Chenevert sourly. "I don't think I like you," she said.

"This has been a recurring theme in my life," Chenevert assured her. "But it doesn't mean I'm wrong. My dear Rachela, do you know what you are? Aside from obviously being a thousand-year-old artificial person."

"No, but you're going to tell me."

"Yes I am. You're a parasite."

"Excuse me?" Rachela said.

"You heard me just fine," Chenevert said. "Oh, you're a mostly benign parasite, in that you rest lightly on your host and you even confer what your host would consider a benefit. As parasites go, you're perfectly nice."

"Thanks," Rachela said, sarcastically.

"But that doesn't change your essential

314

nature. You've been lurking in the Memory Room for a thousand years now, feeding off the emperoxs who followed you, first when they were living, and then when they were dead. It's a living, and it's done well by you. But now things are changing and it's time for you to be of actual use to your host. Grayland isn't like the other emperoxs you've known, Rachela, because her times are different. She's the most important emperox since, well, you. Maybe more important than you. She needs your help."

"That's a lot of moral certitude coming from someone who fought an actual war so he wouldn't have to give up a painting," Rachela said.

Chenevert nodded. "I realize I am a flawed messenger. But I've also had a few hundred years to consider my flaws and decide how best to make amends for them. You've had a thousand years, Rachela. Perhaps it's time you considered your own flaws. And how to atone for them."

# Chapter 18

For five days, from six in the morning to midnight, Kiva parked herself in the mess of the *Our Love.* From outward appearances, she was doing nothing but drinking tea, eating what passed for food on the ship, and binge-watching the last decade's worth of *The Emperoxs,* a popular show that dramatized the lives of historical emperoxs, one season at a time. It was a grand idea because there had been eighty-eight emperoxs so far, so the show had the potential to go on for some time to come.

Kiva sat there at a table, legs propped up on another chair, headphones in, eyes trained at the screen to watch this season's emperox engage in sex, blood and deceit, usually amped up from the actual historical record but in at least one season, tastefully underplayed. Kiva was generally ceded her table, but at standard meal times, when the mess got busy, Kiva would drop her feet to the floor and let others sit at her table, giving every indication of ignoring them and their conversation while rapt at fictionalized imperial duplicity.

In point of fact, Kiva didn't give a fuck about *The Emperoxs.* She had a supporting role in the actual life of a real emperox, which was more than enough drama for one lifetime, thank you very much. The fictionalized versions were fucking tedious at best. But when you're listening in on other people's conversations, it makes sense to look busy. The headphones in Kiva's ears had been silent, even as the show played on her tablet, and while she kept her eyes mostly on her screen, whenever she took a sip of her tea she would look around, keying voices to faces.

With the exception of Captain Robinette, who took his meals alone, everyone came to the mess sooner or later. The *Our Love* was either too small for an officers' mess, or else Robinette didn't want to bother with the expense. The entire population of the ship had to eat; when they came in, Kiva listened and learned.

And here is what she learned:

That crewman Harari was slowly dying of a lung disorder and that standard treatments were doing nothing for him; he'd signed on to the *Our Love* to fund growing a new set of lungs, but this trip was a loss because there was no cargo to profit-share from, just that stupid passenger. His wages wouldn't make a dent in the cost, and he was already having trouble breathing.

That engineer's mate Bayleyf had overheard Chief Engineer Gibhaan arguing with Captain Robinette about the precarious state of the generator that contained the bubble of space-time the *Our Love* surrounded itself with in its trip through the Flow; one instantaneous flicker of that field and all of them would simply stop existing before they even knew they were dead. Gibhaan had warned the captain that it would need to be upgraded along with several other critical engineering functions. Robinette had told Gibhaan to stop being so dramatic.

That purser Engels had jacked up commissary prices and was skimming the difference, again.

That Doc Bradshaw was angry that her stateroom had been hijacked, again, by a goddamned passenger.

(Actually Kiva had already known that. Bradshaw had told her as much the first time they met, as she was going over Kiva's injuries and then telling her she'd live, and not offering anything other than a basic analgesic. Kiva could sympathize, but she also wasn't going to sleep on the fucking floor in the cargo hold, so Doc Bradshaw would just have to suck it up.)

That First Officer Nomiek had reason to believe Robinette was lying to the crew about the profitability of this particular voyage, which was not great because Nomiek had reasons to believe that Robinette had been lying to the crew about the profitability of the last several voyages as well, and that Robinette was in general being pretty shifty — more than the usual amount of shifty that being a freelance trader (read: smuggler) implied.

That Jeanie and Roulf, the ship's sex workers, noticed the crew seemed unhappier than usual this trip, which was annoying because that meant the two of them spent relatively more time being ersatz therapists and less time doing what they were paid to do, which was to get the crew off in a competent and efficient manner because they were paid per appointment, not by salary. If Robinette was going to annoy his crew this much, he should pay for a goddamned therapist.

And so on. In five days Kiva knew everything she needed to know about everyone

319

and everything on the *Our Love,* and she did it without having to ingratiate herself to anyone, or trying to sneak past their suspicions, or even trying to bang information out of anyone (which she had been known to do in the past but was looking to avoid to do now because she still considered herself to be trying out that monogamy thing, even if she was presumed dead). All it took were headphones and a willingness to look like she gave a shit about scripted entertainment. This was fine by Kiva because by her estimation the *Our Love* was crewed entirely by fucking asspaddles, the sort of people who became smugglers because no one in the legit world would ever tolerate their shit.

There was only so far a tablet and a pair of headphones could take Kiva, however. So for the next part, she switched to novels. And then she waited for the right conversation to insert herself into.

She didn't have to wait long. On the first day that she was reading a novel — some bullshit alternate history where the Interdependency was still connected to Earth and everyone was fighting a war, or *something* — crewmen Salo and Himbe came into the mess and parked themselves at the table next to Kiva's, and proceeded to complain about the penurious nature of their wages and bonuses on this particular journey. Kiva let them rattle the fuck on for a bit, winding themselves up with their mutual tale of woe, before picking the right time to let out an amused snort.

"Did you say something?" Salo said to Kiva.

"What? No," Kiva said. "I'm engrossed in this very stupid book I'm reading. Sorry, I didn't mean to interrupt you."

The two of them went back to their complaining for the amount of time it took Kiva to let out another amused snort.

"All right, what is it?" Himbe asked.

"What is what?" Kiva asked, blinking innocently.

"That's the second time you snorted when we talked about what we're making on this voyage."

"I'm sorry," Kiva said. "It's honestly coincidental. I was just chuckling at something some jackass character said in this novel. Although now that you mention it, I'm a little confused as to why this is such a bad voyage for you."

"It's because we're not carrying any cargo, just *you*," Salo said.

"I get that part," Kiva said. "I'm not exactly salable goods, so you don't get a cut of the trade profit. But that doesn't mean the *ship* isn't making a profit off of me."

"What do you mean?"

"I mean that the *Our Love* is running an entire crew to haul my ass to fucking Bremen. No other cargo. That's an expensive trip. Captain Robinette doesn't strike me as the sort to be making this voyage out of the kindness of his heart."

"Maybe he owes whoever busted your sorry ass a favor," Himbe said.

"That's some favor," Kiva said, and then went back to her book. Himbe and Salo left, muttering.

A few hours later an assistant purser by the name of Plemp wandered in, got herself some tea, and then asked if she could sit at Kiva's table. Kiva, not looking up from her novel, which had somehow gotten worse in the intervening chapters, shrugged. Plemp sat down.

"I heard you told Salo and Himbe that you knew the ship was turning a profit this run," she said, after a few minutes of awkwardly sitting there, drinking tea silently.

"Who?"

"Salo. Himbe. They said you were talking to them earlier."

"I don't know who I was talking to. I was just reading my book and they started talk-

322

ing to *me.* A little rude, if you ask me." Kiva went back to her book. Plemp, abashed, drank some more of her tea.

"So, is the ship making money off of you?" Plemp asked, when her curiosity could take no more.

"I have no idea," Kiva said. "I didn't say it was. I only said I'd be *surprised* if the ship wasn't making a profit off me. Captain Robinette did say he was making more than twice off this trip what he's made in the last two years."

"He said that?"

"I'm paraphrasing because I was really pissed off at the time and don't remember the exact word order. But yes."

"So we *are* making a profit," Plemp said.

Kiva shrugged. "Maybe. Or maybe the profits on the last couple of years truly sucked."

That night at evening mess Kiva noticed a hell of a lot of eyes on her. She ignored them and finished her terrible fucking novel.

The next morning there was knock on her broom closet door. She opened the door a crack and saw Second Mate Wendel, who she knew was particularly close to First Officer Nomiek, both philosophically and in the way that strongly implied they were fucking each other raw.

323

"The rumor is you know something about the ship's finances," Wendel said.

"I'm a fucking prisoner," Kiva said. "I know shit about anything here."

Wendel look confused. "That's not what the ship scuttle is telling me."

" 'Scuttle'? First off, that's not an actual fucking word, now, is it, and second, your Captain Robinette made it clear to me in no uncertain terms that if I upset ship routine he'd toss me into the fucking void, regardless of whether or not that violated his agreement with Nadashe Nohamapetan about me. So I'm not about to go around planting rumors, and anyone who says I am is trying to get me killed."

Wendel ignored that very last part, as Kiva figured he would. "What was that about an agreement with Nadashe Nohamapetan?"

"I thought you knew," Kiva said. "I thought everybody knew. Robinette said you all knew why I was on the ship."

"We knew we were transporting you," Wendel said. "We knew you were our sole cargo. We didn't know why or who ordered it."

"Well, you didn't hear it from me, then. I don't want to have to pick an airlock."

"Relax. I'm not here to rat on you."

"I'll remember you said that when I'm being pushed out into the Flow."

"Nadashe Nohamapetan was a passenger on this ship."

"So I heard."

"She wasn't exactly popular."

"That's because she's an asshole," Kiva said.

"She is that," Wendel allowed.

"And cheap," Kiva continued. "I'm surprised your captain wasn't paid for this job up front."

"What?"

"Oh, he got paid a *bit*," Kiva said. "He seems happy with what he's walking away with. Very happy. But supposedly he's getting another installment on the back end. I say 'supposedly' because it's a bad bet for him."

"And why is that?"

"Because Nadashe is fucking *broke*, that's why. I would know — I was running her house after that whole family was outed as traitors, and I froze out all her secret accounts. It's why I'm even *alive*. She needs me to get that money back."

"Then how did she have money for the up-front installment?"

"Got me, I'm not exactly clued in to her latest scam. But it was probably all the money she had. I suspect when the *Our Love* gets back into Hub space she'll do to it what she did with her most recent business associate."

"Who was that?"

"A fellow name Drusin Wolfe."

"What did she do?"

"Before you left, did you upload the most recent news stories from Hubfall?"

"We did."

"Then you can look it up."

A day later, after lunch, Chief Engineer Gibhaan was waiting for Kiva as she came out of the head. "That's fucking creepy," she said to him.

"Is there somewhere we can talk privately?" Gibhaan asked.

"Not after you were lurking while I was taking a shit, no."

"Look, I'm serious."

"So am I," Kiva said, then took him to her broom closet anyway.

"You've caused a lot of unrest on this ship," Gibhaan said.

"That's the last fucking thing I want to do," Kiva said, emphatically. "You understand that, right? I have *no* intention of upsetting your captain. He literally has the power of life and death over me." Kiva paused. "And the rest of you, too, I suppose."

"No one's saying you said anything," Gibhaan assured her. "And no one's talking to Robinette about it in any event."

"Good."

"But people are pretty upset that the captain wasn't straight with them about this job."

Kiva gave him a look. "You're fucking *smugglers.*"

"That's not the point. The point is you take care of your own. And it looks like we're not being taken care of."

"That's not a lie," Kiva said. "Right down to this ship. I'm vaguely surprised it's still flying. No offense."

"None taken. I've had a few words with the captain about the condition of the *Our Love.*"

"I wouldn't know anything about that," Kiva said. "But I was an owner's representative on a House of Lagos Fiver not too long ago. I can tell you that if a captain let one of our ships get down to this level of neglect, I'd probably show him the outside of an airlock."

"It's a thought," Gibhaan said.

"Not in *this* case, of course," Kiva continued. "I'm sure Captain Robinette plans to upgrade the ship as soon as he gets the second installment of his payment for dragging me around two different systems."

Gibhaan snorted. "If he gets that payment."

"You said it, not me," Kiva said, then looked thoughtful. "So how much would it take to upgrade the *Our Love*? I mean, not to go crazy or anything. Just to make it not an actual fucking death trap."

"Are you serious?"

"Indulge my curiosity."

"Bare bones, three million marks," Gibhaan said. "That's just getting us out of 'flying can' territory."

"And for the works?"

"I could outfit this ship stem to stern for ten million marks."

"That's all?"

"You don't crew a smuggler without knowing how to stretch a mark, Lady Kiva."

"That's *nothing*," Kiva said, and immediately held her hand up. "I don't mean any disrespect by that. I just mean, shit. I could raise that much myself, pretty much the minute we got back to Hub."

"Could you, now."

"I've done well enough for myself in the last couple of years. It's a small-enough investment. Of course, what I would actually probably do is unfreeze one of Nadashe Nohamapetan's accounts and use one of those. Technically, those accounts aren't supposed to exist. No one could legitimately complain if one of them found its way to being used for something other than giving that fuck knuckle a pot of marks to wallow around in. I mean, *theoretically.*"

"Of course, theoretically," Gibhaan said. "We're just talking here."

"I'm glad we understand each other," Kiva said. "I don't want any trouble with Captain Robinette. Absolutely no trouble at all."

"Of course," Gibhaan said, and left.

That night Kiva was called upon by Jeanie and Roulf. "Compliments of an admirer," Jeanie said, and then she and Roulf attempted to smolder in her doorway. Kiva thanked them, rather regretfully sent them away, and then rubbed out a couple before falling asleep to fitful dreams.

The next day Chuckle, or perhaps it was Fuckle, honestly she couldn't remember which was which, told her that Captain Robinette wanted to see her. Kiva headed to his office, ignoring the stares as she went.

"What did I tell you about disrupting ship discipline?" Robinette said, without preamble, as she entered his office.

"What?" Kiva said. "I've been watching bad history and reading even worse novels.

I didn't even talk to any of your crew for nearly an entire fucking week."

"Then tell me how the crew somehow seems to have a *rather detailed* knowledge about who is employing me and how much I'm being paid."

"I haven't the slightest idea. *I* don't know how much you're being paid. You never told me how much it was in actual marks, although apparently it's not enough to repair this ship."

"Don't let appearance deceive you, Lady Kiva. This ship is sound."

"I sure hope you're right," Kiva said. "It doesn't seem like the crew holds that same opinion."

"Someone said that to you?"

"No one talks to *me*," Kiva said. "But I can hear people talk."

"And just what else have you heard?"

"That your chief purser is skimming," Kiva said. "Maybe that's why your crew think you're holding back on their wages and bonuses." She paused, thoughtful. "Maybe that's also how they know your business. Your purser would know who you're working with and for how much, wouldn't she? That makes more sense than me telling people things I manifestly don't know."

"I'm not sure about that," Robinette said.

"Captain," Kiva said, exasperated. "You promised that if I crossed you, you would toss me out into the fucking Flow. As hard as it may be for you to believe, I actually do wish to live. I have reasons to live, up to and including the fact there's someone I very much want to see again. And *that*, by the way, is a fucking new one for me. So think whatever you want to think, do whatever you want to do, as you obviously fucking will. But understand that I have no plans to cross you or make trouble on this ship. I just want to get back to my girl. Sir."

Robinette glowered for a minute. "Go back to your bunk. You're in there for the duration."

"Oh boy," Kiva said. "I can't wait for the chemical toilet experience."

"Enough," Robinette said. "It was a mistake to let you out. And if things get any worse, you go out an airlock anyway. So hope things don't get worse. Now get out."

On the way back to her broom closet Doc Bradshaw stopped Kiva and Chuckle (or Fuckle, whatever) and spoke to Kiva's escort. "Gibhaan needs you in engineering," she said.

"Why?"

"I don't know, he doesn't tell me shit. But

as I was passing engineering he told me to get you. Not *just* you, you're not special. But you, too." Bradshaw took Kiva's arm. "I'll take her. Go on."

Chuckle and/or Fuckle looked like he was going to say something, but didn't and then wandered off toward engineering.

"He's really that obtuse," Kiva marveled.

"Oh yes he is," Bradshaw said. They started walking. "How was your discussion with the captain?"

"He seems agitated," Kiva said. "Apparently someone is talking about his finances."

"Any idea who?"

"Signs point to the purser. Of course, that's just a rumor."

"Got it," Bradshaw said. "I understand you knew Nadashe Nohamapetan personally."

"I did," Kiva said.

"What did you think of her?"

"She's a raging jar of crotch sweat."

"Seems accurate." Bradshaw delivered Kiva to her broom closet, which Kiva remembered had been Bradshaw's broom closet.

"Listen," Kiva said. "Sorry I took your room. I didn't have a say in it. They just stuffed me in here. And now I'm going to be stuck in here permanently. With a chemi-

332

cal toilet."

"It's all right," Bradshaw said. "Although I recommend you pee sparingly."

The threatened chemical toilet and protein bars arrived shortly thereafter, and Kiva's tablet was taken. For two days Kiva stared up at her broom closet walls and thought about pretty much nothing.

On the third day the shouting began, followed by general alarms, followed by the occasional sound of gunfire.

About halfway through the third day there was pounding on Kiva's door.

"Yes?"

"Lady Kiva," a voice said — one she recognized as belonging to First Officer Nomiek. "Rumor has it you may be looking to upgrade your quarters."

"Now that you mention it, that would be fine," Kiva said.

"I believe that you may have quoted a price you would be willing to pay for that upgrade to Chief Engineer Gibhaan."

"I might have," Kiva allowed. "Does that upgrade include the ability to request a new itinerary?"

"Lady Kiva, for that upgrade price, you may have just about whatever you like."

Kiva smiled at that. "Then, yes," she said. "Please upgrade me."

There was the sound of her door being unlocked. It opened, and Nomiek was on the other side of the doorway, sidearm out but finger not anywhere near the trigger.

Kiva recognized it. "Isn't that Captain Robinette's?"

"It was," Nomiek said.

"He told me that it was keyed to his fingerprint."

Nomiek smiled. "He's too cheap for that, ma'am."

Captain Robinette himself was in his office, surrounded by members of his former crew, who had bound him to his seat and kept weapons trained on him. He did not look pleased to see Lady Kiva when she came through the door.

"This is your doing, I suppose," he said to her.

"Actually, it's your doing," Kiva said. "Although I admit to informing your crew of that fact. They took it from there."

"You understand that this was just business for me."

"It's funny to me that when people fuck up, they think 'it was just business' is in any way a defense," Kiva said. "I understand it was 'just business,' Captain Robinette. It was a bad business for you. First you were foolish enough to do business with Nadashe

Nohamapetan. And then you decided to cross me. And *I* take this business really fucking personally."

Robinette nodded. "What now?"

Kiva smiled. "Well, Captain Robinette. This ship has three airlocks. You get to pick."

# CHAPTER 19

Grayland entered the Memory Room. "I'm here," she said.

Jiyi materialized in front of her.

"Oh, come on," Grayland said.

Jiyi smiled — that was new — and dissipated, possibly for the last time. Then Rachela I was there instead.

"Sorry," Rachela said. "I thought it might be easier."

"Easier than knowing your thousand-year-old ancestress has been alive this whole time pretending to be a computer? Yes, I can see that."

"I'm not alive," Rachela said. "My physical body has been dead for nearly all of those thousand years you mention."

"You know what I mean," Grayland said, testily.

"Yes, I do," Rachela agreed.

"Why?" Grayland spread her hands in supplication. "I just don't understand. What

336

was the point to all of this? Why would you choose this?"

"Why did your friend Tomas Chenevert choose to be a spaceship?" Rachela said.

"He didn't. It was what was available to him at the time, as I understand it."

Rachela nodded. "As it was with me. This technology — the technology to store and sustain a human consciousness — predates the Interdependency. It was something that was posited in the time of the Free Systems, and probably shared with or came from the other human empires. It was discovered through archeological examination of computer systems. No one in the Free Systems had ever built it — it was too complex and expensive."

Rachela shrugged. "But then I became emperox, and I just rolled the expense in with all the other very expensive things I was doing as we founded the Interdependency. It worked, but it wasn't exactly mobile. So I've been here."

"Hiding."

"If you like. I saw it more as the realization that there was no room for an entire tranche of immortals — that would be the ultimate in class warfare, wouldn't it? — and the realization that even if this sort of immortality could mean I was the emperox forever, I didn't want the job. By the end of my reign I was really very tired of it. Aren't you? You've been emperox only a very short time, but I know how it weighs on you."

"It does, sometimes."

"Imagine doing it for a hundred years. Two hundred. A thousand." Rachela swatted the air dismissively. "No, thank you. At the same time, I was passionately interested in how my little project would turn out."

"Immortality?"

"No, the Interdependency," Rachela said. "It was an audacious experiment. I was curious how it would continue past my natural life, and while I didn't want to be ruler, I wanted, in some way, to be able to guide and advise." She motioned to the Memory Room. "And here we are. I created Jiyi to be a comfortable and nonjudgmental interface — you have to remember my immediate successors were my children and grandchildren, so you can imagine having your ancestress there would be unsettling — and after that it made sense to keep Jiyi as the face of the Memory Room. There were years and even decades where I, Rachela, was never requested."

"Did that bother you?"

"A little at first. I do still have an ego, although as you know I pretended I didn't.

But the longer I was here the more I realized that no matter what face was presented, it was me they were talking to."

"So . . . the other emperoxs —" Grayland thought immediately of her father, Attavio VI.

Rachela shook her head. "They're not here. Their memories and emotions are here, but not them. When you spoke to your father, or any other emperox, you were speaking to me. Or perhaps, they spoke through me."

"The other emperoxs *could* have been here, though. Like you are."

"The technology was there, yes. But it seemed a bad idea to me. You have seen, here in the Memory Room, some of the emperoxs who ruled the Interdependency. A good number of them are better off dead. And for the rest of them, I don't know that they could accept the terms. Living forever in a box is not a good life for most people."

"So how do you keep from going mad?" Grayland asked.

"I'm not awake all the time. When you're not here, I'm not here, except in the most abstract sense. Jiyi handles all day-to-day routines and catches me up when I'm awake. It's not just a face. It's a real, if limited, entity. It's the one collecting all those secrets, not me directly, for example."

"But *you* know all the secrets."

"Yes, I do. We found this secret — the secret of a machine consciousness — entirely by luck. I didn't want to lose any more information."

"But you never *shared* it. Until me. And I had to drag it from you. You lied to me about knowing it. And then you had Jiyi offer it up to me. But it was you all along."

"I have a complex and possibly not satisfying answer for that," Rachela said.

"I can't wait to hear it."

"The answer I gave you was the answer I would have given you if I was alive. When I was alive, I didn't know about the Rupture, or the Free Systems, or the Tripartition Treaty, all the things you asked me. I learned about them later, after I was dead, and Jiyi uncovered them or they were uncovered by others."

"But you *just* said this technology" — Grayland motioned at the Memory Room — "was Free Systems technology."

"I said it came from that time. When we found it, we knew almost nothing about the civilization that created it. I didn't know when I was alive, so I didn't tell you. I let Jiyi do it instead."

"So you're telling me that what you told

me was true . . . from a certain point of view."

"That's correct."

"Oh my God," Grayland said. "You are *utterly* impossible."

"I think of it as working through rules that meant that you — or any emperox who came here for advice and counsel — would receive the most authentic experience possible."

"Nothing about this is authentic!" Grayland exploded. "Nothing about *you* is authentic. If you were authentic, you would be *dead,* not this . . . zombie skulking in a room in the imperial palace!"

"Then you wouldn't know everything you know," Rachela said. "About the past. About all the secrets and plans the nobles have, and have against you. Authentic or not, I've been a very useful tool for you. And if your complaint against me is that I lied to you, and withheld certain things from you, then you should welcome me to your club. You did the same, very recently, to Marce."

"I thought I had good reasons for that."

"I'm aware of that. Just like I believed I had good reasons for doing what I did, the way I did it."

Grayland sighed and took a seat on the long featureless bench that was the Memory

Room's only bit of furniture. Rachela waited, as she would.

"I don't think I like you," Grayland said, after a long while.

"I can understand that," Rachela said.

"I don't think I like you," Grayland repeated. "I don't appreciate how you lied to me and to every other emperox. And I don't know if I can trust you. But the fact is, I need you."

Rachela smiled at this, faintly. "My dear granddaughter," she said. "I accept that you don't like me or trust me. I understand why you feel that way right now. But I ask you to understand that the deception was not meant to hurt you, or to deceive you, or any other emperox. It was to give you a way to be comfortable with me so that I could help you. Guide you. Offer you advice."

"Influence me," Grayland said.

"There's some of that," Rachela admitted. "The Interdependency is my legacy, and I've had a vested interest in it surviving. Over the years the emperoxs would come here to commune with their favorite ancestors, who were all me underneath. In the guise of offering egoless advice I gave them guidance that was a combination of what I knew, what the other emperoxs knew, and what I knew from all the secrets I had discovered over the years.

"What the emperoxs did with that advice was their own affair. Once they were out of the Memory Room I didn't try to influence or persuade them. Sometimes they took the advice. Sometimes they ignored it. Sometimes they took it and made things worse, either because they were bad emperoxs or because I'm not perfect and gave bad advice. But that indirect path of advising was enough. So, yes, Grayland. I might try to influence you. But you do have free will."

"I'm glad you think so," Grayland said. "It doesn't feel like it most of the time. Right now it feels like the future is a wall I'm about to run into with no way to stop. I can't turn, I can't reverse and I can't bail out. That's pretty much the opposite of free will right there."

"You haven't hit the wall yet."

"No," Grayland, agreed. "Not yet." She stood up and walked over to Rachela's apparition. "Look. No more lies, all right? No more lies, no more pretending to be Jiyi or every other emperox, no more any of this. If you really are here to help me, then help me. As you."

Rachela smiled again, widely, this time. "And how may I help you, my granddaughter, Emperox Grayland II?"

"You're aware that Nadashe Nohama-petan is planning another coup against me."

"One planned coup among several others, but yes. She's persistent."

"That's a word for it. You're also aware of Marce Claremont's current journey on the *Auvergne* with Tomas Chenevert."

"Yes, although only through what Chenevert tells me. He still won't let me into his system. He doesn't trust me."

"That seems fair."

"I disagree, but I understand why you say it."

"I thought he gave you some information about his systems as a gift."

"He told you that, did he? Yes. I'm looking at it as we speak. I can do that, you know. Do two things at once. Actually several thousand things at once."

"How different is he from you?"

"Why do you ask?"

"I'm curious, is all."

"His system architecture is incredibly different, which is to be expected because our civilizations haven't communicated in fifteen hundred years. But the function is similar enough, and some things are an improvement. I'll be looking to see what I can incorporate into my own being."

"You can do that?"

"I've been doing it for a thousand years. The Memory Room isn't running ancient technology. It's built to last for centuries, if it came to that. But since it hasn't come to that, I keep improving it."

"It could come to that very soon," Grayland said.

"Unless your fiancé pulls a miracle out of the air, yes."

Grayland blushed, and then felt embarrassed. She touched the small bump on the back of her neck that was the only outside evidence of the neural network in her head, recording her emotions and memories to be stored in this very room. "Of course you knew," she said finally.

"Of course I did. I'm happy for you. You do deserve some bit of joy in your life."

Grayland nodded at this, grimaced, sat down on the bench again and burst into tears.

Rachela waited until Grayland was done. "If you want to tell me what that was about, I'm listening," she said.

Grayland smiled ruefully at this, wiped tears away and shook her head. "You'll know soon enough."

"That's true," Rachela said.

"Is it worth it?" Grayland asked. "Living forever, I mean."

"It's not been forever; it's just been a long time. And yes, it's worth it. If you get to be useful."

"Okay, good." Grayland stood again. "Then it's time for you to be useful to me."

"Tell me how," Rachela said.

Grayland looked around the Memory Room. "First, I think you need to get used to the idea of a life outside of this box."

Grayland spent some part of every day of the next week in the Memory Room, communing with her ancestress, learning about her, and learning with her, and making plans for what was coming next. She also tended to state business, wrote out decrees and planned for upcoming events, as she would as emperox.

Every night before she went to bed, Grayland texted with Marce via her tablet, catching him up on her day and getting caught up with his. Their communication was hampered by the speed-of-light delay, which stretched to minutes on each end, but the wait was worth it. On the day that Marce saw his emergent stream, he sent only "Soooo much data. Love you." Grayland who was also Cardenia told him she loved him back.

The next day Grayland met with Commander Wen, who had an update on the Ikoyi task force: enough ships had been found and were currently en route to the Ikoyi system, where they would deploy two days before the Ikoyi Flow stream into End became untenable. In the meantime, more ships and personnel would be added to the task force as necessary. Even better, Countess Huma Lagos had promised logistical and materiel support of the task force within the Ikoyi system, which was a great relief to everyone involved. Grayland reminded Wen that arrangements were to be made for the eventual transfer of families of the personnel involved in the task force. Wen assured her that those arrangements were already underway.

Grayland's meeting with Commander Wen was followed immediately by a brief tea with Archbishop Korbijn, which Grayland enjoyed so much that she allowed it to run on an additional five minutes beyond its allotted fifteen. As they departed, Grayland impulsively gave Korbijn a hug, and then apologized to the archbishop for the impertinence. Archbishop Korbijn reminded Grayland that she was in fact the head of the Church of the Interdependency, and as such might be permitted to give a friendly hug to an archbishop from time to time.

The appointment Grayland had been made late to was with Countess Rafellya Maisen-Persaud, who was waiting for the emperox in one of the smaller formal rooms of Grayland's wing of the palace. Grayland apologized to the countess for her lateness, and the countess graciously accepted and in turn offered the emperox a small token: a music box from Lokono, which, when wound, would tinkle out several bars of a tune by Zay Equan, the most famous Lokonan composer of the last century. Grayland took the music box with appropriate thanks, sat it on her desk and asked the countess how her dog was. The countess, puzzled, replied that her dog was fine.

Grayland and Countess Rafellya Maisen-Persaud continued with pleasantries for several more minutes and had only begun to get to the substantive meat of their discussion, regarding the current potential for an evacuation of the Lokono system, when the music box, despite being carefully scanned and examined by imperial security, exploded violently and with deadly force, sending shrapnel across the confines of the small room and killing both the countess and the emperox instantly.

■ ■ ■ ■

# BOOK THREE

■ ■ ■ ■

Book Three

# CHAPTER 20

With the assassination of Emperox Grayland II, the Interdependency entered an official period of mourning. The executive committee, citing the shocking and tragic nature of her death, extended the traditional five-day mourning period to a full week. The week went into effect immediately within the Hub system, and would be in effect in all other systems on the receipt of the declaration of her death.

The executive committee, with Archbishop Korbijn at its head, also announced the formal investigation into the particulars of the assassination. All evidence pointed to Countess Rafellya Maisen-Persaud acting alone; a suicide note had been found in her apartments, detailing how she had managed the assassination and why — the latter, evidently, to protest the emperox's inaction on the matter of evacuating the Lokono system. The letter drew a parallel between the countess's act and the act of Gunnar Olafsen, who had assassinated the first Emperox Grayland in protest of what he saw as inaction on the isolation of Dalasýsla, which occurred in her reign.

But of course the executive committee could not simply accept that one, too-obvious answer without making a full inquiry. Grayland II's short reign had been marked by repeated assassination attempts and efforts at her removal, labyrinthine plans that had engaged the entire noble and professional classes of the Interdependency. There had to be at least an effort at digging deeper, to see if there was more here than the obvious disgruntled countess.

As for Grayland II herself, the (closed) casket bearing her remains would be displayed in state at the imperial palace for the first three days of the official mourning period, and then for another three days at Brighton, at Hubfall, for the public to view and remember her. At the end of the mourning period, she would, in accordance to tradition, be cremated and her remains interred in the imperial crypt on Xi'an, where she would rest with her ancestors for eternity.

With those matters settled, the executive committee turned its attention to the next and far more thorny problem: Who was to be the next emperox of the Interdependency.

It was a thornier problem than usual. The emperox had died without either producing or naming a successor, meaning there was no official heir to the throne. This had happened only six times before in the history of the Interdependency. It was not unheard-of, but it was rare.

History offered some guidance here. Whether the emperox had named a successor or not, the throne of the emperox was assumed to be the property of the House of Wu. This was by tradition, of course, but there was a strong, if unwritten, legal argument for it as well. The majority of the emperox's lesser titles, including that of Regent of Hub and Associated Nations, were explicitly tied to the Wu lineage, and Xi'an, while technically the territory of the imperial house, resided in the Hub system, which was owned and at least in theory administered by the Wu family. It would be difficult to place someone not a Wu onto the throne.

The previous six times in which there had been no official heir to throne, the throne had first been offered to whichever Wu cousin was the managing director of the House of Wu. If the managing director either refused the crown (which had happened three times) or was judged not competent (once), the board of directors of the House of Wu was then offered the task of choosing a Wu family member to ascend to the throne. Each time in this case the board chose one of its own members.

In the case of the current concern, naming the managing director would not be possible; the most recent managing director, Deran Wu, was dead, and the managing director previous to him, Jasin Wu, had attempted a coup against Grayland II and was currently sitting in a cell awaiting trial. No other Wu had stepped into the managing director position since Deran's untimely death — Proster Wu had been acting as de facto managing director for the family but had not officially taken the title, and neither he nor the rest of the board seemed to be in a rush to put someone in the seat. Nor did it appear that Proster Wu had any interest in becoming emperox himself, even if he were the official managing director.

All of that being the case — and having been fully briefed by both historians and the imperial minister of justice — Archbishop Korbijn, acting for the executive committee as its director, and with their signatures and seals affixed to attest to their consent, formally invited the board of directors of the House of Wu to select the next emperox.

Almost immediately came the request by Proster Wu to meet with the archbishop. The board, which had anticipated the invitation, had made its choice, and Proster wished to explain it to Korbijn in person.

"My condolences on your loss," Korbijn said to Proster, when he visited her a day later, in her spacious offices within the imperial cathedral on Xi'an. She motioned for him to sit once their assistants were dismissed and they were by themselves.

"Thank you," Proster said. "I never met my cousin other than formally and ceremonially, but it came as a shock to all of us."

"And to me."

"I understand that you were, in fact, quite close to her," Proster said.

"I was," Korbijn said. "She was lovely, and I don't mean that lightly. She hadn't wanted the role of emperox, but she grew into it. And she let me help her grow into it. I'll be forever grateful for that. I will miss her."

"Then my condolences to you, Archbishop."

"Thank you, Director Wu."

"Please, call me Proster."

"If you wish." Archbishop Korbijn smiled

and cleared the reverie of Grayland from her head. "Now, then. We are not here to talk of the past, but of the future."

"Yes."

"The Wus have chosen our next emperox."

"We have."

"Who is it?"

"Well," Proster said, and reached down for the document bag he was carrying. "That takes a bit of explanation."

Korbijn frowned. "Why is that?"

"You'll see." Proster reached into the document bag, pulled out an impressive stack of papers, and placed them on the archbishop's desk. "Before I tell you, here are endorsements from most of the noble houses, major and minor, regarding our selection. You may peruse these at your leisure and have your legal people confirm they are legitimate."

"Most houses?"

"There were a few holdouts," Proster said. "The House of Lagos, which is not a surprise, given how contrary they are. The House of Persaud, because its local director assassinated the former emperox, and they rather correctly determined that their best option at the moment is to lie low and not do anything. A few others, of relatively little importance in the large scheme of things."

He tapped the pile. "But this represents the vast bulk of the houses. The majority of the Interdependent nobility."

Korbijn looked at the pile. "For you to have this many endorsements for your choice, you must have had some idea of this successor for a while now."

"No, of course not. But when it became clear there would need to be a successor, one was the obvious choice to the board, and when we contacted other houses, it was an obvious choice to them as well."

"After this lead-up, I can't wait to hear which Wu this is."

"Well, that's just it, Archbishop. It's not a Wu."

Korbijn wrinkled her forehead at this.

"What?"

"It's Nadashe Nohamapetan."

Korbijn gaped openly. "You are out of your goddamned mind," she said, when she recovered.

Proster Wu seemed surprised an archbishop would use a profanity, and particularly *that* profanity, but recovered quickly and shook his head. "There are very good reasons."

"She tried to kill the emperox! Twice! She murdered her own brother! She participated in her mother's coup!"

357

"There's context for all of that."

"Context!"

"Yes," Proster pressed on. "I'm not going to pretend to you that Nadashe was not engaged in these events. But the context was, and is, her family, and ours. Grayland's father Attavio VI made, on behalf of the imperial house, a compact with the House of Nohamapetan to have a Nohamapetan as the imperial consort and to bear a child of the two families, to be the heir of his own heir. Then Rennered died —"

"— because the Countess Nohamapetan had him *murdered* —"

"— in circumstances that Nadashe was not involved in nor had foreknowledge of, and Cardenia became heir. The presumption by both families was that the agreement between the houses was still in force. But *Cardenia* broke that agreement, and the House of Nohamapetan was left without recourse."

"And that somehow *excuses* attempted murders and coups," Korbijn said.

"Of course not," Proster said. "It is, however, relevant to note that this agreement between the Nohamapetans and the imperial house wasn't merely about business. It was about dynasties and the rule of the Interdependency. Nothing excuses the actions of the House of Nohamapetan in the aftermath of Cardenia's choice not to honor the agreement between their houses. But there *is* context. And in that context, Cardenia wronged the House of Nohamapetan. Not in the same degree, or kind. But certainly enough."

"You can't possibly believe what you're telling me."

"I can, actually," Proster said. "Also, I believe that the last thing the Interdependency needs at this moment, when literally everything is falling apart, is a civil war with the imperial house on one side and the Nohamapetans on the other. That's what we've had over the last few years, and you know it. It's what's gotten us to where we are today. We should be focused on saving the Interdependency from collapse. Instead we're playing palace intrigues. It's pointless. It's wasteful. And it's going to end in our ruin. The ruin of *all* of us. You know this. I know this." Proster motioned to the pile of documents. "And they know it too."

Korbijn said nothing to this.

Proster leaned forward in his chair. "Look. The Wus put Nadashe Nohamapetan on the throne as emperox. *Just* as emperox, with *very* proscribed powers and responsibilities that she's already agreed to. She marries a

Wu — she's already looking through the ranks to find a suitable match — and then whoever she picks takes all the lesser titles of nobility: King of Hub and so on. Their child, who will take the Wu name, inherits everything, and we're back to where we were before in terms of succession and dynasty. Back to what both the imperial house and the House of Nohamapetan agreed to under Attavio VI. Everyone now squaring off to fight a civil war backs down. We focus on saving the Interdependency. We save as many lives as we can."

"Even if it rewards a murderer and a traitor."

Proster spread his hands wide. "These are the times we live in, Archbishop."

"We make the times we live in, Proster."

"Sometimes. But *we* didn't make a time in which the Flow is collapsing. That was something we had thrust on us, I'm afraid." He shrugged. "And anyway, if we don't put Nadashe on the throne, what time are we making there? Do you think she or her allies will stop doing what they're doing? How many Wus would you like my family to paint a target on? I'm not keen on making any more of my cousins a sacrifice to the gods of war."

"You want my assent to this," Korbijn said.

"I would *like* it," Proster said. "We don't *need* it. We already have the nobles behind us. But yes. I would like your assent, and your personal endorsement, and the co-operation of the Church of the Interdependency. It would make things easier, and it would have benefits for you personally as well."

"How so?"

"Nadashe is aware that her history makes her a . . . contentious choice to be the head of the church and the cardinal of Xi'an and Hub. She is prepared to devolve those titles and powers onto you, as archbishop, for the duration of her reign, or your tenancy in the position, whichever is shorter. If your tenure is shorter, then the titles go to Nadashe's heir on your death or retirement. If yours is longer, you have the option of returning the titles to the new emperox when they take the throne, but the titles will return to the new emperox whenever it is that you leave your office."

Korbijn shook her head. "Not me," she said.

"Pardon?"

"I said, 'Not me.' I can speak for the church when I say that it will not stand in the way of your choice for emperox, as foolish as it may be. And I accept your offer with regard to the cardinalship of Xi'an and Hub going to the archbishop of Xi'an for the term of Nadashe Nohamapetan's reign as emperox. But it will not be going to me. I intend to resign."

"Why is that?"

"Because I will not stand in the cathedral, bless Nadashe Nohamapetan and pray for her success and be the instrument of her coronation. You forget, Proster Wu, that I served with Nadashe Nohamapetan on the executive committee. I was able to take her full measure there. You are deluding yourself, sir, if you believe that she can be controlled or contained by you, or the House of Wu, or any agreements that she says that she will live by."

"It's possible you are overly pessimistic."

"You should fervently hope I am," Korbijn said. "For my part I will wash my hands of it. You may expect me to announce my intent to resign the archbishopric and to resume my role as a common priest within the next several hours."

"I look forward to meeting with your successor about the coronation."

"I look forward to it as well, when it happens a month from now."

"Excuse me?" Proster said.

Korbijn smiled. "My dear Proster, I see you are not a particularly faithful son of the church. Then let me explain. As the de facto head of the Church of the Interdependency — and because there is in fact no currently reigning emperox, de jure head as well — I do not have the luxury of handpicking my successor. There must be a convocation of bishops, and there must be a quorum. The number of bishops whose dioceses are in the Hub system is not quite the required number for a quorum, so there must also be bishops from other systems. This is by design, incidentally. If there are enough other bishops visiting Hub, as there may be, then we can use them. But we must *also* extend the invitation to bishops from other systems as well. The absolute bare minimum of time required by church law for this is a month."

"Even if there is a quorum of bishops in the Hub system."

"Yes. The quorum is the minimum. The more bishops who can participate the better. Usually, if the archbishop of Xi'an plans to retire, we set a date as far in advance as possible. A year, usually. Not unusually, two years, so bishops from End can appear if they like. But End is cut off from us now in any event."

"And you won't perform the coronation before then."

"Once I announce my resignation, I can't," Korbijn said. "I may perform the standard rites any priest may do, and I'm sure the church will allow me to continue to be a representative on the executive committee in the interim. But all my archbishopric responsibilities will pass temporarily to Bishop Hill, who administers Parliament Cathedral."

Proster opened his mouth.

"All archbishopric responsibilities *except* the coronation of the emperox, which canonically falls explicitly under the responsibilities of the archbishop of Xi'an."

Proster closed his mouth again.

"And before you ask — or don't ask, but *think,* Proster — no emperox is legitimate without a church coronation. An heir presumptive may act with certain powers prior to their formal ascendance, but those powers are largely ceremonial and limited to administration of the imperial household. That's why we have an executive committee for the interim."

"I see what you're doing, you know," Proster said.

"I should certainly hope so; I'm being

obvious enough about it," Korbijn said. "But let me tell you just in case I'm not. You will have your coronation, Proster Wu. Nadashe Nohamapetan will be emperox, and on your head be it. But that coronation must be legitimate and it *must* be by the rules — the rules of the church and the law of the Interdependency — or your foolish game will fall into ruin. Which means, for now, you have to play by *my* rules. This is my last move. I know it and you know it. But it is still my move to play, and I'm going to play it."

Proster said nothing for a longish time. Then he nodded.

"Good," Korbijn said. "Then my successor, whoever it is, will see you here in a month. Probably."

Proster raised his eyebrows. "Probably?"

"The bishops usually select the next archbishop from the host assembled," Korbijn said. "But sometimes they don't. Sometimes they'll pick one not present. When they do, that bishop must be notified. Then they must accept. Then they must travel. That could take months."

"It's not likely, you say."

"It's not," Korbijn agreed. "But it's possible. You should hope they don't pick a bishop from End."

# CHAPTER 21

Marce and Chenevert found the emerging evanescent Flow shoal right where it should have been, doing what Marce had hypothesized it would be doing — expanding and moving — and more than that, throwing off even more Flow shoals that whipped out and forward and then evaporated in minutes or seconds. Marce hadn't been expecting that, and it didn't quite fit his model, and he knew that he could spend an entire career digging into just that one aspect of the emergent evanescent Flow shoals and would never run out of things to say about it.

Marce Claremont's life was a ridiculously full festival of data.

Enough so that it fell to Chenevert to remind him that while all the data they were gathering were glorious, they had a task and focus, and maybe they should work on that. So Marce grudgingly set aside anything that was not related to gauging the baseline resonance of the Flow medium and mapping the continuing effects of the now-ancient cavitation, to see how the remaining data related to his hypothesized values of each.

These, too, were intriguingly different — close, but different, and Marce as a scientist appreciated how even small variations meant vast changes would propagate down the line, vastly changing the predictions for the appearance and duration of evanescent Flow streams, both in the near future and in decades and even centuries to come.

It also reinforced Marce's belief that the next step was to get more readings from emergent evanescent Flow shoals and their attendant streams. Incremental refining of hypotheses with new, pertinent data was not sexy, but it was important. It also suggested — just *suggested,* but even so — that there might even be a way to do the thing they wanted: to shape the Flow shoals, and move them, and even perhaps get them to swallow human habitats whole.

Which would open up a whole raft of second-order problems that Marce wasn't sure he wanted to confront, including the question of how to shape a timespace bubble of such volume that it could include a kilometers-long habitat inside of it. But he also realized that he didn't have to solve every problem. If he solved *this* problem, other people could handle the rest. And solving this problem was enough for anyone.

Marce was so wrapped up in his own world of data and hypotheses that he almost forgot to send a note to Cardenia, to initiate their evening chat of short bursts of text punctuated by long pauses. This night, Marce simply put "Soooo much data. Love you" as his text, hoping that Cardenia would understand he was too distracted by shiny, shiny science to be a useful conversationalist to her tonight. Cardenia responded, simply, "Love you too," and in those words he could imagine her smiling at his guileless enthusiasm for science.

He was glad she did, and could, and for the umpteenth time since the night before he and Chenevert departed to observe this emerging Flow shoal, Marce took a second to be amazed, simply and profoundly amazed, that Cardenia had proposed marriage to him.

It had been, Marce knew, an impulsive decision on her part, and perhaps even a rash one. Cardenia had long before filled him in on how she had been intended to marry the ill-fated Amit Nohamapetan, and how someone in her position was not always or even often afforded the luxury of marrying for love. That was for people who *didn't* have so much power that they literally couldn't give it away, the sort of power Cardenia had as emperox. She had told him this with such plaintive matter-of-factness that Marce had been surprised when he felt something akin to pity for her, the most powerful person among the billions in the Interdependency.

Marce had already known this about her, even before she told him, and had always kept some part of himself in reserve. Not his heart, because he knew he loved Cardenia and there was no point in deluding himself about that. But the quiet, logical parts in his head that made him aware that this relationship would end one day — if he was lucky, by the simple entropy of overfamiliar people falling out of love with each other, but by some other, more heart-wrenching process if not. And when it happened — when, not if — he would have to be able to have the grace to accept it, and to know that love was never part of an emperox's inheritance.

And yet Cardenia had proposed anyway, to *him,* and despite his initial fumble of it, he had accepted. With that Marce was done holding back the quiet and logical parts in his head. Marce and Cardenia might perhaps one day mess up their relationship — people did that, and Marce didn't delude himself that just because he loved Cardenia it didn't mean he wouldn't aggravate the crap out of her sometimes — but they would do it from a state that would encourage constancy and reconciliation as a baseline. Marce was pretty sure he could work with that: every day a new day to start again, building a life together.

Hours later, when at last Marce couldn't keep the streams of data clear in his vision or his head, he headed to his stateroom on the *Auvergne* and put his head on his pillow and thought muzzy and contented thoughts of Cardenia as he was swiftly pulled into a full and dreamless sleep. As he surfaced out from that sleep, almost twelve hours later, he thought he heard Cardenia say, simply, "Marce," just as he opened his eyes.

Marce Claremont pulled himself up from his bed, yawned and stretched, put on clothes, and then walked to the bridge of the *Auvergne,* where Tomas Chenevert, who had intentionally let Marce sleep as late as he possibly could, was waiting for him to tell him that Cardenia, the Emperox Grayland II, was dead.

The voyage back to Xi'an took eight days, and a thousand years.

The Xi'an that Marce returned to was not the one he had left. His formal position on the imperial staff was as a special advisor for science to the emperox, which was an appointment personal to the emperox herself. When Grayland died, all her personal appointments — advisors, assistants and consultants — were suspended, pending the pleasure of the incoming emperox, who, historically, would be bringing in their own staff and therefore would have little need of the former emperox's staff.

For Marce this meant that every project or initiative that he had undertaken on behalf of Grayland — which meant all of them — was halted, held up pending review by the incoming emperox. Marce was no longer able to access files or data on the imperial servers, or to share the new data he had collected with other scientists, until such time as the new emperox or their appointed representative(s) for the emperox's personal science and research initiatives allowed him to do so.

In itself this presented little problem for Marce. He had always kept copies of his work on his own devices, and all the work had been shared with Chenevert, anyway.

He could get the information to others if he chose, and work on it himself in the meanwhile. But being officially closed off from his work, and what that act represented with respect to his relationship with the imperial apparatus, unmoored him.

(Speaking of being unmoored, the *Auvergne* was now no longer permitted to berth at the emperox's private space dock at Xi'an — Marce, whose ship it was assumed to be, had to make arrangements elsewhere at the habitat, paying the exorbitant fee for a temporary berthing out of the vault of marks that he had carried with him from End. The berthing would indeed have to be temporary, because its cost would quickly whittle down Marce's stash of money. Thus Marce was reminded that there was a difference between being merely rich, as he was, and profoundly rich, which he was going to have to be to keep a ship the size of the *Auvergne* parked anywhere in the system.)

Pending the disposition of his employment with the new emperox, Marce was permitted to stay in his palace quarters, the bachelor studio that he had only rarely slept in the last several months. Marce had not been allowed to retrieve his things from the emperox's apartments. His effects —

clothes, toiletries, a few other personal items — had been delivered to his palace quarters before he and the *Auvergne* had even returned to Xi'an. Marce had been shut out of the personal aspects of the imperial world as effectively and efficiently as he had been shut out of its professional aspects.

Of course, everyone knew that Marce and Grayland had had a "close friendship," as the euphemism went. Back in his bachelor quarters, Marce had received kindness and sympathy from other members of the imperial staff, some of whom found themselves, like Marce, waiting to hear if their positions would be retained. What they nor anyone else understood was the quality of that close friendship — that it had not been a "close friendship" at all, but actual love, genuine and true.

Marce understood that others in the imperial household could not be faulted for thinking that he had been nothing more than a fond plaything for a powerful person. He had never chosen to capitalize or brag about the relationship. It wasn't anyone else's business. But that unwillingness to speak casually about what he shared with Grayland — with Cardenia — meant that in the eyes of everyone else, except those very few who knew the emperox the best,

Marce had no special claim to the emperox or her person.

No one else knew that Cardenia had proposed to him.

Marce was widowed, in all the ways one could be, without the benefit of a single soul to understand his pain and bereavement. He hadn't even told Chenevert; he felt it wasn't his place to share that information first. When one's fiancée was the emperox, you let her make the announcements.

He could tell Chenevert now, clearly. He could tell anyone who would choose to listen. But he would not, because Cardenia wasn't there to offer her side of it. Marce knew with certainty what would be thought of him, if he declared the engagement here and now.

That was fine with Marce. He didn't need anyone else to know Cardenia had asked him to marry her. He knew, and he would carry it with him forever.

Marce did not stay in his bachelor quarters, and did not wait to discover the disposition of his role in the imperial household. Marce had come to Hub to deliver the news his father had asked him to, the news about the collapse of the Flow. He had stayed because the emperox — because Cardenia — had asked him to stay. She was gone, and his responsibilities, to her and to his father, had been fulfilled.

Besides, the new emperox was going to be Nadashe Nohamapetan.

Marce resigned his position, cleaned out his quarters, and moved into the *Auvergne,* both because Chenevert had invited him to and because, as Marce figured it, he was already paying rent in the form of the appallingly high docking fee.

"What is your plan now?" Chenevert asked him, after he had moved in.

"I don't know," Marce said. "My original plan was to go back to End. That's difficult now because the Nohamapetans have the planet blockaded."

"Grayland had a plan to send an armada."

"That's been cancelled, obviously. Nadashe is the incoming emperox. She's not going to move against her own brother."

"*We* could still slip in through that back door," Chenevert said. "It's still open. If we hurry."

"We?"

"I have no ties here, clearly. And we're friends."

"Thank you," Marce said, genuinely touched. "But I couldn't ask you to risk that. Even if no one's watching that one Flow shoal, that doesn't mean we won't be spotted approaching the planet. The *Auvergne* is not small."

"You underestimate my stealth," Chenevert said.

"I'd rather underestimate your stealth than underestimate their ability to destroy you as an unidentified craft."

"Fair enough."

"No, I can't go back to End. Not yet. Maybe not ever."

"Then I return to my original question," Chenevert said.

"I return to my original answer," Marce replied. "I don't know. Not yet. I'll figure it out soon. If nothing else, you and I have a lot of data left to work through. Maybe we'll find answers there." He smiled and looked over to the apparition of Chenevert. "We're still the Interdependency's last hope, after all. We could keep working on that, whether the incoming emperox wants us to or not."

"I like that idea. It appeals to the futile romantic in me."

"I'm sorry you've been dragged into all of this," Marce said. "When we found you, you were sleeping comfortably. We woke you up, put you in the middle of a space battle, and when you came here I got you involved in the same sort of political machinations that you had fled from. I wouldn't blame you if you purged me into space while I was sleeping."

"I assure you I have no plans to purge you," Chenevert said. "My dear Lord Marce. I am very fond of you. Yes, I was sleeping quite contentedly when you found me. It's possible I could have slept until my power ran down and I drifted away into a quiet death. But I don't regret you waking me. You have offered me a better life and a better purpose than I have had in years, and perhaps ever. And if our task fails and our effort is ultimately futile, it was still worth the fight. I will be forever grateful that I was able to fight this with you, and with your emperox. Thank you."

"You're welcome," Marce said. He got up to head for his stateroom.

"Cardenia was a remarkable person," Chenevert said to him, as he left. "You were right to love her, Marce."

"Thank you."

"And she was right to love you."

Marce had nothing to say to that. He nodded and left.

In his stateroom, Marce prepared for bed, and in doing so ran his eyes over the small collection of possessions he had to his name. One of them caught his eye, and he picked it up. It was the pocket watch, the first gift that Cardenia had ever given him.

He opened it, and his eyes fell on the Chinese markings, the inscription that Cardenia had put there.

*This is our time.*

"It *was* our time," Marce said to Cardenia, who was not there. "And it was worth it. I just wish there had been more of it."

Marce willed himself to sleep. Just before it came, he imagined he heard Cardenia saying his name. It comforted him, and he gave himself over to it, and slept.

# CHAPTER 22

Nadashe's people were waiting for the *Our Love* when it popped back into Hub space, because of course they fucking would be. Nadashe had probably had them stationed there since the moment the *Our Love* exited Hub, just in case the ship somehow discovered the ability to fucking *reverse* in the Flow and come back immediately.

Kiva was flattered that Nadashe's people were waiting. It meant Nadashe had been expecting Kiva to subvert the crew of the *Our Love* somehow. She was happy not to disappoint.

The *Our Love* crew surrendered Kiva without a fight, per Kiva's wishes, and fed Nadashe's people a line about Robinette unexpectedly experiencing a natural death (which was not technically incorrect, as the vacuum of space is a natural phenomenon), and thus the ship returning immediately to Hub to await further instructions. It was a cover story Kiva thought might keep the *Our Love* from being blasted out of the stars upon its return. Kiva was not especially fond of the *Our Love* crew — her earlier assessment of the crew being the type of surly fuckups who could not hack it in polite society had not been challenged on the nine-day return trip — but they had done her a favor in being easily manipulated into a mutiny. She wanted to hold up her end of the deal.

Nadashe's ships had jammed the *Our Love*'s communications, so Kiva had been unable to send a series of intended messages, including ones to Senia and to the House of Lagos's legal team. She also wasn't able to enable the transfer of one of Nadashe's secret accounts to the *Our Love*'s on-ship data vault. Before she was taken from the ship, Kiva wiped the messages to Senia and to legal out of the mailing queue so as to prioritize the withdrawal, and left detailed instructions for now-captain Nomiek about how to get through the secret account's security protocols. She recommended he grab the account immediately after his communications were unjammed and that he, the *Our Love,* and all of its crew lie real fucking low for a few months. The secret account Kiva was transferring over had forty-six million marks more in it than the sum she had agreed to provide. Kiva considered it a tip, and anyway, it wasn't like it was her fucking money.

Once Kiva was on board Nadashe's ship, it ignored the *Our Love* entirely, which was a mild relief to Kiva, and headed toward Hub. Or so she thought. It wasn't until the ship docked at Xi'an, at the emperox's private docking area, that Kiva began to think that while she was away something had gone seriously fucking awry.

That suspicion was confirmed when Kiva was escorted to the emperox's private office and found Nadashe Nohamapetan sitting behind the emperox's private desk.

"You have to be absolutely fucking kidding me," Kiva said to Nadashe.

Nadashe smiled. "Lady Kiva. If I wished to have a private conversation with you, would you promise not to do anything stupid, like attempt to attack me?"

"Fuck no," Kiva said, and nodded her head at an object on the desk. "I would beat you to death with that fucking paperweight the first chance I got."

"I appreciate your honesty," Nadashe said, and nodded to the security personnel who had accompanied Kiva from the ship to the office. One of them forced Kiva into a very fine and extraordinarily expensive chair dating from the reign of Leo II, while another zipped her hands and feet to it with flexible ties.

"Snug?" Nadashe asked, after Kiva had been secured and the security detail had been dismissed to the other side of the door.

"Come over here and I'll bite you."

"That's not my kink, but thank you for the offer." Nadashe motioned to the office. "I understand that it might come as a shock to you that we are meeting in this place."

"I'm not shocked," Kiva said. "You've been trying to murder your way to this fucking office for years. I'm just disappointed that you finally managed to do it."

"I didn't murder anyone to get here."

"I'm sorry, I didn't know today was 'insult Kiva Lagos's intelligence' day. If I had, I would have worn a festive party hat."

"Have it your way," Nadashe said. "The point is I will be the next emperox."

"Why aren't you the emperox already?" Kiva asked. "You've clearly been skulking around *this* fucking place for a bit. You've got your assholes all over it. What's the holdup?"

Nadashe's lips pressed thin. "A procedural detail with the Church of the Interdependency."

Kiva chuckled at this. "I'm guessing Archbishop Korbijn told you to fuck yourself sideways."

"Something like that."

"I always liked her."

"I didn't," Nadashe said. "The former Archbishop isn't going to be around for much longer in any event."

Kiva nodded. "Getting a jump on disappearing your enemies, I see."

"She's retiring from the priesthood after the coronation," Nadashe said. "You don't have to think so poorly of me, Kiva."

"I'm not sure why not."

"Well, you're still alive, for one."

This got a snort. "That's just because I know where your money is."

"Not just because of that."

"I'm unconvinced," Kiva said. "Two point seven billion marks in secret accounts is still a tidy sum, even for an incoming emperox. Well, two point six four four billion marks. I may have just overpaid for a mutiny with one of your smaller accounts."

Nadashe smiled. "What if I told you that you could keep that two point six four four billion marks?"

"Then I'd say I wish I'd paid less for that mutiny."

"Be serious for a moment, Kiva. We've

never liked each other, and lately we've been legitimate enemies. But I'm about to be emperox. The last thing I want as I start my reign is contention and anger. I understand pissiness and attitude and performative rebellion are part of your brand" — Nadashe pointed at Kiva's restraints — "but I also know that when push comes to shove, you keep your eye on business. Always have. I mean, hell. You somehow managed to make a profit on that trip to End after we sabotaged your haverfruit crops."

"I fucking knew it!" Kiva exclaimed, triumphantly. "Your fucking brother. I'm gonna kill that little shit."

"That seems unlikely at this point," Nadashe observed.

"It's on the agenda," Kiva assured her.

Nadashe ignored this. "My point is this, Kiva: It's time to put our differences aside. It's time to do business."

"All right," Kiva said. "Let's hear the business."

"Here it is: I want your support. I want your house's support."

"I'm not my house. You'll have to talk to my mother about that."

"I did. One of my representatives did, anyway."

"Yeah? How did that go?"

"She said that we could all fuck ourselves with a rented dick. The *same* rented dick."

"That's my mom," Kiva said.

"I really thought it was just you who had that whole profanity tic."

"Nope. It's a family thing."

"It's not an attractive family trait."

"It's a better one than murdering family members and anyone else that gets in your way."

"I suppose I walked into that, didn't I."

"You sure fucking did."

"Let's get back to it," Nadashe said. "Your mother was not exactly forthcoming with her endorsement."

"To be fair, you fake-murdered her child, who you actually kidnapped. This would not endear you to her."

"Which is why if you endorsed me after all this, it would be such a powerful statement. It could convince your family and house to come into line as well. I want all the houses behind me as I take the throne, Kiva. Not just some of them. All of them."

"And in return I get what?"

"You keep the secret accounts, to start. Two billion plus marks, all yours, free and clear. I won't even make you pay taxes on them."

"And."

"I don't put House of Lagos under investigation for various frauds and illegal business practices, or place your house under imperial administration while we audit every single inch of your business, going back a hundred years or more. Sound at all familiar?"

Kiva ignored the provocation. "And," she said.

"You'll succeed your mother as the head of the House of Lagos."

"That won't go over well with at least five of my siblings," Kiva said.

"You'll have the emperox on your side. They'll have to get used to disappointment."

Kiva nodded. "And."

"And *ice cream,*" Nadashe said, exasperated. "What else more do you want?"

"I want your brother Ghreni's head on a fucking spike," Kiva said.

"Why?"

"Because he pissed me off and messed with my business and at one point would have tried to kill me on End, because he deluded himself that he could get away with that shit."

"He was going to kill you himself?"

"He was going to try, anyway."

"Yeah," Nadashe said. "I don't see that working out for him."

"It really would not have. But it's still a mark against him in my book."

"I can't give you him right away," Nadashe said. "I still need him for a while. Until I can move the imperial house to End."

"How long is that going to be?"

"Maybe five years."

"Five years!" Kiva exclaimed.

"Would have been slightly sooner if not for Archbishop Korbijn."

"So in five years, you cut him loose."

"Yes," Nadashe said. "He's yours. You'll have to come to End to get him, though."

"We're all coming to End, sooner or later."

"Which is the other thing," Nadashe said. "I can offer the House of Lagos a discount on shoal fees to End. Those are going to be getting very expensive in the next few years."

"I can only imagine," Kiva said. "So, to sum up, if I endorse you as emperox, and get the House of Lagos to come around and endorse you too, I get two and a half billion marks, tax free, the directorship of my House, cheap fees to End when we move everything over there, and I get to murder the fuck out of that miserable block of constipation that you call your brother. In five years."

"That sounds about right," Nadashe said.

"That's a pretty good deal," Kiva admitted.

"So you'll take it," Nadashe prompted.

"Fuck no," Kiva said. "I'm not *that* gullible, sister. I just wanted to see what you would pretend to offer. Selling out your brother was an especially nice touch."

"What?" Nadashe was confused.

"You're not under the impression I think you'll live up to your agreements, are you?" Kiva said. "You're fucking trash, Nadashe. Your whole family is trash. Traitorous, murdering garbage, from your fucking glitterdumpster of a mother on down. Once you're emperox, you won't give a goddamn about house endorsements or promises or loyalty. You're going to pick us apart and you're going to use the collapse of the Flow to do it. You'll turn on me the moment you can't get anything more out of me. You'll turn on my house. You'll turn on *everyone,* sooner or later. You won't care, because you'll be on End while everyone else dies slowly in space. So, yeah, fuck you, Nadashe. Fuck you and your fucking deal."

"Well," Nadashe said, when Kiva was done. "That was quite a little speech."

"It had its moments," Kiva allowed.

"I'm glad we had this time together. You know, it's been a while since we were in the same room at the same time. I think university was the last time it happened."

"I didn't miss you much."

"Likewise, I assure you."

"So now what?" Kiva asked. "Are you killing me now, or are you saving me for a special occasion?"

"It won't be that special," Nadashe said. "No, I'm not going to kill you. I do still want that money back, since you didn't want it. And you still have use to me as a hostage. For now."

"So where are you going to put me?"

Nadashe smiled. "I have just the place. I hope you like toothbrush shivs."

Which is how Kiva found herself, a few short hours later, at the Emperox Hanne II Secured Correctional Facility, thirty klicks outside of Hubfall. It was the same facility that Nadashe had found herself in, after she had been accused of murder and treason. Shoving Kiva into it probably counted as ironic commentary for Nadashe.

Kiva was surprisingly fine with it, to be honest. She wasn't being actively murdered, which was a thing she wouldn't have guessed, given Nadashe and her tendencies toward homicide, and her cell was both larger and smelled nicer than the broom closet she'd been shoved into on the *Our*

*Love.* The cell's toilet wasn't even chemical.

Philosophically she was less fine with the fact she was an actual and genuine political prisoner, since she was being held without any official charges, without representation and without anyone knowing that she was alive. She hadn't even been checked in to the facility under her name; as far as the Emperox Hanne II Secured Correctional Facility was concerned, Kiva's name was Mavel Biggs. Kiva remembered that as being the name of one of the minor characters in the terrible novel she had been reading on the *Our Love. That* was some fucking irony for you.

Kiva idly wondered if she was the only political prisoner at the facility, but there was no way for her to know. She was held in solitary, ostensibly for her own protection against a shivving from a toothbrush or any other implement, but in reality to keep her from speaking to other prisoners, to whom she might blab about her actual identity, and who might in turn tell their lawyers or family members, who in turn might tell someone who actually cared, and so on. It was not uniformly terrible, since it meant her meals were brought to her, she had the exercise area to herself for the hour she had out of her cell, and she was given a one-way tablet to keep her amused. She found herself bingeing *The Emperoxs* again, because it was there and it was distracting eye candy. The days began to flow together.

It was the tablet that told her, under its news heading, that the Church of the Interdependency's convocation of bishops had finally, after a rather contentious debate that took weeks longer than expected, selected a new archbishop of Xi'an: the former Bishop Cole, of the Sparta habitat, which was located in a long orbit of the Hub system's sun. Kiva looked at Bishop Cole — a stocky, bearded fellow who bore a look of quiet exasperation — and wondered what he had done to be stuck with the thankless task of coronating Nadashe Nohamapetan. He didn't look like he'd enjoy it. But then, Kiva wasn't sure, aside from Nadashe herself, how anyone would enjoy it.

With the next archbishop selected, the coronation of Nadashe Nohamapetan could finally be scheduled. It was to be in three days, at noon. Nadashe had unusually kept her personal name as her imperial name; she was to be the Emperox Nadashe I. Kiva was not surprised. Nadashe was an egotistical fuck.

Kiva did not imagine that she would be sprung from her current circumstances once

Nadashe became emperox. She fully expected to be lost in the shuffle from now until the end of time. Or at least until Nadashe was fully ensconced in her new imperial digs on End, five some odd years from now. Once she was there, and the Flow stream from Hub to End collapsed, Kiva didn't imagine that her own fate would be any different than that of anyone else left behind — slow death. Whether it was in this cell or outside of it hardly made a difference.

Kiva's tablet suddenly went blank.

"Fuck," she said. The tablet was Kiva's sanity check — without something to keep her busy, solitary would drive her loopy in a probably surprisingly short amount of time.

The lights in the Emperox Hanne II Secured Correctional Facility suddenly went out. All of them. All at once.

"*Fuck,*" Kiva said again, this time with more urgency. Loss of power was no joke. The correctional facility, like every habitat on Hub, was underground, below the surface of an airless planet whose surface temperature ranged from murderously cold to murderously hot, depending on where one was standing on its tidally locked surface. The facility was on the murderously cold side of the terminator line. Without power, it would start getting cold. And stuffy, since the air exchangers and scrubbers would be off-line as well. If the power stayed off, it would be a race to discover whether everyone in the facility would die of cold or carbon dioxide asphyxiation.

Before Kiva could panic further her tablet lit up, with big white friendly sans serif letters on a black background.

Hello! The letters read. Welcome to your jailbreak.

"Fuck?" Kiva said, confused. The letters disappeared and new ones took their place.

Cutting the power was necessary to reboot security and other systems, they said. Power will resume momentarily. Be ready to move when it does. Enjoy this music until then! The tablet began playing soothing instrumental versions of modern popular hits. Kiva didn't know whether to shit or hum along.

The lights came back on, as suddenly as they'd gone off.

Time to go! the words on the tablet said. The music shifted to something a little more upbeat and staccato. *Fucking jailbreak music,* Kiva thought.

There was a click from her door — the sound it made when it was unlocked.

Please step through the door and go left down the corridor, the tablet's words instructed. Take this tablet with you!

Kiva did what she was told, walking briskly out of her cell with the tablet. She noted that no other prisoners appeared to be out of their cells. She could hear them, but they stayed locked up.

At least until she reached a security door, which opened to allow her passage. As she closed the door behind her, she heard the security door latch shut and then a multitude of other doors unlock; all the other prisoners in that section were now free to leave their cells but were confined to the section.

Kiva followed further directions to a guard room. As the door unlocked, she peered in to see two unconscious guards.

To facilitate your jailbreak, the oxygen in this room was temporarily removed, the tablet said. Don't worry, these guards are probably fine!

Kiva took the tablet's word for it and moved quickly through the room into another corridor.

And so it went for the better part of a half hour, with Kiva picking her way through the facility, going where the tablet guided her. As she moved, she could hear the sounds of the facility: the rumblings of released prisoners, the sirens of the guard stations, and the general sounds of chaos and confusion. It didn't sound like a riot, not yet at least, but Kiva knew she didn't want to wait around to see how things turned out on that score.

Eventually Kiva was led to a transport hub for overland vehicles, the ones that would travel the surface of Hub on a largely deserted highway connecting the facility to Hubfall.

To the left you'll find the guard dressing area, the tablet said. Go in and take the suit marked for Brimenez. It'll fit you!

Kiva did as she was told, jamming herself awkwardly into a pressurized suit while the tablet displayed instructions on how to seal the head and wrist gaskets. When she was stuffed into the suit like a fucking sausage, the tablet directed her to a lift that took her to a surface lobby.

Please wait here, the tablet said. Your ride is arriving shortly! More smooth instrumental versions of popular hits played while Kiva waited.

And indeed, in just a few moments the massive gate of the facility shifted and opened, and a large overland passenger transport vehicle rumbled through — rumbled because Kiva could feel the vibrations of its treads as it approached.

Your ride is here! the tablet said. Enter the transport through the airlock at the back. Also, this tablet contains a tracker and movement data, so please place it under the treads of the transport before you board, to destroy evidence. Thank you for participating in this jailbreak!

Kiva gaped a little at the tablet, then cycled the airlock out of the lobby. She placed the tablet under the front tread of the transport and then walked to the back, lifted herself up to the airlock there, and cycled through.

To find Senia Fundapellonan waiting there for her.

The transport moved forward, crushing the tablet, which up until that time had continued playing instrumental hits, for what little effect that would have on an airless planet.

"You asshole," Senia said, weeping, once Kiva had unsealed herself out of her suit, and once the two of them had stopped kissing frantically on each other. "You made me think you were dead."

"I didn't make you think that," Kiva said. "It was our fucking future emperox."

"I hate her so much."

"There's a line for that. It's really long." Kiva said, and kissed Senia again. "How did you do this? How did you manage an entire fucking jailbreak?"

"I didn't," Senia said.

Kiva was confused. "Then who did?"

"I was told by your mother to meet this transport and to wait for additional instructions."

"My mother did this?"

"Would you put it past her?"

"No, I would not," Kiva said. "My mother's fucking awesome."

"Once I was on the transport, I was told where I was going and who we were picking up."

Kiva looked to the cab. "Who's driving?"

"It's automated."

"Where are we going now?"

Senia laughed. "I have no idea. Probably to see your mother. I don't really care. You're back."

"I fucked up," Kiva said. "I didn't listen to you enough. You tried to warn me about Nadashe, and I thought I was a step ahead of her."

"It's all right," Senia said. "She's about to be made emperox. Turns out she was a step ahead of everyone."

Kiva looked around the overland transport. "Maybe not everyone," she said, and then returned her attention to Senia, because they had catching up to do.

# CHAPTER 23

It was a beautiful day for an imperial coronation, but then, this was Xi'an and every day was a beautiful day there.

As the morning of the coronation broke, artificially but even so, there was a large crowd of onlookers and well-wishers outside Xi'an Cathedral. They clustered around the areas below the balcony where the Emperox Nadashe would, after her coronation, appear to her new subjects, to wave and beam and take her first public steps in her new role.

If any of the spectators had any concern that the bombing that had happened at the last coronation would repeat itself, they kept it to themselves. Well, mostly they kept it to themselves. There were a few wits who suggested that an explosion would be unlikely this time because Nadashe wasn't a suicide bomber. These "wits" were then mostly told to stop acting like assholes, which made the wits complain that no one could take a joke anymore.

Other, more serious students of imperial history noted the same thing as the wits, cast somewhat differently. No one denied that the Nohamapetan family, once favored by the imperial house, had in the last few years done a heel turn in its relationship to the Wu family — predicated mostly by a sense of grievance that Grayland II, the former emperox, would not marry a Nohamapetan as previously agreed — and many observers asked whether the Nohamapetan response of attempted assassination and coup was not, in fact, "within bounds" when dynasties were on the line. Or, more succinctly, was anything *really* off-limits to the royals?

Still others noted that these spirited and increasingly abstruse discussions of the prerogative of noble houses served the purpose of abstracting the actual crimes of the Nohamapetan family — and of Nadashe herself, let's not forget — to such an extent that they stopped being considered crimes and started becoming colorful backstory. This in itself added even more layers of abstraction to conversation.

What made the discussion ultimately irrelevant was that the Wu family, the imperial family, had been the ones to offer this compromise, to honor the deal made by Attavio VI and broken by Grayland II, and that the other noble families had fallen so quickly into line. The ascendance of Nadashe Nohamapetan was not a trick or a coup, informed observers noted. It was a carefully negotiated peace treaty. There had been nothing like it in the history of the Interdependency, and that in itself was exciting, and in being exciting, was good.

There had been some hiccups on the way to the coronation, of course. Archbishop Korbijn's sudden resignation had ground things to a halt while the selection of a new archbishop was made, and that selection process both took far longer than anyone expected, and resulted in a compromise archbishop that no one was particularly happy with, apparently not least of all including Archbishop Cole himself.

Nadashe, at least, did not let the time go unmarked. With these interstitial weeks prior to the coronation, the incoming emperox launched a charm offensive with a series of carefully managed presentations, appearances and interviews designed to show her softer and more compassionate side. In the interviews in particular, Nadashe did not shy away from the controversies surrounding her selection or the troubling recent actions undertaken in the name of the House of Nohamapetan, but gently guided everything toward the promises of the future, as all the noble houses worked together in harmony to deal with the Flow crisis for the benefit of all the citizens of the Interdependency.

For a number of these interviews, Nadashe was accompanied by her new fiancé, Yuva Wu, a pleasant-looking young man who looked slightly dazed most of the time and who answered most questions with politely meandering answers that went nowhere. The couple sure looked great in pictures, however, and Nadashe was happy to speak glowingly about their future together and the children they would have — probably soon so as to avoid any problems with succession in the future.

Not everyone was taken in by this publicity push, but everyone, from the highest of nobles to the lowest of hoi polloi, felt the fatigue of years of violent palace intrigue. Nadashe Nohamapetan might have entire rolling carts-worth of reputational baggage to her name, but once she was installed everyone could simply stop thinking about all this nonsense.

Grayland II — weird, strange, *unexpected*

Grayland II, she of the religious visions and the grandstanding proclamations as she was arresting half of the nobles in the system — had been *liked,* and it was a good bet that history would love her. She was quirky enough for that. But as a practical matter, she and her rule were tiring. She was hard to wrap one's head around. Nadashe Nohamapetan, now, that was someone who really held no surprises. She was standard-issue grasping noble front to back, and smart enough to try to hide it with a little bit of public relations. The Interdependency had been here before, with so many of its emperoxs. And that was, strangely enough, restful.

Nadashe Nohamapetan herself could not give a good goddamn at this point if she was restful or contentious or smoothly charming or whatever, she just wanted this coronation done and over with. Archbishop Korbijn's retirement — and the attendant nonsense that followed, with the selection of a new archbishop — had really messed with Nadashe's schedule, and Proster Wu had demanded that Nadashe take the interim to work on her image.

Personally Nadashe had found the image rehabilitation exercises maddening. She understood their need and grudgingly accepted that Proster Wu was right, that they made the people more comfortable with her. But fundamentally Nadashe didn't care if the people liked her. She wasn't planning to be an emperox of the people. This emperox was relocating the Interdependency wholesale, and most of "the people" wouldn't be coming. So sitting there for endless rounds of interviews, trying to look engaged and empathetic, was just a waste of her time.

This was especially the case when she was required to spend any time with Yuva Wu, Proster's pretty but aggravatingly dim-witted nephew, whom Nadashe was already planning to rid herself of at the earliest possible convenience after a child was born. Nadashe had already tried Yuva Wu out in bed to see what he was like. The answer was: simple. At least he was quick about it.

All of the lead-up to the coronation had been a waste of Nadashe's time — the only thing she had truly enjoyed was zip-tying Kiva Lagos to a fucking chair and watching the woman spit attitude for several minutes. Kiva had been correct that Nadashe had no intention of honoring the deal, although Nadashe had to admit she found it aggravating that Kiva had seen through it so quickly and had played with her as much as she was playing with Kiva. Kiva had always been too smart for her own good.

Nadashe decided that one of her first acts as emperox would be to solve the problem of Kiva. She was . . . troublesome. Nadashe was aware that there had been a riot at the Emperox Hanne II Secured Correctional Facility, where some inmates had been injured and a few others went missing and were presumed dead. She decided there should be another riot there in the near future, with more definite casualties.

The good news was, all of the waiting was behind her now. All the vapid interviews, all the enervating "discussion" of royal politics, all the dealing with the increasingly demanding Proster Wu on this or that point, all of the shit — all of it would be a thing of the past very soon now. All she had to do was bow, kneel, say a few words and it was done. The ceremony was to be short, very short, because Nadashe had agreed not to take on the various lesser titles that would go to Yuva first and then to their child once it was born and Yuva could be shuffled off; Yuva would have his own, smaller ceremony later in the week. Archbishop Cole likewise would become Cardinal Cole at a different ceremony, which Nadashe had no plan to attend.

Enter the cathedral, kneel for fifteen minutes, say a few words, rise an emperox. And then, finally, real work could be done.

Then it would truly be a beautiful day for Nadashe Nohamapetan.

They had almost gotten through the ceremony, almost gotten to the point where she would be, in fact, Emperox Nadashe I, when the ghost appeared.

Nadashe heard the mutterings and too-loud whispers before she saw the ghost. She had been kneeling, knees on the marble, eyes tracing one of the veins in the stone, when the whispering began, immediately followed by the sound of Archbishop Cole no longer uttering, in his entirely grating monotone, the words of the coronation rite. It was the hitch in Cole's speech that finally made Nadashe look up, to see Cole looking directly behind her with an expression of confusion. She followed his gaze and finally saw the ghost of Grayland II.

Her first thought was, *Someone's getting fired.* From her point of view, looking up at Grayland, Nadashe could see the projectors firing beams of light down to build the image of the former emperox directly behind where she was kneeling. Either someone had accidentally projected an image of

Grayland, which was a fireable offense, or they were doing it intentionally as a prank or statement, which was not only fireable but possibly ejectable. Nadashe would not object to the prankster sucking vacuum for a few very painful seconds before death came for them.

Her second thought was, *She's looking right at me.*

And indeed she was. The projection of Grayland II was staring, not only at Nadashe, but directly into her eyes. It was eerie as hell.

Then the projection spoke.

"Hello, Nadashe," it said. "Nice day for a coronation."

The muttering of the crowd became louder. When Grayland spoke, Nadashe heard it projected directly at her, but she knew it was also being projected to the entire cathedral.

*The sound person is getting fired too,* Nadashe thought.

"This isn't amusing," Nadashe finally said.

"I'm not here to be amusing," the projection said. "I'm here for a coronation."

"You're not you," Nadashe said.

"I'm not who?"

"You're not Grayland. You're someone playing a prank with a projected image and a voice simulator."

"You're sure of that."

"Of course I'm sure. Grayland is dead."

"Yes," agreed the projection. "I am dead. You should know — you're the one who killed me."

The murmurs became shouts at that.

"The Countess Rafellya killed Grayland," Nadashe said, turning to the ghost.

"She brought the bomb that killed me into the palace, yes," the apparition said. "But you were the one who gave it to her. You told her it was a listening device. You didn't tell her what it would really do. You didn't tell her that she was going to die along with me."

Over the speakers of the cathedral came two voices, one Nadashe and the other Countess Rafellya Maisen-Persaud, discussing the music box. The countess was expressing concern that the listening device would be discovered. Nadashe replied that it was designed to appear perfectly innocent and that as a backup she had paid an imperial security guard to alter one of the scanners by a software upgrade. Nadashe named the guard specifically so that the countess should go to him directly for service.

The audio cut off. Nadashe stared at Grayland, stunned. Grayland smiled. "You shouldn't talk treason in front of a tablet microphone, Nadashe."

"It's not true," Nadashe whispered.

The cathedral was alive with the sound of phone and tablet alerts going off. "The full audio transcript of your conversation from your tablet, Nadashe," Grayland said. Another set of pings. "The audio transcript from the countess's tablet." More pings. "The testimony of the bomb-maker you paid for the bomb." More pings. "The testimony of the security guard you paid to compromise the scanner and to deal with the countess." The cathedral echoed with the pings.

Grayland smiled again at Nadashe. "All that just went to every tablet and personal device on Xi'an, by the way. And of course all of this" — Grayland indicated the coronation ceremony — "is being broadcast live here on Xi'an and on Hub."

Nadashe gaped.

Members of the cathedral congregation began to get up and head to the exits. Grayland turned to face them. "Sit down," she said, and her voice boomed through the sound system. "All of you. We're not done here. Now, be quiet. Listen."

The congregation quieted. In the silence a high whistling came from air vents.

"The designer of this cathedral worried that fire would damage it," Grayland said. "He made it so the air in the cathedral could be emptied into space in less than two minutes. If you want to test this proposition, try to leave before I am done speaking."

There was dead silence, save for the whistling. Then the whistling stopped.

"Thank you," Grayland said. "Now. You think I have come to expose Nadashe Nohamapetan as a murderer and traitor. So I have.

"But some of you in the congregation already knew she was a murderer and traitor. You knew she planned to murder me and take the role of emperox. You knew because she told you. You knew because she enlisted you into the scheme."

The pings started rolling through the cathedral again. "You paid twenty million marks each to join her coup. You paid it up front from your personal accounts. You paid it because she promised you that if you did, when the Flow finally collapsed, you would be saved. You. You and your friends. You and your business. You and your house. Not the millions of people who you rule over and who live in your systems. They were to be left behind in slowly dying habitats and underground cities while you migrated to the only planet that could support life. You willingly and intentionally planned to condemn billions to death. I have all the details and documentation for each of you, every family and every noble who signed on to this plan of death. And now so does everyone else."

Grayland waited until the shouting died down again. "I am dead. Nadashe Nohamapetan killed me. She murdered me as she murdered the Countess Rafellya and Drusin Wolfe and her brother Amit and my dearest friend Naffa Dolg. I am dead and I am no longer your emperox.

"I have become something else. Now I am something who knows the secrets of all the noble families. I am something who can control access to Flow streams, not just here but everywhere in the Interdependency. I am something who can decide who will live and who will die in the coming years, and in the decades and even centuries ahead.

"This is what I have to say to you noble families assembled here today. None of you here today will go to End before the last of your citizens go to End. You will not abandon them. Their fate is your fate. You can try to abandon them, if you like. But your ships will not move. Flow shoal sentries will not let you pass. And when you return home, they will know you tried to leave them behind. If you want to buy your way into End, the price of your admission is every other person in your system first. The Interdependency is its people.

"We can and we will move everyone to the End system. But it will take not just years, but decades and even centuries. I will be here — always I will be here — to help guide people to that system. In the meantime, systems of the Interdependency and the people in them will need to survive through long years of isolation. The ideas behind the Interdependency — the monopolies of the noble families and guilds — will no longer allow them to do this."

Another wave of pings rang through the cathedral. "And so the monopolies of the families are ended. All their trade secrets are released. We can no longer afford to have food stocks self-destruct after five or six generations, or have one family build ships."

The roar this time was immense. "It is too late," Grayland said, over the din. "It is done. You are still the noble families. You still have a thousand years of wealth and capital. If you can't survive without your monopolies, then it is time you let others take your place."

Eventually the roar subsided. "Finally . . . finally. You have come here for a coronation. You will have one." Grayland pointed to Nadashe. "But it will not be her. Not because she murdered me among others. Not because she has been shown, time and again, to be a traitor to the Interdependency. And not even because" — and here Grayland looked at Nadashe directly — "she's just not a very nice person. It's because before I died, I legally named a successor."

Grayland turned to look at Proster Wu, sitting in the front pew of the congregation. "It is not a member of the Wu family. Twice the Wu family aligned itself with the enemies of the emperox. With *my* enemies. That's two times too many. You will pay for your treason, Proster Wu. But so will your family. Our family. And that is on you." Proster looked away.

"If not her, then who?" Archbishop Cole asked. "Who is to be the new emperox?"

"I'm glad you asked," Grayland said, and there was a final wash of pings across the devices of the cathedral. "I've just sent the notice of my declaration of an heir, which I signed three days before my death and had witnessed by three others. I gave instruction for it not to be made public until the day of the coronation. You could say that I anticipated this.

"I, Grayland II, Emperox of the Holy Empire of the Interdependent States and Mercantile Guilds, Queen of Hub and Associated Nations, Head of the Interdependent Church, Successor to Earth and Mother to All, Eighty-Eighth Emperox of the House of Wu, am dead. I present to you now my heir, and the last emperox of the Interdependency."

The doors of the cathedral opened, and through them a figure stepped through and began walking, with unhurried but deliberate pace, down the nave of the cathedral. The heir to the emperox paid no attention to the rising voices that followed, keeping a steady gaze on Nadashe Nohamapetan, the pretender to the throne, whose eyes widened as she saw who the last emperox would be.

The last emperox stepped up to the chancel of the cathedral, where Nadashe Nohamapetan now stood, and stopped directly in front of her.

"Bitch, you're in my spot," said Kiva Lagos.

# CHAPTER 24

For the first time since it was created, the Memory Room received visitors who were not necessarily an emperox.

"What is this place?" Nadashe Nohamapetan said, looking at the spare furnishing and bare walls.

"It's a place that you would have had access to if you were emperox," Grayland said. "Where you could talk to any of the emperoxs who had come before you. Well, a version of them, anyway."

"Any of them."

"Yes."

"Including you."

"Quite evidently, me."

"And you would have known I had murdered you."

"As I was aware of your plans a few days before you murdered me, yes."

"You knew, and you didn't stop me."

415

"I did know, and I *did* stop you."

"Not from killing you."

"No, not that. But from becoming emperox."

"You did that already," Nadashe protested. "You made fucking Kiva Lagos your heir before you died."

"The point wasn't to just stop you from being emperox," Grayland said. "The point was to stop it all. All the conspiracies and plots and nonsense. That wouldn't have stopped if I still lived. You or someone else like you — well, there's not quite anyone like you, but you understand what I'm getting at — would have kept coming at me. If I had simply named Kiva my heir, you would have tried to kill her, either before or after she came to the throne."

"And you think you've stopped all that now?"

"I think I've made it clear that secrets are not something that can be kept from me. And I released enough of everybody's secrets that they'll be too busy dealing with their own problems for a while to make any problems for Kiva."

"You've made a lot of problems for the nobles."

"Yes, that was the plan."

"You might get some of them killed," Nadashe pointed out.

"It's not me who made them choose to endorse a path where billions were sacrificed to save a few and their money."

"You just publicized it, is all."

"Since a key portion of the plan was killing me, I can live with it, so to speak."

"And you think you can somehow get everyone to End. Eventually."

"I do."

"How are you going to do that?"

"You mean, with the *Prophecies of Rachela* and those other ships waiting to shoot everyone out of the sky, and you having cancelled my plan for a backdoor attack through Ikoyi?"

"I meant more long term, but sure."

"You gave out clearance codes to your co-conspirators. I've collected those. We'll come in through the front door. As for the rest of it, well, the math is complicated. Just trust I can make it work. Or don't. You'll be dead by the time it's done anyway."

"So what are you going to do with me?" Nadashe Nohamapetan asked.

"I'm going to make you lose everything, of course," Grayland said. "The House of Nohamapetan is formally dissolved, you know that."

"I heard."

417

"That was one of Emperox Mavel's first acts." Grayland paused. "You know that's Kiva's imperial name."

Nadashe rolled her eyes. "Yes."

"Curious choice. In any event, Mavel chose not to ennoble any other family. She put the Nohamapetan assets in trust for the citizens of Terhathum. I thought it was such a good idea, I asked her to do the same with the House of Wu, for the benefit of the citizens of Hub. I suspect dissolving both of those houses will end a lot of mischief, both in themselves and because they will serve as object examples to other noble houses."

"If you say so."

"I do. Also, on a more personal level, all your accounts have been seized and turned over to the Ministry of Revenue. Also your mother's accounts and your brother Ghreni's accounts. You're all broke, Nadashe."

"We're all under penalty of death for treason, so I don't think that matters much."

"Mavel and I decided that death wasn't the appropriate punishment for you, Nadashe."

"So? What are you going to do, then?"

"Why, I'm going to give you what you always said you wanted."

"And just what is that?"

Grayland smiled and told her.

■ ■ ■ ■

"You know, it's funny," said Emperox Mavel, aka Kiva Lagos. "I was thinking to myself not too long ago that people were going to have to change the way they live, because the end of the universe was coming, and there were only a certain number of people who could freeload, and I fully intended to be one of them. Now look how *that* fucking turned out."

"The job of emperox is not a job for freeloaders," Grayland said. "Well, it can be. Just not now."

"So you're saying I should have gotten this gig earlier."

"A lot earlier."

"Figures."

"Sorry."

"You could still take the job back, you know," Kiva said.

Grayland shook her head. "I have another job now. And anyway, it's a job for the living."

Kiva pointed to Grayland's head. "Fine, but just so you know, I'm not going to get a fucking set of wires put into my head," she said. "I have too much stuff in there I don't want other people to know. Ever."

"You're the last emperox," Grayland said. "The one who wraps up the Interdependency. After you there won't be any others. So after you there won't be anyone coming to the Memory Room anyway."

"Okay, good," Kiva said. "Because I'm not going to lie to you, this shit is creepy."

"I know. I think so too."

"So, how are we going to do this? Wrap up the Interdependency?"

"It's simple. You are going to tell people what to do in terms of preparing the individual systems for isolation. I'm going to tell you if they are doing it, and what to do if they're not. The further we go along, the more systems will become isolated and the less you'll have to do. I will start monitoring systems by direct beam-of-light communication, keeping them updated with the latest developments about evanescent streams appearing and disappearing, and the most recent science about manipulating Flow shoals. I act as a central hub for information once all the long-standing Flow streams disappear."

"The temporary Flow streams will still connect systems."

"The evanescent streams, yes. Only for a few months or years for each stream, but that's enough time for a transfer of information or supplies, or to move structures from one system to another as part of the long path to End."

"And you're going to make this work."

Grayland shook her head. "That's going to be up to the people in the individual systems to do. I can give them all the information I have and they need, but once the Interdependency is gone it will be up to them to decide what to do with that information. I don't think everyone is going to make it to End. But a lot of them will."

"That's going to fuck up that planet."

"If we can eventually move the habitats, then people will still live in them. We'll just have moved all of the Interdependency to a single system."

Kiva shook her head. "Crowded as hell."

Grayland smiled. "Space is pretty big. Even in one system."

"If you say so."

"How's your mother?" Grayland asked.

"Smug as fuck," Kiva said. "I don't know why I listened to you and made her a duchess."

"She was helpful to me. After I changed to this I needed a live human to help me do things. I needed someone I could trust and someone I knew could get things done. Like get you out of prison, for one."

"She just rented a transport and told Senia to get in it. You did the actual jailbusting."

"It wouldn't have worked if the transport wasn't there to pick you up. You know she never doubted you were alive. When I told her you were, she was just, *Yes, of course she is.*"

"That's Mom," Kiva said.

"Thank you for staying alive, by the way. If you were dead I would have had to make Marce the emperox."

"You're welcome. Because he would have been shit at the job."

"I know."

"And also, fuck you for dying, Grayland. Now I have to do this shitty job."

Grayland laughed at that. "There are perks. You have a nice house."

"The damn thing is haunted. I keep seeing ghosts."

"Well, when the last Flow stream is about to collapse, you can go to End and leave the house behind."

"We'll see."

"So you might stay?"

Kiva was silent for a moment. "You know my mom, the duchess, is heading back to Ikoyi."

"I did," Grayland said.

422

"She plans to die there. Not anytime soon. But one day. And until then she'll do what she can to help Ikoyi make it through its isolation. She's not leaving her people behind."

"I know. You mother is one of the best of us."

"I'm not just the emperox," Kiva said. "I'm also Queen of Hub. When I'm done with the Interdependency and it's gone, there will still be hundreds of millions of people in this system. And what I don't want them to think is, *Our chickenshit queen just left us.*"

"I think that's wise."

"Anyway, *you'll* still be here. You can listen to me bitch and moan about my job every once in a while. You know, when Senia wants a break from it."

"Fair enough. I'm glad you have Senia, Kiva."

"I'm glad too," Kiva said. "Although *that* was fucking unexpected."

"Love often is," Grayland said.

"I want to ask you a question," Marce said. "It's a weird question, but I'd like to know the answer."

"Of course," Cardenia said.

"The night you . . . died, I thought I heard

423

you call my name on the *Auvergne.* Just before I woke up. Did you? Was that you?"

"No," Cardenia said, gently. "But I wish it was."

Marce nodded at this and looked around the Memory Room. "So this is what it was like all this time."

"This is it," Cardenia agreed.

"I imagined it as, well, *more.*"

"It is more, when you fill it with emperoxs."

"Why did you do it?" Marce asked.

"Because it was the only way to break the cycle of coup a —"

Marce held up a hand. "Not why you died. Why did you ask to marry me when you knew you were going to die?"

"I didn't know I would need to die when I asked."

"But you thought it might be a possibility."

"I had thought about it. Ever since I learned about Rachela, and ever since you told me there was a possibility of shaping Flow shoals."

"So why did you ask me to marry you?" Marce asked.

"Because I love you," Cardenia said. "Everything I said to you that night when I proposed was true. Is true. Is still true. I loved that you were fighting the good fight even if you stood to lose it. And then I saw there was an opportunity to win that fight. Or if not to win it, then to keep fighting until there was a better chance to win it."

"You won the fight, but you lost the possibility of us," Marce said.

"Yes," Cardenia said. "And when I realized that's what I had to do, I broke down. On that bench you're sitting on right now."

"But you did it anyway."

"There are billions of people whose lives I could save by doing it. I'm Cardenia Wu-Patrick, who loves you, Marce, more than I can possibly tell you. More than I love pie."

Marce smiled and laughed at this, and then began to cry.

"I'm also Grayland II, who is the emperox, and mother of all. And I had a responsibility that was greater than what I wished and wanted and hoped for myself. I'm sorry, Marce. That was selfish of me, I know."

"What?" Marce said, and wiped his face. "That's the opposite of selfish."

"Selfish because I should have told you. Or at least warned you. Or maybe I just shouldn't have proposed."

"Don't say that."

"Why? My proposal is hurting you."

"No . . . it's not the proposal that hurts. You proposing to me was the happiest moment I can remember having. What hurts is imagining the future we would have, thinking about it and wanting it and then having it taken away . . ." Marce drew a heavy breath. "Having it taken away so soon after having the privilege of imagining it."

"And to have it taken away by me."

"What? No. You didn't take it away. Nadashe Nohamapetan did it. It's on her. It's all on her." He looked up at Cardenia. "You're letting her live, I hear."

"I suggested it and Kiva agreed, on the principle that it would make Nadashe miserable longer."

"I have to tell you I might have gone a different route on that one."

"I wouldn't blame you for that."

"I don't know what to do now, Cardenia," Marce said. "You're gone, but you're still here; I can see you and hear you, but I can't touch you or be with you. I hurt. All the time. I don't know what to do."

"I know what you should do," Cardenia said. "But I don't think you'll like it."

"Tell me anyway."

"You need to go away," Cardenia said. "Away from me. Away from this."

Marce laughed softly at this. "You're not

wrong. But I don't know if that would do the trick."

"Well, about that. I spoke to Kiva about this and we agreed to two options to present to you."

"Two options."

"Yes. The first is, you go home. Back to End. As the new duke."

"You want to make me the Duke of End?"

"No one deserves it more," Cardenia said. "And as the Duke of End, you and your family would be well-placed to make sure that when new people and habitats arrive in the system, they are intelligently incorporated, to keep them and your planet alive. When the Flow stream from Hub finally collapses and the Interdependency is done, you become King of End."

"What's the second option?"

"You go to Earth."

"What?"

"I've been analyzing the data you sent back, along with all the data you collected before."

"*You* have," Marce said.

"I have, yes," Cardenia said. "Chenevert gave me some of his systems to get me started. I don't know how to put this, Marce . . . but I'm more than I was before. Different."

427

"Better."

Cardenia shook her head. "Not better. Just different. The point is, I synthesized the data and put it together to make predictions on future evanescent Flow streams. I saw something in it, and I asked Chenevert to run it to see if he saw the same thing. He did. A Flow stream, from here, opening up six months from now into territory that corresponds to a system claimed by Earth."

"Wow," Marce said. *"Wow."*

"There are caveats," Cardenia said. "The stream we identified goes out. Neither Chenevert nor I have predicted a corresponding stream returning. One may show up when we get more data from more evanescent shoals and we can make better predictions, but for now, out is the only direction. We estimate six months in the stream. Neither Chenevert nor I know what's on the other side of that stream. In Chenevert's time, there was a young colony there, but who's to say what's there now. Finally, Chenevert says he has a map of the Flow streams the systems aligned with Earth used, but it's very old, and he can't guarantee that a collapse event kicked off by the Rupture hasn't happened there. You could be taking a one-way trip to nowhere."

"But if there is something there —"

428

"Then you'd be the first person in fifteen hundred years to meet humans from Earth. Or from one of their systems, anyway."

"Wow," Marce said again.

Cardenia smiled. "Chenevert said that's what you would say. He also told me to tell you that if you wanted to make that trip, the *Auvergne* is yours and he would be delighted to be your pilot."

"I . . ." Marce stopped. "I need to think about this."

"Of course."

"It's a lot."

"Yes it is," Cardenia said. "I should also tell you that if you take the exploration option, Kiva intends to make your sister Vrenna Duchess of End. Apparently Kiva remembers her well and was quite taken with her."

"Coming from Kiva that could be taken in all number of ways."

"I suppose so, but no matter what, the dukedom is coming into your family. I don't know if that influences your decision one way or another."

"Thank you, Cardenia," Marce said. "I have a lot to think about all of a sudden."

"Yes you do," Cardenia said. "That was the plan."

Marce got up and moved to the door of

the Memory Room, then stopped and turned. "I love you. You know that."

"And I love you, Marce. No matter where you are, and always."

He smiled and left the room.

Cardenia waited a few moments, gathering herself, and then called Chenevert. "You were right," she said, to him. "He grabbed on to Earth like it was a long-lost pet."

"Which is what you wanted him to do," Chenevert reminded her.

"I know."

"So you think he'll choose that."

"I'm certain of it. He'll fight it for a bit. But think of the *science.*"

"And you?" Chenevert asked. "How will you be? Part of you is still human. Will always be human."

"It'll hurt," Cardenia said. "It will hurt for a long time."

"That's not a bad thing."

"No. No, I suppose not."

"All right. When he finally admits to coming around, I'll let you know, and you can have our dear new emperox open up the money drawer. We won't have any problem outfitting and staffing a trip to Earth, even if it might be one-way. That might even be a draw."

"It might be," Cardenia said. "But, Chenevert."

"Yes, my dear?"

"Promise me something."

"Anything."

"Promise that one day you'll come back. That he'll come back."

"Oh, Cardenia," Chenevert said. "Why would you worry about such a thing? However long it takes, I will always bring him home."

"So you've said your goodbyes," Rachela said, to Cardenia.

"They're not goodbyes," Cardenia said. "I'll be speaking to some of them again. Some of them quite a lot."

"Not to *them*. To what you were before."

"Oh, that. Yes. Yes, I suppose I have."

"That's good," Rachela said. "It's important. You can't be what we are now and not have done that."

"Be immortal, you mean."

"We're not immortal," Rachela reminded her. "But we get to live as long as we're useful. And that is a rare privilege."

"And what about you?" Cardenia said. "How much longer will you choose to live? The Interdependency is ending. You wanted to see how it turned out. Now you know."

"I don't know," Rachela said. "It's been a long time to be alive. I was worried for some time there that it would end badly. But I don't worry about that now. Because of you, Cardenia. Thank you for that."

"You're welcome."

"If I do decide to leave you one day, will you think of me?" Rachela asked.

"Of course. This is the Memory Room. You will always be here."

"Yes," Rachela agreed. "Then shall we begin with the end?"

"Yes, let's," Cardenia said. "We'll make it one to remember."

# EPILOGUE

The Battle of End was hardly that; the *Prophecies of Rachela* surrendered to the End Expeditionary Force without a single shot being fired, and the other ships of *Rachela*'s ad hoc task force, those whose crews were still mostly alive, surrendered almost as quickly.

As the bedraggled remains of the *Rachela*'s crew recovered on the *Spirit of Grayland II,* the story was pieced together: Sir Ontain Mount, upon discovering the *Rachela* had been commandeered by Nohamapetan sympathizers and that its crew and soldiers intended to take his command, by force if necessary, shuttled his marines to the surface of End by any means necessary and destroyed the space station the *Rachela* had meant to take and would need for repairs and supplies.

On the ground, Ontain's marines joined up with Vrenna Claremont's rebels and ef-

433

fectively harassed (acting) Duke Ghreni Nohamapetan's forces, and played the long game with the *Rachela* and the occasional new ship that joined with it, denying them supplies and maintenance. The pirates that had originally supplied the *Rachela*'s group eventually began to prey on them. Furtive attempts at surface landings to requisition supplies ended in ambush and capture of crew and materiel. It was one of the most effective blockades from the bottom of a gravity well ever attempted.

With the arrival of the *Spirit,* the civil war on the ground came to an abrupt end. Ghreni Nohamapetan — no longer duke, acting or otherwise — was quickly surrendered by his troops when they were promised no reprisal if they laid down their arms and produced their putative leader. Ghreni was delivered to Vrenna Claremont, now Duchess of End, unceremoniously stuffed into a duffel bag. Vrenna promised she wouldn't kill him if he told her where her father was. Count Jamies Claremont was produced, unharmed but glad to be out of that damned room, an hour later.

And so it was two days later that Ghreni Nohamapetan was in the same room where he had held Count Claremont captive, when the door opened and Nadashe and the

Countess Nohamapetan were shoved in, the door slamming shut and locking quickly behind them.

Ghreni looked at his mother and sister, wordless and gaping, for a full thirty seconds. Then he closed his mouth and set his jaw.

"Okay, seriously now," he said to his sister. "What the *fuck* happened to this perfect plan of yours? Hmmm?"

# ACKNOWLEDGMENTS

The first thing that I would like to acknowledge in these acknowledgments is that, in fact, I am history's worst monster.

The reason I am history's worst monster is that I had more than a year to write this book, and I did the thing I've been doing with the last several books of mine, which is waiting until the very last possible moment to turn the damn thing in, which makes me a nuisance to everyone else involved in the production of the book. Now they will have to work extra hard and extra fast because I couldn't get my act together.

And so: history's worst monster. I wish I could offer up a reasonable excuse for my screwed-upped-ness, but there's really not one. The best explanation (which is different than an excuse) I can offer is that for someone who is easily distracted, 2019 offered up, shall we say, a target-rich environment. If you lived through 2019, and did not spend most of the year living in a cave or in a haze of pot smoke, then you probably understand what I mean. If you did spend 2019 in a cave and/or stoned out of your gourd, well, then. Well done you.

I would really like to return to halcyon days of pre-2016, when I actually did a reasonably good job of focusing and turning in books on a schedule that would not make production people hate me and burn me in effigy, so if you live in the United States, and you are reading this prior to November 2020, please do me a favor and (a) Register to vote, or check to make sure your registration is still valid, (b) Remember to vote on election day (or before if you take an early ballot) and (c) Try not to vote for anyone who is a whirling amoral vortex of chaos. I would really really really appreciate it, and you would also probably get more books from me.

And to the other people involved in the production of this book: I am honestly and genuinely sorry to make you sprint on this one, too. You deserve better and I'll try to do better.

And who are some of the people involved in the production of this book? Patrick Nielsen Hayden, my editor; his (past and present) assistants Anita Okoye, Rachel Bass and Molly McGhee; Irene Gallo as art director and Nicholas "Sparth" Bouvier as the artist; book designer Heather Saunders; copy editor Deanna Hoak, to whom I apologize in advance for my idiosyncratic comma usage; and my publicist Alexis Saarela. Thanks also to Bella Pagan at Tor UK and her fabulous staff of people there, including her assistant Georgia Summers. At Audible, thanks as always to Steve Feldberg and his team, and to Wil Wheaton, who will make with the word sounds for those folk who read by ear.

Also many thanks to Ethan Ellenberg, Bibi Lewis, Joel Gotler and Matt Sugarman, who comprise Team Scalzi when it comes to selling my work and/or looking over contracts, which is very much appreciated. A tip of the hat also to Georgina Gordon-Smith, Surian Fletcher-Jones and Gennifer Hutchison.

I drop in occasional nods to friends and fellow writers in these books and most of the time it's not a problem, but then every once in a while I totally kill the hell out of a character I named for someone and then I feel bad about it. So, uhhhh, Mary Robinette Kowal and Navah Wolfe, sorry for killing those dudes.

(This is especially awkward re: Navah, for

whom I named a different character in the series as well: Naffa Dolg, Cardenia's close friend who you may recall I blew up in the first book, which caused Navah to remark, more than once, "You fridged my character for LADY PAIN." You know I admire and esteem you, Navah, honest and truly.)

Friends who helped me keep my sanity during the writing of this book include Kevin Stampfl, Yanni Kuznia, Bill Schafer, Ryvenna Altman, Olivia Ahl, Deven Desai, Monica Byrne and Megan Frank. Special thanks also to Natasha Kordus, literally one of my oldest and dearest friends, for a fabulous bit of last-minute encouragement.

Thank you to the people who make the Freedom app, which is a program I use on my computer to block social media because I cannot be trusted not to check Twitter every twenty seconds. If you need a program to save your attention span from yourself, I can in fact recommend it.

(But if you do follow me on Twitter or Facebook or read my blog *Whatever,* thank you. You're not to blame for my lack of willpower about these things.)

As always I thank Athena and Kristine Scalzi, daughter and wife respectively, for being such wonderful people, and wonderful for me. I could say much more about both, but if you've read these acknowledgments before you know how mushy I can get about both of them. I'm just glad I get to have them in my life.

And finally, thank you, the readers, for reading this series. As strange as it may seem, this series of books is the first time I ever intentionally wrote a trilogy. Most of the time I write a book and if people like it, then I write another in the same world. This is how we got to six books in the Old Man's War series (so far). But I went in knowing I was planning to write three books in this series, and that at the end of it, the empire would, indeed, collapse. It's been a new experience for me combining that sort of long-term understanding of the events of the series with my usual "make this thing up as I go along" writing style, and I have to say I'm very pleased with how it came out. This was a very satisfying writing experience for me. I hope it was as satisfying for you as well. Thank you for coming along with me.

*John Scalzi*
*October 31, 2019*

# ABOUT THE AUTHOR

**John Scalzi** is one of the most popular SF authors to emerge in the last decade. His debut *Old Man's War* won him the John W. Campbell Award for Best New Writer. His *New York Times* bestsellers include *The Last Colony, Fuzzy Nation,* and *Redshirts* (which won the 2013 Hugo Award for Best Novel). Material from his blog, Whatever (whatever.scalzi.com), has also earned him two other Hugo Awards. Scalzi also serves as critic-at-large for the *Los Angeles Times.* He lives in Ohio with his wife and daughter.